Acclaim For the Work of STEPHEN KING!

"Excellent, psychologically textured...Stephen King is so widely acknowledged as America's master of paranormal terrors that you can forget his real genius is for the everyday."

—*New York Times Book Review*

"King has written...a novel that's as hauntingly touching as it is just plain haunted...one of his freshest and most frightening works to date."

—*Entertainment Weekly*

"Extraordinarily vivid...an impressive tour de force, a sensitive character study that holds the reader rapt."

—*Playboy*

"Stephen King is superb."

—*Time*

"Mr. King makes palpable the longing and regret that arise out of calamity, and deftly renders the kindness and pettiness that can mark small-town life."

—*Wall Street Journal*

"King is a master at crafting a story and creating a sense of place."

—*USA Today*

"A thoroughly compelling thriller."

—*Esquire*

"Don't start this one on a school night…You'll be up till dawn."
—*People*

"As brilliant a dark dream as has ever been dreamed in this century."
—*Palm Beach Post*

"A great book…A landmark in American literature."
—*Chicago Sun-Times*

"Stephen King is an immensely talented storyteller of seemingly inexhaustible gifts."
—*Interview*

"A rare blend of luminous prose, thought-provoking themes and masterful storytelling."
—*San Diego Union Tribune*

"Not only immensely popular but immensely talented, a modern-day counterpart to Twain, Hawthorne, Dickens."
—*Publishers Weekly*

"He's a master storyteller. Gather around the pages of his literary campfire and he'll weave you a darn good yarn."
—*Houston Chronicle*

"King surpasses our expectations, leaves us spellbound and hungry for the next twist of plot."
—*Boston Globe*

"Top shelf. You couldn't go wrong with a King book."
—*Michael Connelly*

"Stephen King is the Winslow Homer of blood."
—*New Yorker*

"King has invented genres, reinvented them, then stepped outside what he himself has accomplished…Stephen King, like Mark Twain, is an American genius."

—*Greg Iles*

"Stephen King is much more than just a horror fiction writer. And I believe that he's never been given credit for taking American literature and stretching its boundaries."

—*Gloria Naylor*

"To my mind, King is one of the most underestimated novelists of our time."

—*Mordechai Richler, Vancouver Sun*

"King possesses an incredible sense of story…[He is] a gifted writer of intensely felt emotions, a soulful writer in control of a spare prose that never gets in the way of the story…I, for one (of millions), wait impatiently to see where this king of storytellers takes us next."

—*Ridley Pearson*

"An absorbing, constantly surprising novel filled with true narrative magic."

—*Washington Post*

"It grabs you and holds you and won't let go…a genuine page turner."

—*Chattanooga Times*

"Blending philosophy with a plot that moves at supersonic speed while showcasing deeply imagined characters…an impressive sensitivity to what has often loosely been called the human condition."

—*Newsday*

"You surrender yourself... King engulfs you... and carries you away to 4AM page-turning."

—*A.P. Wire*

"Enthralling... superb."

—*Dallas Times Herald*

"A spellbinder, a compulsive page-turner."

—*Atlanta Journal*

"Faultlessly paced... continuously engrossing."

—*Los Angeles Times*

"A literary triumph... Read this book."

—*Milwaukee Journal*

"Superbly crafted... extraordinary."

—*Booklist*

"His writing has a lyricism, an evocative descriptive sweep... It's a gift."

—*Columbia State*

"Dazzlingly well written."

—*The Indianapolis Star*

"King is a terrific storyteller."

—*San Francisco Chronicle*

"By far the world's most popular author... He never seems to use up the magic."

—*Chicago Tribune*

I stashed my basket of dirty rags and Turtle Wax by the exit door in the arcade. It was ten past noon, but right then food wasn't what I was hungry for. I walked slowly along the track and into Horror House.

I had to duck my head when I passed beneath the Screaming Skull, even though it was now pulled up and locked in its home position. My footfalls echoed on a wooden floor painted to look like stone. I could hear my breathing. It sounded harsh and dry. I was scared, okay? Tom had told me to stay away from this place, but Tom didn't run my life any more than Eddie Parks did.

Between the Dungeon and the Torture Chamber, the track descended and described a double-S curve where the cars picked up speed and whipped the riders back and forth. Horror House was a dark ride, but when it was in operation, this stretch was the only completely dark part. It had to be where the girl's killer had cut her throat and dumped her body. How quick he must have been, and how certain of exactly what he was going to do!

I walked slowly down the double-S, thinking it would not be beyond Eddie to hear me and shut off the overhead work-lights as a joke. To leave me in here to feel my way past the murder site with only the sound of the wind and that one slapping board to keep me company. And suppose...just suppose...a young girl's hand reached out in that darkness and took mine...?

SOME OTHER HARD CASE CRIME BOOKS YOU WILL ENJOY:

FIFTY-TO-ONE *by Charles Ardai*
KILLING CASTRO *by Lawrence Block*
THE DEAD MAN'S BROTHER *by Roger Zelazny*
THE CUTIE *by Donald E. Westlake*
HOUSE DICK *by E. Howard Hunt*
CASINO MOON *by Peter Blauner*
FAKE I.D. *by Jason Starr*
PASSPORT TO PERIL *by Robert B. Parker*
STOP THIS MAN! *by Peter Rabe*
LOSERS LIVE LONGER *by Russell Atwood*
HONEY IN HIS MOUTH *by Lester Dent*
QUARRY IN THE MIDDLE *by Max Allan Collins*
THE CORPSE WORE PASTIES *by Jonny Porkpie*
THE VALLEY OF FEAR *by A.C. Doyle*
MEMORY *by Donald E. Westlake*
NOBODY'S ANGEL *by Jack Clark*
MURDER IS MY BUSINESS *by Brett Halliday*
GETTING OFF *by Lawrence Block*
QUARRY'S EX *by Max Allan Collins*
THE CONSUMMATA
by Mickey Spillane and Max Allan Collins
CHOKE HOLD *by Christa Faust*
THE COMEDY IS FINISHED *by Donald E. Westlake*
BLOOD ON THE MINK *by Robert Silverberg*
FALSE NEGATIVE *by Joseph Koenig*
THE TWENTY-YEAR DEATH *by Ariel S. Winter*
THE COCKTAIL WAITRESS *by James M. Cain*
SEDUCTION OF THE INNOCENT *by Max Allan Collins*
WEB OF THE CITY *by Harlan Ellison*

JOYLAND

by **Stephen King**

A HARD CASE CRIME BOOK
(HCC-112)
First Hard Case Crime edition: June 2013

Published by

Titan Books
A division of Titan Publishing Group Ltd
144 Southwark Street
London
SE1 0UP

in collaboration with Winterfall LLC

ISBN 978-1-78116-264-4

Design direction by Max Phillips
www.maxphillips.net

Typeset by Swordsmith Productions

Printed in the United States of America

Visit us on the web at www.HardCaseCrime.com

For Donald Westlake

♥

I had a car, but on most days in that fall of 1973 I walked to Joyland from Mrs. Shoplaw's Beachside Accommodations in the town of Heaven's Bay. It seemed like the right thing to do. The only thing, actually. By early September, Heaven Beach was almost completely deserted, which suited my mood. That fall was the most beautiful of my life. Even forty years later I can say that. And I was never so unhappy, I can say that, too. People think first love is sweet, and never sweeter than when that first bond snaps. You've heard a thousand pop and country songs that prove the point; some fool got his heart broke. Yet that first broken heart is always the most painful, the slowest to mend, and leaves the most visible scar. What's so sweet about that?

♥

Through September and right into October, the North Carolina skies were clear and the air was warm even at seven in the morning, when I left my second-floor apartment by the outside stairs. If I started with a light jacket on, I was wearing it tied around my waist before I'd finished half of the three miles between the town and the amusement park.

I'd make Betty's Bakery my first stop, grabbing a couple of still-warm croissants. My shadow would walk with me on the sand, at least twenty feet long. Hopeful gulls, smelling the croissants in their waxed paper, would circle overhead. And when I walked back, usually around five (although sometimes I stayed later—there was nothing waiting for me in Heaven's Bay, a town that mostly went sleepybye when summer was over), my shadow walked with me on the water. If the tide was in, it would waver on the surface, seeming to do a slow hula.

Although I can't be completely sure, I think the boy and the woman and their dog were there from the first time I took that walk. The shore between the town and the cheerful, blinking gimcrackery of Joyland was lined with summer homes, many of them expensive, most of them clapped shut after Labor Day. But not the biggest of them, the one that looked like a green wooden castle. A boardwalk led from its wide back patio down to where the seagrass gave way to fine white sand. At the end of the boardwalk was a picnic table shaded by a bright green beach umbrella. In its shade, the boy sat in his wheelchair, wearing a baseball cap and covered from the waist down by a blanket even in the late afternoons, when the temperature lingered in the seventies. I thought he was five or so, surely no older than seven. The dog, a Jack Russell terrier, either lay beside him or sat at his feet. The woman sat on one of the picnic table benches, sometimes reading a book, mostly just staring out at the water. She was very beautiful.

Going or coming, I always waved to them, and the boy waved back. She didn't, not at first. 1973 was the year of the OPEC oil embargo, the year Richard Nixon announced he was not a crook, the year Edward G. Robinson and Noel Coward died. It was Devin Jones's lost year. I was a twenty-one year-old virgin with literary aspirations. I possessed three pairs of bluejeans, four pairs of Jockey shorts, a clunker Ford (with a good radio), occasional suicidal ideations, and a broken heart.

Sweet, huh?

♥

The heartbreaker was Wendy Keegan, and she didn't deserve me. It's taken me most of my life to come to that conclusion, but you know the old saw; better late than never. She was from Portsmouth, New Hampshire; I was from South Berwick, Maine. That made her practically the girl next door. We had begun "going together" (as we used to say) during our freshman year at UNH—we actually met at the Freshman Mixer, and how sweet is that? Just like one of those pop songs.

We were inseparable for two years, went everywhere together and did everything together. Everything, that is, but "it." We were both work-study kids with University jobs. Hers was in the library; mine was in the Commons cafeteria. We were offered the chance to hold onto those jobs during the summer of 1972, and of course we did. The money wasn't great, but the togetherness was priceless. I assumed that would also be the deal during the summer of 1973, until Wendy announced that her friend Renee had gotten them jobs working at Filene's, in Boston.

"Where does that leave me?" I asked.

"You can always come down," she said. "I'll miss you like mad, but really, Dev, we could probably use some time apart."

A phrase that is very often a death-knell. She may have seen that idea on my face, because she stood on tiptoe and kissed me. "Absence makes the heart grow fonder," she said. "Besides, with my own place, maybe you can stay over." But she didn't quite look at me when she said that, and I never did stay over. Too many roommates, she said. Too little time. Of course such problems can be overcome, but somehow we never did, which should have told me something; in retrospect, it tells me a lot. Several times we had been very close to "it," but "it" just never quite happened. She always drew back, and I never pressed her. God help me, I was being gallant. I have wondered often since what would have changed (for good or for ill) had I not been. What I know now is that gallant young men rarely get pussy. Put it on a sampler and hang it in your kitchen.

♥

The prospect of another summer mopping cafeteria floors and loading elderly Commons dishwashers with dirty plates didn't hold much charm for me, not with Wendy seventy miles south, enjoying the bright lights of Boston, but it was steady work, which I needed, and I didn't have any other prospects. Then, in late February, one literally came down the dish-line to me on the conveyor belt.

Someone had been reading *Carolina Living* while he or she snarfed up that day's blue plate luncheon special, which happened to be Mexicali Burgers and Caramba Fries. He or she had left the magazine on the tray, and I picked it up along with the dishes. I almost tossed it in the trash, then didn't. Free reading material was, after all, free reading material. (I was a work-study kid, remember.) I stuck it in my back pocket and forgot about it until I got back to my dorm room. There it flopped onto the floor, open to the classified section at the back, while I was changing my pants.

Whoever had been reading the magazine had circled several

job possibilities...although in the end, he or she must have decided none of them was quite right; otherwise *Carolina Living* wouldn't have come riding down the conveyor belt. Near the bottom of the page was an ad that caught my eye even though it hadn't been circled. In boldface type, the first line read: WORK CLOSE TO HEAVEN! What English major could read that and not hang in for the pitch? And what glum twenty-one-year-old, beset with the growing fear that he might be losing his girlfriend, would not be attracted by the idea of working in a place called Joyland?

There was a telephone number, and on a whim, I called it. A week later, a job application landed in my dormitory mailbox. The attached letter stated that if I wanted full-time summer employment (which I did), I'd be doing many different jobs, most but not all custodial. I would have to possess a valid driver's license, and I would need to interview. I could do that on the upcoming spring break instead of going home to Maine for the week. Only I'd been planning to spend at least some of that week with Wendy. We might even get around to "it."

"Go for the interview," Wendy said when I told her. She didn't even hesitate. "It'll be an adventure."

"Being with you would be an adventure," I said.

"There'll be plenty of time for that next year." She stood on tiptoe and kissed me (she always stood on tiptoe). Was she seeing the other guy, even then? Probably not, but I'll bet she'd noticed him, because he was in her Advanced Sociology course. Renee St. Claire would have known, and probably would have told me if I'd asked—telling stuff was Renee's specialty, I bet she wore the priest out when she did the old confession bit—but some things you don't want to know. Like why the girl you loved with all your heart kept saying no to you, but tumbled into bed with the new guy at almost the first opportunity. I'm not sure anybody ever gets completely over their first love, and that still rankles. Part of me still wants to know what was *wrong* with me. What I was lacking. I'm in my sixties now, my hair is gray and I'm a prostate cancer survivor, but I still want to know why I wasn't good enough for Wendy Keegan.

♥

I took a train called the Southerner from Boston to North Carolina (not much of an adventure, but cheap), and a bus from Wilmington to Heaven's Bay. My interview was with Fred Dean, who was—among many other functions—Joyland's employment officer. After fifteen minutes of Q-and-A, plus a look at my driver's license and my Red Cross life-saving certificate, he handed me a plastic badge on a lanyard. It bore the word VISITOR, that day's date, and a cartoon picture of a grinning, blue-eyed German Shepherd who bore a passing resemblance to the famous cartoon sleuth, Scooby-Doo.

"Take a walk around," Dean said. "Ride the Carolina Spin, if you like. Most of the rides aren't up and running yet, but that one is. Tell Lane I said okay. What I gave you is a day-pass, but I want you back here by…" He looked at his watch. "Let's say one o'clock. Tell me then if you want the job. I've got five spots left, but they're all basically the same—as Happy Helpers."

"Thank you, sir."

He nodded, smiling. "Don't know how you'll feel about this place, but it suits me fine. It's a little old and a little rickety, but I find that charming. I tried Disney for a while; didn't like it. It's too…I don't know…"

"Too corporate?" I ventured.

"Exactly. Too corporate. Too buffed and shiny. So I came back to Joyland a few years ago. Haven't regretted it. We fly a bit more by the seat of our pants here—the place has a little of the old-time carny flavor. Go on, look around. See what you think. More important, see how you *feel*."

"Can I ask one question first?"

"Of course."

I fingered my day pass. "Who's the dog?"

His smile became a grin. "That's Howie the Happy Hound, Joyland's mascot. Bradley Easterbrook built Joyland, and the original Howie was his dog. Long dead now, but you'll still see a lot of him, if you work here this summer."

I did...and I didn't. An easy riddle, but the explanation will have to wait awhile.

♥

Joyland was an indie, not as big as a Six Flags park, and nowhere near as big as Disney World, but it was large enough to be impressive, especially with Joyland Avenue, the main drag, and Hound Dog Way, the secondary drag, almost empty and looking eight lanes wide. I heard the whine of power-saws and saw plenty of workmen—the largest crew swarming over the Thunderball, one of Joyland's two coasters—but there were no customers, because the park didn't open until June fifteenth. A few of the food concessions were doing business to take care of the workers' lunch needs, though, and an old lady in front of a star-studded tell-your-fortune kiosk was staring at me suspiciously. With one exception, everything else was shut up tight.

The exception of the Carolina Spin. It was a hundred and

seventy feet tall (this I found out later), and turning very slowly. Out in front stood a tightly muscled guy in faded jeans, balding suede boots splotched with grease, and a strap-style tee shirt. He wore a derby hat tilted on his coal-black hair. A filterless cigarette was parked behind one ear. He looked like a cartoon carnival barker from an old-time newspaper strip. There was an open toolbox and a big portable radio on an orange crate beside him. The Faces were singing "Stay with Me." The guy was bopping to the beat, hands in his back pockets, hips moving side to side. I had a thought, absurd but perfectly clear: *When I grow up, I want to look just like this guy.*

He pointed to the pass. "Freddy Dean sent you, right? Told you everything else was closed, but you could take a ride on the big wheel."

"Yes, sir."

"A ride on the Spin means you're in. He likes the chosen few to get the aerial view. You gonna take the job?"

"I think so."

He stuck out his hand. "I'm Lane Hardy. Welcome aboard, kid."

I shook with him. "Devin Jones."

"Pleased to meet you."

He started up the inclined walk leading to the gently turning ride, grabbed a long lever that looked like a stick shift, and edged it back. The wheel came to a slow stop with one of the gaily painted cabins (the image of Howie the Happy Hound on each) swaying at the passenger loading dock.

"Climb aboard, Jonesy. I'm going to send you up where the air is rare and the view is much more than fair."

I climbed into the cabin and closed the door. Lane gave it a shake to make sure it was latched, dropped the safety bar, then returned to his rudimentary controls. "Ready for takeoff, cap'n?"

"I guess so."

"Amazement awaits." He gave me a wink and advanced the control stick. The wheel began to turn again and all at once he was looking up at me. So was the old lady by the fortune-telling booth. Her neck was craned and she was shading her eyes. I waved to her. She didn't wave back.

Then I was above everything but the convoluted dips and twists of the Thunderball, rising into the chilly early spring air, and feeling—stupid but true—that I was leaving all my cares and worries down below.

Joyland wasn't a theme park, which allowed it to have a little bit of everything. There was a secondary roller coaster called the Delirium Shaker and a water slide (Captain Nemo's Splash & Crash). On the far western side of the park was a special annex for the little ones called the Wiggle-Waggle Village. There was also a concert hall where most of the acts—this I also learned later—were either B-list C&W or the kind of rockers who peaked in the fifties or sixties. I remember that Johnny Otis and Big Joe Turner did a show there together. I had to ask Brenda Rafferty, the head accountant who was also a kind of den mother to the Hollywood Girls, who they were. Bren thought I was dense; I thought she was old; we were both probably right.

Lane Hardy took me all the way to the top and then stopped the wheel. I sat in the swaying car, gripping the safety bar, and looking out at a brand-new world. To the west was the North Carolina flatland, looking incredibly green to a New England kid who was used to thinking of March as nothing but true spring's cold and muddy precursor. To the east was the ocean, a deep metallic blue until it broke in creamy-white pulses on the beach where I would tote my abused heart up and down a few months hence. Directly below me was the good-natured jumble of Joyland—the big rides and small ones, the concert hall and concessions, the souvenir shops and the Happy Hound Shuttle, which took customers to the adjacent motels and, of course, the beach. To the north was Heaven's Bay. From high above the park (upstairs, where the air is rare), the town looked like a nestle of children's blocks from which four church steeples rose at the major points of the compass.

The wheel began to move again. I came down feeling like a kid in a Rudyard Kipling story, riding on the nose of an elephant. Lane Hardy brought me to a stop, but didn't bother to unlatch the car's door for me; I was, after all, almost an employee.

"How'd you like it?"

"Great," I said.

"Yeah, it ain't bad for a grandma ride." He reset his derby so it slanted the other way and cast an appraising eye over me. "How tall are you? Six-three?"

"Six-four."

"Uh-huh. Let's see how you like ridin all six-four of you on the Spin in the middle of July, wearin the fur and singin 'Happy Birthday' to some spoiled-rotten little snothole with cotton candy in one hand and a meltin Kollie Kone in the other."

"Wearing what fur?"

But he was headed back to his machinery and didn't answer. Maybe he couldn't hear me over his radio, which was now blasting "Crocodile Rock." Or maybe he just wanted my future occupation as one of Joyland's cadre of Happy Hounds to come as a surprise.

♥

I had over an hour to kill before meeting with Fred Dean again, so I strolled up Hound Dog Way toward a lunch-wagon that looked like it was doing a pretty good business. Not everything at Joyland was canine-themed, but plenty of stuff was, including this particular eatery, which was called Pup-A-Licious. I was on a ridiculously tight budget for this little job-hunting expedition, but I thought I could afford a couple of bucks for a chili-dog and a paper cup of French fries.

When I reached the palm-reading concession, Madame Fortuna planted herself in my path. Except that's not quite right, because she was only Fortuna between May fifteenth and Labor Day. During those sixteen weeks, she dressed in long skirts, gauzy, layered blouses, and shawls decorated with various cabalistic symbols. Gold hoops hung from her ears, so heavy they dragged the lobes down, and she talked in a thick Romany accent that made her sound like a character from a 1930s fright-flick, the kind featuring mist-shrouded castles and howling wolves.

During the rest of the year she was a widow from Brooklyn who collected Hummel figures and liked movies (especially the weepy-ass kind where some chick gets cancer and dies beautifully). Today she was smartly put together in a black pantsuit and low heels. A rose-pink scarf around her throat added a touch of color. As Fortuna, she sported masses of wild gray locks, but that was a wig, and still stored under its own glass dome in her little Heaven's Bay house. Her actual hair was a cropped cap of dyed black. The *Love Story* fan from Brooklyn and Fortuna the Seer only came together in one respect: both fancied themselves psychic.

"There is a shadow over you, young man," she announced.

I looked down and saw she was absolutely right. I was standing in the shadow of the Carolina Spin. We both were.

"Not that, stupidnik. Over your future. You will have a hunger."

I had a bad one already, but a Pup-A-Licious footlong would soon take care of it. "That's very interesting, Mrs…um…"

"Rosalind Gold," she said, holding out her hand. "But you can call me Rozzie. Everyone does. But during the season…" She fell into character, which meant she sounded like Bela Lugosi with breasts. "Doorink the season, I am…*Fortuna*!"

I shook with her. If she'd been in costume as well as in character, half a dozen gold bangles would have clattered on her wrist. "Very nice to meet you." And, trying on the same accent: "I am…*Devin*!"

She wasn't amused. "An Irish name?"

"Right."

"The Irish are full of sorrow, and many have the sight. I don't know if you do, but you will meet someone who does."

Actually, I was full of happiness…along with that surpassing desire to put a Pup-A-Licious pup, preferably loaded with chili, down my throat. This was feeling like an adventure. I told myself I'd probably feel less that way when I was swabbing out toilets at the end of a busy day, or cleaning puke from the seats of the Whirly Cups, but just then everything seemed perfect.

"Are you practicing your act?"

She drew herself up to her full height, which might have been five-two. "Is no act, my lad." She said *ect* for *act*. "Jews are the most psychically sensitive race on earth. This is a thing everyone knows." She dropped the accent. "Also, Joyland beats hanging out a palmistry shingle on Second Avenue. Sorrowful or not, I like you. You give off good vibrations."

"One of my very favorite Beach Boys songs."

"But you are on the edge of great sorrow." She paused, doing the old emphasis thing. "And, perhaps, danger."

"Do you see a beautiful woman with dark hair in my future?" Wendy was a beautiful woman with dark hair.

"No," Rozzie said, and what came next stopped me dead. "She is in your past."

Ohh-kay.

I walked around her in the direction of Pup-A-Licious, being careful not to touch her. She was a charlatan, I didn't have a single doubt about that, but touching her just then still seemed like a lousy idea.

No good. She walked with me. "In your future is a little girl and a little boy. The boy has a dog."

"A Happy Hound, I bet. Probably named Howie."

She ignored this latest attempt at levity. "The girl wears a red hat and carries a doll. One of these children has the sight. I don't know which. It is hidden from me."

I hardly heard that part of her spiel. I was thinking of the previous pronouncement, made in a flat Brooklyn accent: *She is in your past*.

Madame Fortuna got a lot of stuff wrong, I found out, but she *did* seem to have a genuine psychic touch, and on the day I interviewed for a summer at Joyland, she was hitting on all cylinders.

♥

I got the job. Mr. Dean was especially pleased by my Red Cross life-saving certificate, obtained at the YMCA the summer I turned sixteen. That was what I called my Boredom Summer.

In the years since, I've discovered there's a lot to be said for boredom.

I told Mr. Dean when my finals ended, and promised him that I'd be at Joyland two days later, ready for team assignment and training. We shook hands and he welcomed me aboard. I had a moment when I wondered if he was going to encourage me to do the Happy Hound Bark with him, or something equivalent, but he just wished me a good day and walked out of the office with me, a little man with sharp eyes and a lithe stride. Standing on the little cement-block porch of the employment office, listening to the pound of the surf and smelling the damp salt air, I felt excited all over again, and hungry for summer to begin.

"You're in the amusement business now, young Mr. Jones," my new boss said. "Not the carny business—not exactly, not the way we run things today—but not so far removed from it, either. Do you know what that means, to be in the amusement business?"

"No, sir, not exactly."

His eyes were solemn, but there was a ghost of a grin on his mouth. "It means the rubes have to leave with smiles on their faces—and by the way, if I ever hear *you* call the customers rubes, you're going to be out the door so fast you won't know what hit you. I can say it, because I've been in the amusement business since I was old enough to shave. They're rubes—no different from the redneck Okies and Arkies that rubbernecked their way through every carny I worked for after World War II. The people who come to Joyland may wear better clothes and drive Fords and Volkswagen microbuses instead of Farmall pickups, but the place turns em into rubes with their mouths hung open. If it doesn't, it's not doing its job. But to you, they're the conies. When *they* hear it, they think Coney Island. We know better. They're rabbits, Mr. Jones, nice plump fun-loving rabbits, hopping from ride to ride and shy to shy instead of from hole to hole."

He dropped me a wink and gave my shoulder a squeeze.

"The conies have to leave happy, or this place dries up and blows away. I've seen it happen, and when it does, it happens fast. It's an amusement park, young Mr. Jones, so pet the conies and give their ears only the gentlest of tugs. In a word, *amuse* them."

"Okay," I said...although I didn't know how much customer amusement I'd be providing by polishing the Devil Wagons (Joyland's version of Dodgem cars) or running a street-sweeper down Hound Dog Way after the gates closed.

"And don't you dare leave me in the lurch. Be here on the agreed-upon date, and five minutes before the agreed-upon time."

"Okay."

"There are two important showbiz rules, kiddo: always know where your wallet is...and *show up*."

♥

When I walked out beneath the big arch with WELCOME TO JOYLAND written on it in neon letters (now off) and into the mostly empty parking lot, Lane Hardy was leaning against one of the shuttered ticket booths, smoking the cigarette previously parked behind his ear.

"Can't smoke on the grounds anymore," he said. "New rule. Mr. Easterbrook says we're the first park in America to have it, but we won't be the last. Get the job?"

"I did."

"Congratulations. Did Freddy give you the carny spiel?"

"Sort of, yeah."

"Tell you about petting the conies?"

"Yeah."

"He can be a pain in the banana, but he's old-time showbiz, seen it all, most of it twice, and he's not wrong. I think you'll do okay. You've got a carny look about you, kid." He waved a hand at the park with its landmarks rising against the blameless blue sky: the Thunderball, the Delirium Shaker, the convoluted twists and turns of Captain Nemo's water slide, and—of course—the Carolina Spin. "Who knows, this place might be your future."

"Maybe," I said, although I already knew what my future was going to be: writing novels and the kind of short stories they publish in *The New Yorker*. I had it all planned out. Of course, I also had marriage to Wendy Keegan all planned out, and how we'd wait until we were in our thirties to have a couple of kids. When you're twenty-one, life is a roadmap. It's only when you get to be twenty-five or so that you begin to suspect you've been looking at the map upside down, and not until you're forty are you entirely sure. By the time you're sixty, take it from me, you're fucking lost.

"Did Rozzie Gold give you her usual bundle of Fortuna horseshit?"

"Um..."

Lane chuckled. "Why do I even ask? Just remember, kid, that ninety percent of everything she says really is horseshit. The other ten...let's just say she's told folks some stuff that rocked them back on their heels."

"What about you?" I asked. "Any revelations that rocked *you* back on your heels?"

He grinned. "The day I let Rozzie read my palm is the day I go back on the road, ride-jocking the tornado-and-chittlins circuit. Mrs. Hardy's boy doesn't mess with Ouija boards and crystal balls."

Do you see a beautiful woman with dark hair in my future? I'd asked.

No. She is in your past.

He was looking at me closely. "What's up? You swallow a fly?"

"It's nothing," I said.

"Come on, son. Did she feed you truth or horseshit? Live or Memorex? Tell your daddy."

"Definitely horseshit." I looked at my watch. "I've got a bus to catch at five, if I'm going to make the train to Boston at seven. I better get moving."

"Ah, you got plenty of time. Where you staying this summer?"

"I hadn't even thought about it."

"You might want to stop at Mrs. Shoplaw's on your way to the bus station. Plenty of people in Heaven's Bay rent to summer help, but she's the best. She's housed a lot of Happy Helpers over the years. Her place is easy to find; it's where Main Street ends at the beach. Great big rambler painted gray. You'll see the sign hanging from the porch. Can't miss it, because it's made out of shells and some're always falling off. MRS. SHOPLAW'S BEACHSIDE ACCOMMODATIONS. Tell her I sent you."

"Okay, I will. Thanks."

"If you rent there, you can walk down here on the beach if you want to save your gas money for something more important, like stepping out on your day off. That beach walk makes a pretty way to start the morning. Good luck, kid. Look forward to working with you." He held out his hand. I shook it and thanked him again.

Since he'd put the idea in my head, I decided to take the beach walk back to town. It would save me twenty minutes waiting for a taxi I couldn't really afford. I had almost reached the wooden stairs going down to the sand when he called after me.

"Hey, Jonesy! Want to know something Rozzie won't tell you?"

"Sure," I said.

"We've got a spook palace called Horror House. The old Roz-ola won't go within fifty yards of it. She hates the pop-ups and the torture chamber and the recorded voices, but the real reason is that she's afraid it really might be haunted."

"Yeah?"

"Yeah. And she ain't the only one. Half a dozen folks who work here claim to have seen her."

"Are you serious?" But this was just one of the questions you ask when you're flabbergasted. I could see he was.

"I'd tell you the story, but break-time's over for me. I've got some power-poles to replace on the Devil Wagons, and the safety inspection guys are coming to look at the Thunderball around three. What a pain in the ass those guys are. Ask Shoplaw. When it comes to Joyland, Emmalina Shoplaw knows more than I do. You could say she's a student of the place. Compared to her, I'm a newbie."

"This isn't a joke? A little rubber chicken you toss at all the new hires?"

"Do I look like I'm joking?"

He didn't, but he did look like he was having a good time. He even dropped me a wink. "What's a self-respecting amusement park without a ghost? Maybe you'll see her yourself. The rubes never do, that's for sure. Now hurry along, kiddo. Nail down a room before you catch the bus back to Wilmington. You'll thank me later."

♥

With a name like Emmalina Shoplaw, it was hard not to picture a rosy-cheeked landlady out of a Charles Dickens novel, one who went everywhere at a bosomy bustle and said things like *Lor' save us*. She'd serve tea and scones while a supporting cast of kind-hearted eccentrics looked on approvingly; she might even pinch my cheek as we sat roasting chestnuts over a crackling fire.

But we rarely get what we imagine in this world, and the gal who answered my ring was tall, fiftyish, flat-chested, and as pale as a frosted windowpane. She carried an old-fashioned beanbag ashtray in one hand and a smoldering cigarette in the other. Her mousy brown hair had been done up in fat coils that covered her ears. They made her look like an aging version of a princess in a Grimm's fairy tale. I explained why I was there.

"Going to work at Joyland, huh? Well, I guess you better come in. Do you have references?"

"Not apartment references, no—I live in a dorm. But I've got a work reference from my boss at the Commons. The Commons is the food-service cafeteria at UNH where I—"

"I know what a Commons is. I was born at night, but it wasn't last night." She showed me into the front parlor, a house-long room stuffed with mismatched furniture and dominated by a big table-model TV. She pointed at it. "Color. My renters are welcome to use it—and the parlor—until ten on weeknights and midnight on the weekends. Sometimes I join the kids for a movie or the Saturday afternoon baseball. We have pizza or I make popcorn. It's jolly."

Jolly, I thought. *As in jolly good*. And it sounded jolly good.

"Tell me, Mr. Jones, do you drink and get noisy? I consider that sort of behavior antisocial, although many don't."

"No, ma'am." I drank a little, but rarely got noisy. Usually after a beer or two, I just got sleepy.

"Asking if you use drugs would be pointless, you'd say no whether you do or not, wouldn't you? But of course that sort of thing always reveals itself in time, and when it does, I invite my renters to find fresh accommos. Not even pot, are we clear on that?"

"Yes."

She peered at me. "You don't *look* like a pothead."

"I'm not."

"I have space for four boarders, and only one of those places is currently taken. Miss Ackerley. She's a librarian. All my rents are single rooms, but they're far nicer than what you'd find at a motel. The one I'm thinking of for you is on the second floor. It has its own bathroom and shower, which those on the third floor do not. There's an outside staircase, too, which is convenient if you have a lady-friend. I have nothing against lady-friends, being both a lady and quite friendly myself. Do you have a lady-friend, Mr. Jones?"

"Yes, but she's working in Boston this summer."

"Well, perhaps you'll meet someone. You know what the song says—love is all around."

I only smiled at that. In the spring of '73, the concept of loving anyone other than Wendy Keegan seemed utterly foreign to me.

"You'll have a car, I imagine. There are just two parking spaces out back for four tenants, so every summer it's first come, first served. You're first come, and I think you'll do. If I find you don't, it's down the road you'll go. Does that strike you as fair?"

"Yes, ma'am."

"Good, because that's the way it is. I'll need the usual: first month, last month, damage deposit." She named a figure that also seemed fair. Nevertheless, it was going to make a shambles of my First New Hampshire Trust account.

"Will you take a check?"

"Will it bounce?"

"No, ma'am, not quite."

She threw back her head and laughed. "Then I'll take it, assuming you still want the room once you've seen it." She stubbed out her cigarette and rose. "By the way, no smoking upstairs—it's a matter of insurance. And no smoking in here, once there are tenants in residence. That's a matter of common politeness. Do you know that old man Easterbrook is instituting a no-smoking policy at the park?"

"I heard that. He'll probably lose business."

"He might at first. Then he might gain some. I'd put my money on Brad. He's a shrewd guy, carny-from-carny." I thought to ask her what that meant, exactly, but she had already moved on. "Shall we have a peek at the room?"

A peek at the second floor room was enough to convince me it would be fine. The bed was big, which was good, and the window looked out on the ocean, which was even better. The bathroom was something of a joke, so tiny that when I sat on the commode my feet would be in the shower, but college students with only crumbs in their financial cupboards can't be too picky. And the view was the clincher. I doubted if the rich folks had a better one from their summer places along Beach Row. I pictured bringing Wendy here, the two of us admiring the view, and then...in that big bed with the steady, sleepy beat of the surf outside...

"It." Finally, "it."

"I want it," I said, and felt my cheeks heat up. It wasn't just the room I was talking about.

"I know you do. It's all over your darn face." As if she knew what I was thinking, and maybe she did. She grinned—a big wide one that made her almost Dickensian in spite of her flat bosom and pale skin. "Your own little nest. Not the Palace of Versailles, but your own. Not like having a dorm room, is it? Even a single?"

"No," I admitted. I was thinking I'd have to talk my dad into putting another five hundred bucks into my bank account, to keep me covered until I started getting paychecks. He'd grouse but come through. I just hoped I wouldn't have to play the Dead Mom card. She had been gone almost four years, but Dad carried half a dozen pictures of her in his wallet, and still wore his wedding ring.

"Your own job and your own place," she said, sounding a bit dreamy. "That's good stuff, Devin. Do you mind me calling you Devin?"

"Make it Dev."

"All right, I will." She looked around the little room with its sharply sloping roof—it was under an eave—and sighed. "The thrill doesn't last long, but while it does, it's a fine thing. That sense of independence. I think you'll fit in here. You've got a carny look about you."

"You're the second person to tell me that." Then I thought of my conversation with Lane Hardy in the parking lot. "Third, actually."

"And I bet I know who the other two were. Anything else I can show you? The bathroom's not much, I know, but it beats having to take a dump in a dormitory bathroom while a couple of guys at the sinks fart and tell lies about the girls they made out with last night."

I burst into roars of laughter, and Mrs. Emmalina Shoplaw joined me.

♥

We descended by way of the outside stairs. "How's Lane Hardy?" she asked when we got to the bottom. "Still wearing that stupid beanie of his?"

"It looked like a derby to me."

She shrugged. "Beanie, derby, what's the diff?"

"He's fine, but he told me something…"

She was giving me a head-cocked look. Almost smiling, but not quite.

"He told me the Joyland funhouse—Horror House, he called it—is haunted. I asked him if he was pulling my leg, and he said he wasn't. He said you knew about it."

"Did he, now."

"Yes. He says that when it comes to Joyland, you know more than he does."

"Well," she said, reaching into the pocket of her slacks and bringing out a pack of Winstons, "I know a fair amount. My husband was chief of engineering down there until he took a heart attack and died. When it turned out his life insurance was lousy—and borrowed against to the hilt in the bargain—I started renting out the top two stories of this place. What else was I going to do? We just had the one kid, and now she's up in New York, working for an ad agency." She lit her cigarette, inhaled, and chuffed it back out as laughter. "Working on losing her southern accent, too, but that's another story. This overgrown monstrosity of a house was Howie's playtoy, and I never begrudged him. At least it's paid off. And I like staying connected to the park, because it makes me feel like I'm still connected to him. Can you understand that?"

"Sure."

She considered me through a rising raft of cigarette smoke, smiled, and shook her head. "Nah—you're being kind, but you're a little too young."

"I lost my Mom four years ago. My dad's still grieving. He says there's a reason *wife* and *life* sound almost the same. I've got school, at least, and my girlfriend. Dad's knocking around a house just north of Kittery that's way too big for him. He knows he should sell it and get a smaller one closer to where he works—we both know—but he stays. So yeah, I know what you mean."

"I'm sorry for your loss," Mrs. Shoplaw said. "Some day I'll open my mouth too wide and fall right in. That bus of yours, is it the five-ten?"

"Yes."

"Well, come on in the kitchen. I'll make you a toasted cheese and microwave you a bowl of tomato soup. You've got time. And I'll tell you the sad story of the Joyland ghost while you eat, if you want to hear it."

"Is it really a ghost story?"

"I've never been in that damn funhouse, so I don't know for sure. But it's a murder story. That much I *am* sure of."

♥

The soup was just Campbell's out of the can, but the toasted cheese was Muenster—my favorite—and tasted heavenly. She poured me a glass of milk and insisted I drink it. I was, Mrs. Shoplaw said, a growing boy. She sat down opposite me with her own bowl of soup but no sandwich ("I have to watch my girlish figure") and told me the tale. Some of it she'd gotten from the newspapers and TV reports. The juicier bits came from her Joyland contacts, of whom she had many.

"It was four years ago, which I guess would make it around the same time your mother died. Do you know what always comes first to my mind when I think about it? The guy's shirt. And the gloves. Thinking about those things gives me the creeps. Because it means he *planned* it."

"You might be kind of starting in the middle," I said.

Mrs. Shoplaw laughed. "Yeah, I suppose I am. The name of your supposed ghost is Linda Gray, and she was from Florence. That's over South Carolina way. She and her boyfriend—if that's what he was; the cops checked her background pretty closely and found no trace of him—spent her last night on earth at the Luna Inn, half a mile south of here along the beach. They entered Joyland around eleven o'clock the next day. He bought them day passes, using cash. They rode some rides and then had a late lunch at Rock Lobster, the seafood place down by the concert hall. That was just past one o'clock. As for the time of death, you probably know how they establish it...contents of the stomach and so on..."

"Yeah." My sandwich was gone, and I turned my attention to the soup. The story wasn't hurting my appetite any. I was twenty-one, remember, and although I would have told you different, down deep I was convinced I was never going to die. Not even my mother's death had been able to shake that core belief.

"He fed her, then he took her on the Carolina Spin—a slow ride, you know, easy on the digestion—and then he took her into Horror House. They went in together, but only he came out. About halfway along the course of the ride, which takes about nine minutes, he cut her throat and threw her out beside the monorail track the cars run on. Threw her out like a piece of trash. He must have known there'd be a mess, because he was wearing two shirts, and he'd put on a pair of yellow work-gloves. They found the top shirt—the one that would have caught most of the blood—about a hundred yards farther along from the body. The gloves a little farther along still."

I could see it: first the body, still warm and pulsing, then the shirt, then the gloves. The killer, meanwhile, sits tight and finishes the ride. Mrs. Shoplaw was right, it *was* creepy.

"When the ride ended, the son of a bee just got out and walked away. He mopped up the car—that shirt they found was soaking—but he didn't get quite all of the blood. One of the Helpers spotted some on the seat before the next ride started and cleaned it up. Didn't think twice about it, either. Blood on amusement park rides isn't unusual; mostly it's some kid who gets overexcited and has a nose-gusher. You'll find out for yourself. Just make sure you wear your own gloves when you do the cleanup, in case of diseases. They have em at all the first-aid stations, and there are first-aid stations all over the park."

"Nobody noticed that he got off the ride without his date?"

"Nope. This was mid-July, the very height of the season, and the place was a swarming madhouse. They didn't find the body until one o'clock the next morning, long after the park was closed and the Horror House work-lights were turned on. For the graveyard shift, you know. You'll get your chance to experience that; all the Happy Helper crews get cleanup duty one week a month, and you want to catch up on your sleep ahead of time, because that swing-shift's a booger."

"People rode past her until the park closed and didn't see her?"

"If they did, they thought it was just part of the show. But probably the body went unnoticed. Remember, Horror House is a dark ride. The only one in Joyland, as it happens. Other parks have more."

A dark ride. That struck a shivery chord, but it wasn't strong enough to keep me from finishing my soup. "What about a description of him? Maybe from whoever served them at the restaurant?"

"They had better than that. They had pictures. You want to believe the police made sure they got on TV and printed in the newspapers."

"How did that happen?"

"The Hollywood Girls," Mrs. Shoplaw said. "There are always half a dozen working the park when it's going full-blast. There's never been anything close to a cooch joint at Joyland, but old man Easterbrook didn't spend all those years in rolling carnies for nothing. He knows people like a little dash of sex appeal to go with the rides and the corndogs. There's one Hollywood Girl on each Helper team. You'll get yours, and you and the rest of the guys on your team will be expected to keep a big-brotherly eye out in case anyone bothers her. They run around in these short green dresses and green high heels and cutie-pie green hats that always make me think of Robin Hood and his Merry Men. Only they're the Merry Chicks. They tote Speed Graphic cameras, like the kind you see in old movies, and they take pictures of the rubes." She paused. "Although I'd advise you against calling the customers that yourself."

"Already been warned by Mr. Dean," I said.

"Figures. Anyhow, the Hollywood Girls are told to concentrate on family groups and dating couples who look over twenty-one. Kids younger than that usually aren't interested in souvenir photos; they'd rather spend their money on food and arcade games. So the deal is, the girls snap first, then approach." She did a breathy little Marilyn Monroe voice. " 'Hello, welcome to Joyland, I'm Karen! If you'd like a copy of the picture I just took, give me your name and check at the Hollywood Photo Booth on Hound Dog Way as you exit the park.' Like that.

"One of them took a picture of Linda Gray and her boyfriend at the Annie Oakley Shootin' Gallery, but when she approached, the guy gave her the brushoff. A *hard* brushoff. She told the cops later that he looked like he would've taken her camera and broken it, if he thought he could get away with it. Said his eyes gave her chills. Hard and gray, she said." Mrs. Shoplaw smiled and shrugged. "Only it turned out he was wearing sunglasses. You know how some girls like to dramatize."

As a matter of fact, I did. Wendy's friend Renee could turn a routine trip to the dentist into a horror-movie scenario.

"That was the best picture, but not the only one. The cops went through all the Hollywood Girl snaps from that day and found the Gray girl and her friend in the background of at least four others. In the best of those, they're standing in line for the Whirly Cups, and he's got his hand on her keister. Pretty chummy for someone none of her family or friends had ever seen before."

"Too bad there aren't closed-circuit TV cameras," I said. "My lady-friend got a job at Filene's in Boston this summer, and she says they've got a few of those cameras, and are putting in more. To foil shoplifters."

"A day will come when they have em everywhere," she said. "Just like in that science fiction book about the Thought Police. I don't look forward to it, either. But they'll never have them in rides like Horror House. Not even infrared ones that see in the dark."

"No?"

"Nope. There's no Tunnel of Love at Joyland, but Horror House is most definitely the Tunnel of Grope. My husband told me once that a day when the graveyard shift cleanup crew didn't find at least three pairs of panties beside the track was a slow day, indeed.

"But they did have that one great photo of the guy at the shooting gallery. A portrait, almost. It ran in the papers and on TV for a week. Him snuggled up to her hip to hip, showing her how to hold the rifle, the way the guys always do. Everyone in both Carolinas must have seen it. She's smiling, but he looks dead serious."

"With his gloves and knife in his pockets the whole time," I said. Marveling at the idea.

"Razor."

"Huh?"

"He used a straight razor or something like it, that's what the medical examiner figured. Anyway, they had those photos, including the one great one, and you know what? You can't make his face out in any of them."

"Because of the sunglasses."

"For starters. Also a goatee that covered his chin, and a baseball cap, the kind with a long bill, that shaded what little of his face the sunglasses and goatee didn't cover. Could have been anyone. Could have been you, except you're dark-haired instead of blond and don't have a bird's head tattooed on one of your hands. This guy did. An eagle or maybe a hawk. It showed up very clearly in the Shootin' Gallery pic. They ran a blowup of the tat in the paper for five days running, hoping someone would recognize it. Nobody did."

"No leads at the inn where they stayed the night before?"

"Uh-uh. He showed a South Carolina driver's license when he checked in, but it was stolen a year before. No one even saw her. She must have waited in the car. She was a Jane Doe for almost a week, but the police released a full-face sketch. Made her look like she was just sleeping, not dead with her throat cut. Someone—a friend she went to nursing school with, I think it was—saw it and recognized it. She told the girl's parents. I can't imagine how they must have felt, coming up here in their car and hoping against hope that when they got to the morgue, it would turn out to be someone else's well-loved child." She shook her head slowly. "Kids are such a risk, Dev. Did that ever cross your mind?"

"I guess so."

"Which means it hasn't. Me...I think if they turned back that sheet and it was my daughter lying there, I'd lose my mind."

"You don't think Linda Gray really haunts the funhouse, do you?"

"I can't answer that, because I hold no opinion on the afterlife, pro or con. My feeling is I'll find that stuff out when I get there, and that's good enough for me. All I know is that lots of people who work at Joyland claim to have seen her standing beside the track, wearing what she had on when they found her: blue skirt and blue sleeveless blouse. None of them would have seen those colors in the photos they released to the public, because the Speed Graphics the Hollywood Girls use only shoot black-and-white. Easier and cheaper to develop, I guess."

"Maybe the color of her clothes was mentioned in the articles."

She shrugged. "Might have been; I don't remember. But several people have also mentioned that the girl they saw standing by the track was wearing a blue Alice band, and that *wasn't* in the news stories. They held it back for almost a year, hoping to use it on a likely suspect if they came up with one."

"Lane said the rubes never see her."

"No, she only shows up after hours. It's mostly Happy Helpers on the graveyard shift who see her, but I know at least one safety inspector from Raleigh who claims he did, because I had a drink with him at the Sand Dollar. Guy said she was just standing there on his ride-through. He thought it was a new pop-up until she raised her hands to him, like this."

Mrs. Shoplaw held her hands out with the palms upturned, a supplicatory gesture.

"He said it felt like the temperature dropped twenty degrees.

A cold pocket, he called it. When he turned and looked back, she was gone."

I thought of Lane, in his tight jeans, scuffed boots, and tilted tuff-boy derby. *Truth or horseshit?* he'd asked. *Live or Memorex?* I thought the ghost of Linda Gray was almost certainly horseshit, but I hoped it wasn't. I hoped I would see her. It would be a great story to tell Wendy, and in those days, all my thoughts led back to her. If I bought this shirt, would Wendy like it? If I wrote a story about a young girl getting her first kiss while on a horseback ride, would Wendy enjoy it? If I saw the ghost of a murdered girl, would Wendy be fascinated? Maybe enough to want to come down and see for herself?

"There was a follow-up story in the Charleston *News and Courier* about six months after the murder," Mrs. Shoplaw said. "Turns out that since 1961, there have been four similar murders in Georgia and the Carolinas. All young girls. One stabbed, three others with their throats cut. The reporter dug up at least one cop who said all of them could have been killed by the guy who murdered Linda Gray."

"Beware the Funhouse Killer!" I said in a deep announcer-type voice.

"That's exactly what the paper called him. Hungry, weren't you? You ate everything but the bowl. Now I think you'd better write me that check and beat feet to the bus station, or you're apt to be spending the night on my sofa."

Which looked comfortable enough, but I was anxious to get back north. Two days left in spring break, and then I'd be back at school with my arm around Wendy Keegan's waist.

I took out my checkbook, scribbled, and by so doing rented a one-room apartment with a charming ocean view that Wendy Keegan—my lady-friend—never got a chance to sample. That room was where I sat up some nights with my stereo turned down low, playing Jimi Hendrix and the Doors, having those occasional thoughts of suicide. They were sophomoric rather than serious, just the fantasies of an over-imaginative young man with a heart condition...or so I tell myself now, all these years later, but who really knows?

When it comes to the past, *everyone* writes fiction.

♥

I tried to reach Wendy from the bus station, but her stepmom said she was out with Renee. When the bus got to Wilmington I tried again, but she was still out with Renee. I asked Nadine—the stepmom—if she had any idea where they might have gone. Nadine said she didn't. She sounded as if I were the most uninteresting caller she'd gotten all day. Maybe all year. Maybe in her life. I got along well enough with Wendy's dad, but Nadine Keegan was never one of my biggest fans.

Finally—I was in Boston by then—I got Wendy. She sounded sleepy, although it was only eleven o'clock, which is the shank of the evening to most college students on spring break. I told her I got the job.

"Hooray for you," she said. "Are you on your way home?"

"Yes, as soon as I get my car." And if it didn't have a flat tire. In those days I was always running on baldies and it seemed one of them was always going flat. A spare, you ask? Pretty funny, *señor*. "I could spend the night in Portsmouth instead of going straight home and see you tomorrow, if—"

"Wouldn't be a good idea. Renee's staying over, and that's about all the company Nadine can take. You know how *sensitive* she is about company."

Some company, maybe, but I thought Nadine and Renee

had always gotten on like a house afire, drinking endless cups of coffee and gossiping about their favorite movie stars as if they were personal friends, but this didn't seem like the time to say so.

"Ordinarily I'd love to talk to you, Dev, but I was getting ready to turn in. Me n Ren had a busy day. Shopping and…things."

She didn't elaborate on the *things* part, and I found I didn't care to ask about them. Another warning sign.

"Love you, Wendy."

"Love you, too." That sounded perfunctory rather than fervent. *She's just tired*, I told myself.

I rolled north out of Boston with a distinct feeling of unease. Something about the way she had sounded? That lack of enthusiasm? I didn't know. I wasn't sure I wanted to know. But I wondered. Sometimes even now, all these years later, I wonder. She's nothing to me these days but a scar and a memory, someone who hurt me as young women will hurt young men from time to time. A young woman from another life. Still I can't help wondering where she was that day. What those *things* were. And if it was really Renee St. Clair she was with.

We could argue about what constitutes the creepiest line in pop music, but for me it's early Beatles—John Lennon, actually—singing *I'd rather see you dead, little girl, than to be with another man*. I could tell you I never felt that way about Wendy in the aftermath of the breakup, but it would be a lie. It was never a constant thing, but did I think of her with a certain malevolence in the aftermath of the breakup? Yes. There were long and sleepless nights when I thought she deserved something bad—maybe really bad—to happen to her for the way she hurt me. It dismayed me to think that way, but sometimes

I did. And then I would think about the man who went into Horror House with his arm around Linda Gray and wearing two shirts. The man with the bird on his hand and a straight razor in his pocket.

♥

In the spring of 1973—the last year of my childhood, when I look back on it—I saw a future in which Wendy Keegan was Wendy Jones...or perhaps Wendy Keegan-Jones, if she wanted to be modern and keep her maiden name in the mix. There would be a house on a lake in Maine or New Hampshire (maybe western Massachusetts) filled with the clatter-and-yell of a couple of little Keegan-Joneses, a house where I wrote books that weren't exactly bestsellers but popular enough to keep us comfortably and were—*very* important—well reviewed. Wendy would pursue her dream of opening a small clothing boutique (also well reviewed), and I would teach a few creative writing seminars, the kind gifted students vie to get into. None of this ever happened, of course, so it was fitting that the last time we were together as a couple was in the office of Professor George B. Nako, a man who never was.

In the fall of 1968, returning University of New Hampshire students discovered Professor Nako's "office" under the stairs in the basement of Hamilton Smith Hall. The space was papered with fake diplomas, peculiar watercolors labeled Albanian Art, and seating plans with such names as Elizabeth Taylor, Robert Zimmerman, and Lyndon Beans Johnson penciled into the squares. There were also posted themes from students who never existed. One, I remember, was titled "Sex Stars of the Orient." Another was called "The Early Poetry of Cthulhu: An

Analysis." There were three standing ashtrays. A sign taped to the underside of the stairs read: PROFESSOR NAKO SEZ: "THE SMOKING LAMP IS ALWAYS LIT!" There were a couple of ratty easy chairs and an equally ratty sofa, very handy for students in search of a comfy make-out spot.

The Wednesday before my last final was unseasonably hot and humid. Around one in the afternoon, thunderheads began to build up, and around four, when Wendy had agreed to meet me in George B. Nako's underground "office," the skies opened and it began to pour. I got there first. Wendy showed up five minutes later, soaked to the skin but in high good humor. Droplets of water sparkled in her hair. She threw herself into my arms and wriggled against me, laughing. Thunder boomed; the few hanging lights in the gloomy basement hallway flickered.

"Hug me hug me hug me," she said. "That rain is *so* cold."

I warmed her up and she warmed me up. Pretty soon we were tangled together on the ratty sofa, my left hand curled around her and cupping her braless breast, my right far enough up her skirt to brush against silk and lace. She let that one stay there for a minute or two, then sat up, moved away from me, and fluffed her hair.

"Enough of that," she said primly. "What if Professor Nako came in?"

"I don't think that's likely, do you?" I was smiling, but below the belt I was feeling a familiar throb. Sometimes Wendy would relieve that throb—she had become quite expert at what we used to call a "through-the-pants job"—but I didn't think this was going to be one of those days.

"One of his students, then," she said. "Begging for a last-chance passing grade. 'Please, Professor Nako, please-please-*please*, I'll do anything.' "

That wasn't likely, either, but the chances of being interrupted were good, she was right about that. Students were always dropping by to put up new bogus themes or fresh works of Albanian art. The sofa was make-out friendly, but the locale wasn't. Once, maybe, but not since the understairs nook had become a kind of mythic reference-point for students in the College of Liberal Arts.

"How was your sociology final?" I asked her.

"Okay. I doubt if I aced it, but I know I passed it and that's good enough for me. Especially since it's the last one." She stretched, fingers touching the zig-zag of the stairs above us and lifting her breasts most entrancingly. "I'm out of here in…" She looked at her watch. "…exactly one hour and ten minutes."

"You and Renee?" I had no great liking for Wendy's roommate, but knew better than to say so. The one time I had, Wendy and I had had a brief, bitter argument in which she accused me of trying to manage her life.

"That is correct, sir. She'll drop me at my dad and stepmom's. And in one week, we're official Filene's employees!"

She made it sound as if the two of them had landed jobs as pages at the White House, but I held my peace on that, too. I had other concerns. "You're still coming up to Berwick on Saturday, right?" The plan was for her to arrive in the morning, spend the day, and stay over. She'd be in the guest bedroom, of course, but that was only a dozen steps down the hall. Given the fact that we might not see each other again until fall, I thought the possibility of "it" happening was very strong. Of course, little children believe in Santa Claus, and UNH freshmen sometimes went a whole semester believing that George B. Nako was a real professor, teaching real English courses.

"Absoloodle." She looked around, saw no one, and slipped a hand up my thigh. When it reached the crotch of my jeans, she tugged gently on what she found there. "Come here, you."

So I got my through-the-pants job after all. It was one of her better efforts, slow and rhythmic. The thunder rolled, and at some point the sigh of the pouring rain became a hard, hollow rattle as it turned to hail. At the end she squeezed, heightening and prolonging the pleasure of my orgasm.

"Make sure to get good and wet when you go back to your dorm, or the whole world will know exactly what we were doing down here." She bounced to her feet. "I have to go, Dev. I've still got some things to pack."

"I'll pick you up at noon on Saturday. My dad's making his famous chicken casserole for supper."

She once more said *absoloodle*; like standing on her tiptoes to kiss me, it was a Wendy Keegan trademark. Only on Friday night I got a call from her saying that Renee's plans had changed and they were leaving for Boston two days early. "I'm sorry, Dev, but she's my ride."

"There's always the bus," I said, already knowing that wasn't going to work.

"I promised, honey. And we have tickets for *Pippin*, at the Imperial. Renee's dad got them for us, as a surprise." She paused. "Be happy for me. You're going all the way to North Carolina, and I'm happy for *you*."

"Happy," I said. "Roger-wilco."

"That's better." Her voice dropped, became confidential. "Next time we're together, I'll make it up to you. Promise."

That was a promise she never kept but one she never had to break, either, because I never saw Wendy Keegan after that day in Professor Nako's "office." There wasn't even a final phone call filled with tears and accusations. That was on Tom Kennedy's advice (we'll get to him shortly), and it was probably a good thing. Wendy might have been expecting such a call, maybe even wished for it. If so, she was disappointed.

I hope she was. All these years later, with those old fevers and deliriums long in my past, I still hope she was.

Love leaves scars.

♥

I never produced the books I dreamed of, those well-reviewed almost-bestsellers, but I do make a pretty good living as a writer, and I count my blessings; thousands are not so lucky. I've moved steadily up the income ladder to where I am now, working at *Commercial Flight*, a periodical you've probably never heard of.

A year after I took over as editor-in-chief, I found myself back on the UNH campus. I was there to attend a two-day symposium on the future of trade magazines in the twenty-first century. During a break on the second day, I strolled over to Hamilton Smith Hall on a whim and peeked under the basement stairs. The themes, celebrity-studded seating charts, and Albanian artwork were gone. So were the chairs, the sofa, and the standing ashtrays. And yet *someone* remembered. Scotch-taped to the underside of the stairs, where there had once been a sign proclaiming that the smoking lamp was always lit, I saw a sheet of paper with a single typed line in print so small I had to lean close and stand on tiptoe in order to read it:

Professor Nako now teaches at the Hogwarts School of Witchcraft and Wizardry.

Well, why not?

Why the fuck not?

As for Wendy, your guess is as good as mine. I suppose I could use Google, that twenty-first century Magic 8-Ball, to chase her down and find out if she ever realized *her* dream, the one of owning the exclusive little boutique, but to what purpose? Gone is gone. Over is over. And after my stint in Joyland (just down the beach from a town called Heaven's Bay, let's not forget that), my broken heart seemed a lot less important. Mike and Annie Ross had a lot to do with that.

♥

My dad and I ended up eating his famous chicken casserole with no third party in attendance, which was probably all right with Timothy Jones; although he tried to hide it out of respect for me, I knew his feelings about Wendy were about the same as mine about Wendy's friend Renee. At the time, I thought it was because he was a bit jealous of Wendy's place in my life. Now I think he saw her more clearly than I could. I can't say for sure; we never talked about it. I'm not sure men know how to talk about women in any meaningful way.

After the meal was eaten and the dishes washed, we sat on the couch, drinking beer, eating popcorn, and watching a movie starring Gene Hackman as a tough cop with a foot fetish. I missed Wendy—probably at that moment listening to the *Pippin* company sing "Spread a Little Sunshine"—but there are advantages to the two-guy scenario, such as being able to belch and fart without trying to cover it up.

The next day—my last at home—we went for a walk along the disused railroad tracks that passed through the woods behind the house where I grew up. Mom's hard and fast rule had been that my friends and I had to stay away from those tracks. The last GS&WM freight had passed along them ten years before, and weeds were growing up between the rusty ties, but that made no difference to Mom. She was convinced that if we played there, one last train (call it the Kid-Eating Special) would go bulleting through and turn us all to paste. Only she was the one who got hit by an unscheduled train—metastatic breast cancer at the age of forty-seven. One mean fucking express.

"I'll miss having you around this summer," my dad said.

"I'll miss you, too."

"Oh! Before I forget." He reached into his breast pocket and brought out a check. "Be sure to open an account and deposit it first thing. Ask them to speed the clearance, if they can."

I looked at the amount: not the five hundred I'd asked for, but a thousand. "Dad, can you afford this?"

"Yes. Mostly because you held onto your Commons job, and that saved me having to try and make up the difference. Think of it as a bonus."

I kissed his cheek, which was scratchy. He hadn't shaved that morning. "Thanks."

"Kid, you're more welcome than you know." He took a handkerchief from his pocket and wiped his eyes matter-of-factly, without embarrassment. "Sorry about the waterworks. It's hard when your kids go away. Someday you'll find that out for yourself, but hopefully you'll have a good woman to keep you company after they're gone."

I thought of Mrs. Shoplaw saying *Kids are such a risk*. "Dad, are you going to be okay?"

He put the handkerchief back in his pocket and gave me a

grin, sunny and unforced. "Call me once in a while, and I will be. Also, don't let them put you to work climbing all over one of their damned roller coasters."

That actually sounded sort of exciting, but I told him I wouldn't.

"And—" But I never heard what he meant to say next, advice or admonition. He pointed. "Will you look at that!"

Fifty yards ahead of us, a doe had come out of the woods. She stepped delicately over one rusty GS&WM track and onto the railbed, where the weeds and goldenrod were so high they brushed against her sides. She paused there, looking at us calmly, ears cocked forward. What I remember about that moment was the silence. No bird sang, no plane went droning overhead. If my mother had been with us, she'd have had her camera and would have been taking pictures like mad. Thinking of that made me miss her in a way I hadn't in years.

I gave my father a quick, fierce hug. "I love you, Dad."

"I know," he said. "I know."

When I looked back, the deer was gone. A day later, so was I.

♥

When I got back to the big gray house at the end of Main Street in Heaven's Bay, the sign made of shells had been taken down and put in storage, because Mrs. Shoplaw had a full house for the summer. I blessed Lane Hardy for telling me to nail down a place to live. Joyland's summer troops had arrived, and every rooming house in town was full.

I shared the second floor with Tina Ackerley, the librarian. Mrs. Shoplaw had rented the accommodations on the third floor to a willowy redheaded art major named Erin Cook and a stocky undergrad from Rutgers named Tom Kennedy. Erin, who had taken photography courses both in high school and at Bard, had been hired as a Hollywood Girl. As for Tom and me…

"Happy Helpers," he said. "General employment, in other words. That's what that guy Fred Dean checked on my application. You?"

"The same," I said. "I think it means we're janitors."

"I doubt it."

"Really? Why?"

"Because we're white," he said, and although we did our share of clean-up chores, he turned out to be largely correct. The custodial crew—twenty men and over thirty women who dressed in coveralls with Howie the Happy Hound patches sewn on the breast pockets—were all Haitians and Dominicans, and almost surely undocumented. They lived in their own little village ten miles inland and were shuttled back and forth in a pair of retired school buses. Tom and I were making four dollars an hour; Erin a little more. God knows what the cleaners were making. They were exploited, of course, and saying that there were undocumented workers all over the south who had it far worse doesn't excuse it, nor does pointing out that it was forty years ago. Although there was this: they never had to put on the fur. Neither did Erin.

Tom and I did.

♥

On the night before our first day at work, the three of us were sitting in the parlor of *Maison* Shoplaw, getting to know each other and speculating on the summer ahead. As we talked, the moon rose over the Atlantic, as calmly beautiful as the doe my father and I had seen standing on the old railroad tracks.

"It's an amusement park, for God's sake," Erin said. "How tough can it be?"

"Easy for you to say," Tom told her. "No one's going to expect you to hose down the Whirly Cups after every brat in Cub Scout Pack 18 loses his lunch halfway through the ride."

"I'll pitch in where I have to," she said. "If it includes mopping up vomit as well as snapping pictures, so be it. I need this job. I've got grad school staring me in the face next year, and I'm exactly two steps from broke."

"We all ought to try and get on the same team," Tom said—and, as it turned out, we did. All the work teams at Joyland had doggy names, and ours was Team Beagle.

Just then Emmalina Shoplaw entered the parlor, carrying a tray with five champagne flutes on it. Miss Ackerley, a beanpole with huge bespectacled eyes that gave her a Joyce Carol Oatesian look, walked beside her, bottle in hand. Tom Kennedy brightened. "Do I spy French ginger ale? That looks just a leetle too elegant to be supermarket plonk."

"Champagne it is," Mrs. Shoplaw said, "although if you're expecting *Moet et Chandon*, young Mr. Kennedy, you're in for a disappointment. This isn't Cold Duck, but it's not the high-priced spread, either."

"I can't speak for my new co-workers," Tom said, "but as someone who educated his palate on Apple Zapple, I don't think I'll be disappointed."

Mrs. Shoplaw smiled. "I always mark the beginning of summer this way, for good luck. It seems to work. I haven't lost a seasonal hire yet. Each of you take a glass, please." We did as we were told. "Tina, will you pour?"

When the flutes were full, Mrs. Shoplaw raised hers and we raised ours.

"Here is to Erin, Tom, and Devin," she said. "May they have a wonderful summer, and wear the fur only when the temperature is below eighty degrees."

We clinked glasses and drank. Maybe not the high-priced spread, but pretty damned good, and with enough left for us all to have another swallow. This time it was Tom who offered the toast. "Here's to Mrs. Shoplaw, who gives us shelter from the storm!"

"Why, thank you, Tom, that's lovely. It won't get you a discount on the rent, though."

We drank. I set my glass down feeling just the tiniest bit buzzy. "What is this about wearing the fur?" I asked.

Mrs. Shoplaw and Miss Ackerley looked at each other and smiled. It was the librarian who answered, although it wasn't really an answer at all. "You'll find out," she said.

"Don't stay up late, children," Mrs. Shoplaw advised. "You've got an early call. Your career in show business awaits."

♥

The call *was* early: seven AM, two hours before the park opened its doors on another summer. The three of us walked down the beach together. Tom talked most of the way. He always talked. It would have been wearisome if he hadn't been so amusing and relentlessly cheerful. I could see from the way Erin (walking in the surf with her sneakers dangling from the fingers of her left hand) looked at him that she was charmed and fascinated. I envied Tom his ability to do that. He was heavyset and at least three doors down from handsome, but he was energetic and possessed of the gift of gab I sadly lacked. Remember the old joke about the starlet who was so clueless she fucked the writer?

"Man, how much do you think the people who own those

places are worth?" he asked, waving an arm at the houses on Beach Row. We were just passing the big green one that looked like a castle, but there was no sign of the woman and the boy in the wheelchair that day. Annie and Mike Ross came later.

"Millions, probably," Erin said. "It ain't the Hamptons, but as my dad would say, it ain't cheeseburgers."

"The amusement park probably brings the property values down a little," I said. I was looking at Joyland's three most distinctive landmarks, silhouetted against the blue morning sky: Thunderball, Delirium Shaker, Carolina Spin.

"Nah, you don't understand the rich-guy mindset," Tom said. "It's like when they pass bums looking for handouts on the street. They just erase em from their field of vision. Bums? What bums? And that park, same deal—what park? People who own these houses live, like, on another plane of existence." He stopped, shading his eyes and looking at the green Victorian that was going to play such a large part in my life that fall, after Erin Cook and Tom Kennedy, by then a couple, had gone back to school. "That one's gonna be mine. I'll be expecting to take possession on...mmm...June first, 1987."

"I'll bring the champagne," Erin said, and we all laughed.

♥

I saw Joyland's entire crew of summer hires in one place for the first and last time that morning. We gathered in Surf Auditorium, the concert hall where all those B-list country acts and aging rockers performed. There were almost two hundred of us. Most, like Tom, Erin, and me, were college students willing to work for peanuts. Some of the full-timers were there, as well. I saw Rozzie Gold, today dressed for work in her gypsy duds and dangly earrings. Lane Hardy was up on stage, placing a mike at the podium and then checking it with a series of thudding finger-taps. His derby was present and accounted for, cocked at its usual just-so angle. I don't know how he picked me out in all those milling kids, but he did, and sketched a little salute off the tilted brim of his lid. I sent him one right back.

He finished his work, nodded, jumped off the stage, and took the seat Rozzie had been saving for him. Fred Dean walked briskly out from the wings. "Be seated, please, all of you be seated. Before you get your team assignments, the owner of Joyland—and your employer—would like to say a few words. Please give a hand to Mr. Bradley Easterbrook."

We did as we were told, and an old man emerged from the wings, walking with the careful, high-stepping strides of someone with bad hips, a bad back, or both. He was tall and amazingly thin, dressed in a black suit that made him look more like an undertaker than a man who owned an amusement park. His face was long, pale, covered with bumps and moles. Shaving must have been torture for him, but he had a clean one. Ebony hair that had surely come out of a bottle was swept back from his deeply lined brow. He stood beside the podium, his enormous hands—they seemed to be nothing but knuckles—clasped before him. His eyes were set deep in pouched sockets.

Age looked at youth, and youth's applause first weakened, then died.

I'm not sure what we expected; possibly a mournful foghorn voice telling us that the Red Death would soon hold sway over all. Then he smiled, and it lit him up like a jukebox. You could almost hear a sigh of relief rustle through the summer hires. I found out later that was the summer Bradley Easterbrook turned ninety-three.

"You guys," he said, "welcome to Joyland." And then, before stepping behind the podium, he actually bowed to us. He took several seconds adjusting the mike, which produced a series of amplified screeks and scronks. He never took his sunken eyes from us as he did it.

"I see many returning faces, a thing that always makes me happy. For you greenies, I hope this will be the best summer of your lives, the yardstick by which you judge all your future employment. That is no doubt an extravagant wish, but anyone who runs a place like this year in and year out must have a wide streak of extravagance. For certain you'll never have another job like it."

He surveyed us, giving the poor mike's articulated neck another twist as he did so.

"In a few moments, Mr. Dean and Mrs. Brenda Rafferty, who is queen of the front office, will give you your team assignments. There will be seven of you to a team, and you will be expected to act as a team and work as a team. Your team's tasks will be assigned by your team leader and will vary from week to week, sometimes from day to day. If variety is the spice of life, you will find the next three months very spicy, indeed. I hope you will keep one thought foremost in your mind, young ladies and gentlemen. Will you do that?"

He paused as if expecting us to answer, but nobody made a sound. We only looked at him, a very old man in a black suit and a white shirt open at the collar. When he spoke again, it might have been himself he was talking to, at least to begin with.

"This is a badly broken world, full of wars and cruelty and senseless tragedy. Every human being who inhabits it is served his or her portion of unhappiness and wakeful nights. Those of you who don't already know that will come to know it. Given such sad but undeniable facts of the human condition, you have been given a priceless gift this summer: you are here to sell fun. In exchange for the hard-earned dollars of your customers, you will parcel out happiness. Children will go home and dream of what they saw here and what they did here. I hope you will remember that when the work is hard, as it sometimes will be, or when people are rude, as they often will be, or when you feel your best efforts have gone unappreciated. This is a different world, one that has its own customs and its own language, which we simply call the Talk. You'll begin learning it today. As you learn to talk the Talk, you'll learn to walk the walk. I'm not going to explain that, because it can't be explained; it can only be learned."

Tom leaned close to me and whispered, "Talk the talk? Walk the walk? Did we just wander into an AA meeting?"

I hushed him. I had come in expecting to get a list of commandments, mostly *thou shalt nots*; instead I had gotten a kind of rough poetry, and I was delighted. Bradley Easterbrook surveyed us, then suddenly displayed those horsey teeth in another grin. This one looked big enough to eat the world. Erin Cook was staring at him raptly. So were most of the new summer hires. It was the way students stare at a teacher who offers a new and possibly wonderful way of looking at reality.

"I hope you'll enjoy your work here, but when you don't—when, for instance, it's your turn to wear the fur—try to remember how privileged you are. In a sad and dark world, we are a little island of happiness. Many of you already have plans for your lives—you hope to become doctors, lawyers, I don't know, politicians—"

"*OH-GOD-NO!*" someone shouted, to general laughter.

I would have said Easterbrook's grin could not possibly have widened, but it did. Tom was shaking his head, but he had also given in. "Okay, now I get it," he whispered in my ear. "This guy is the Jesus of Fun."

"You'll have interesting, fruitful lives, my young friends. You'll do many good things and have many remarkable experiences. But I hope you'll always look back on your time in Joyland as something special. We don't sell furniture. We don't sell cars. We don't sell land or houses or retirement funds. We have no political agenda. *We sell fun*. Never forget that. Thank you for your attention. Now go forth."

He stepped away from the podium, gave another bow, and left the stage in that same painful, high-stepping stride. He was gone almost before the applause began. It was one of the best speeches I ever heard, because it was truth rather than horseshit. I mean, listen: how many rubes can put *sold fun for three months in 1973* on their resumes?

♥

All the team leaders were long-time Joyland employees who worked the carny circuit as showies in the off-season. Most were also on the Park Services Committee, which meant they had to deal with state and federal regulations (both very loose in 1973), and field customer complaints. That summer most of the complaints were about the new no-smoking policy.

Our team leader was a peppy little guy named Gary Allen, a

seventy-something who ran the Annie Oakley Shootin' Gallery. Only none of us called it that after the first day. In the Talk, a shooting gallery was a bang-shy and Gary was the bang-shy agent. The seven of us on Team Beagle met him at his joint, where he was setting out rifles on chains. My first official Joyland job—along with Erin, Tom, and the other four guys on the team—was putting the prizes on the shelves. The ones that got pride of place were the big fuzzy stuffed animals that hardly anyone ever won…although, Gary said, he was careful to give out at least one every evening when the tip was hot.

"I like the marks," he said. "Yes I do. And the marks I like the best are the points, by which I mean the purty girls, and the points I like the best are the ones who wear the low-cut tops and bend forrad to shoot like this." He snatched up a .22 modified to shoot BBs (it had also been modified to make a loud and satisfying bang with each trigger-pull) and leaned forward to demonstrate.

"When a guy does that, I notify em that they're foulin the line. The points? Never."

Ronnie Houston, a bespectacled, anxious-looking young man wearing a Florida State University cap, said: "I don't see any foul-line, Mr. Allen."

Gary looked at him, hands fisted on non-existent hips. His jeans seemed to be staying up in defiance of gravity. "Listen up, son, I got three things for you. Ready?"

Ronnie nodded. He looked like he wanted to take notes. He also looked like he wanted to hide behind the rest of us.

"First thing. You can call me Gary or Pops or come here you old sonofabitch, but I ain't no schoolteacher, so can the mister. Second thing. I never want to see that fucking schoolboy hat on your head again. Third thing. The foul line is wherever I say the foul line is on any given night. I can do that because it's in my *myyyyynd*." He tapped one sunken, vein-gnarled temple to make this point perfectly clear, then waved at the prizes, the targets, and the counter where the conies—the rubes—laid down their mooch. "This is all in my *myyyyynd. The shy is mental.* Geddit?"

Ronnie didn't, but he nodded vigorously.

"Now whip off that turdish-looking schoolboy hat. Get you a Joyland visor or a Howie the Happy Hound dogtop. Make it Job One."

Ronnie whipped off his FSU lid with alacrity, and stuck it in his back pocket. Later that day—I believe within the hour—he replaced it with a Howie cap, known in the Talk as a dogtop. After three days of ribbing and being called greenie, he took his new dogtop out to the parking lot, found a nice greasy spot, and trompled it for a while. When he put it back on, it had the right look. Or almost. Ronnie Houston never got the *complete* right look; some people were just destined to be greenies forever. I remember Tom sidling up to him one day and suggesting that he needed to piss on it a little to give it that final touch that means so much. When he saw Ronnie was on the verge of taking him seriously, Tom backpedaled and said just soaking it in the Atlantic would achieve the same effect.

Meanwhile, Pops was surveying us.

"Speaking of good-looking ladies, I perceive we have one among us."

Erin smiled modestly.

"Hollywood Girl, darlin?"

"That's what Mr. Dean said I'd be doing, yes."

"Then you want to go see Brenda Rafferty. She's second-in-command around here, and she's also the park Girl Mom. She'll get you fitted up with one of those cute green dresses. Tell her you want yours extra-short."

"The hell I will, you old lecher," Erin said, and promptly joined him when he threw back his head and bellowed laughter.

"Pert! Sassy! Do I like it? I do! When you're not snappin pix of the conies, you come on back to your Pops and I'll find you something to do…but change out of the dress first. You don't get grease or sawdust on it. *Kapish*?"

"Yes," Erin said. She was all business again.

Pops Allen looked at his watch. "Park opens in one hour, kiddies, then you'll learn while you earn. Start with the rides." He pointed to us one by one, naming rides. I got the Carolina Spin, which pleased me. "Got time for a question or two, but no more'n that. Anybody got one or are you good to go?"

I raised my hand. He nodded at me and asked my name.

"Devin Jones, sir."

"Call me sir again and you're fired, lad."

"Devin Jones, Pops." I certainly wasn't going to call him *come here you old sonofoabitch*, at least not yet. Maybe when we knew each other better.

"There you go," he said, nodding. "What's on your mind, Jonesy? Besides that foine head of red hair?"

"What's carny-from-carny mean?"

"Means you're like old man Easterbrook. His father worked the carny circuit back in the Dust Bowl days, and his grandfather worked it back when they had a fake Indian show featuring Big Chief Yowlatcha."

"You *got* to be *kidding*!" Tom exclaimed, almost exultantly.

Pops gave him a cool stare that settled Tom down—a thing not always easy to do. "Son, do you know what history is?"

"Uh…stuff that happened in the past?"

"Nope," he said, tying on his canvas change-belt. "History is the collective and ancestral shit of the human race, a great big and ever-growin pile of crap. Right now we're standin at the top of it, but pretty soon we'll be buried under the doodoo of generations yet to come. That's why your folks' clothes look so funny in old photographs, to name but a single example. And, as someone who's destined to be buried beneath the shit of your children and grandchildren, I think you should be just a *leetle* more forgiving."

Tom opened his mouth, probably to make a smart comeback, then wisely closed it again.

George Preston, another member of Team Beagle, spoke up. "Are *you* carny-from-carny?"

"Nope. My daddy was a cattle rancher in Oregon; now my brothers run the spread. I'm the black sheep of the family, and damn proud of it. Okay, if there's nothing else, it's time to quit the foolishness and get down to business."

"Can I ask one thing more?" Erin asked.

"Only because you're purty."

"What does 'wearing the fur' mean?"

Pops Allen smiled. He placed his hands on the mooch-counter of his shy. "Tell me, little lady, do you have an idea what it *might* mean?"

"Well…yes."

The smile widened into a grin that showed every yellowing fang in our new team leader's mouth. "Then you're probably right."

♥

What did I do at Joyland that summer? Everything. Sold tickets. Pushed a popcorn wagon. Sold funnel cakes, cotton candy, and a zillion hot dogs (which we called Hound Dogs—you probably knew that). It was a Hound Dog that got my picture in the paper, as a matter of fact, although I wasn't the guy who sold that unlucky pup; George Preston did. I worked as a lifeguard, both on the beach and at Happy Lake, the indoor pool where the Splash & Crash water slide ended. I line-danced in the Wiggle-Waggle Village with the other members of Team Beagle to "Bird Dance Beat," "Does Your Chewing Gum Lose Its Flavor on the Bedpost Overnight," "Rippy-Rappy, Zippy-Zappy," and a dozen other nonsense songs. I also did time—most of it happy—as an unlicensed child-minder. In the Wiggle-Waggle, the approved rallying cry when faced with a bawling kiddie was "Let's turn that frown upside-down!" and I not only liked it, I got good at it. It was in the Wiggle-Waggle that I decided having kids at some point in the future was an actual Good Idea rather than a Wendy-flavored daydream.

I—and all the other Happy Helpers—learned to race from one side of Joyland to the other in nothing flat, using either the alleys behind the shys, joints, rides, and concessions or one of three service-tunnels known as Joyland Under, Hound Dog Under, and the Boulevard. I hauled trash by the ton, usually driving it in an electric cart down the Boulevard, a shadowy and sinister thoroughfare lit by ancient fluorescent bar-lights that stuttered and buzzed. I even worked a few times as a roadie, hauling amps and monitors when one of the acts showed up late and unsupported.

I learned to talk the Talk. Some of it—like bally for a free show, or gone larry for a ride that had broken down—was pure carny, and as old as the hills. Other terms—like points for purty girls and fumps for the chronic complainers—were strictly Joyland lingo. I suppose other parks have their own version of the Talk, but underneath it's always carny-from-carny. A hammer-squash is a cony (usually a fump) who bitches about having to wait in line. The last hour of the day (at Joyland, that was ten PM to eleven) was the blow-off. A cony who loses at some shy and wants his mooch back is a mooch-hammer. The donniker is the bathroom, as in "Hey, Jonesy, hustle down to the donniker by the Moon Rocket—some dumb fump just puked in one of the sinks."

Running the concessions (known as joints) came easy to most of us, and really, anyone who can make change is qualified to push the popcorn wagon or work the counter of a souvenir shop. Learning to ride-jock wasn't much more difficult, but it was scary at first, because there were lives in your hands, many those of little children.

♥

"Here for your lesson?" Lane Hardy asked me when I joined him at the Carolina Spin. "Good. Just in time. Park opens in twenty minutes. We do it the way they do in the navy—see one, do one, teach one. Right now that heavyset kid you were standing next to—"

"Tom Kennedy."

"Okay. Right now Tom's over learning the Devil Wagons. At some point—probably this very day—he's gonna teach you how to run the ride, and you'll teach him how to run the Spin. Which, by the way, is an Aussie Wheel, meaning it runs counterclockwise."

"Is that important?"

"Nope," he said, "but I think it's interesting. There are only a few in the States. It has two speeds: slow and *really* slow."

"Because it's a grandma ride."

"Correctamundo." He demonstrated with the long stick shift I'd seen him operating on the day I got my job, then made me take over the stick with the bicycle handgrip at the top. "Feel it click when it's in gear?"

"Yes."

"Here's stop." He put his hand over mine and pulled the lever all the way up. This time the click was harder, and the enormous wheel stopped at once, the cars rocking gently. "With me so far?"

"I guess so. Listen, don't I need a permit or a license or something to run this thing?"

"You *got* a license, don't you?"

"Sure, a Maine driver's license, but—"

"In North Carolina, a valid DL's all you need. They'll get around to additional regulations in time—they always do—but for this year, at least, you're good to go. Now pay attention, because this is the most important part. Do you see that yellow stripe on the side of the housing?"

I did. It was just to the right of the ramp leading up to the ride.

"Each car has a Happy Hound decal on the door. When you see the Hound lining up with the yellow stripe, you pull stop, and there'll be a car right where the folks get on." He yanked the lever forward again. "See?"

I said I did.

"Until the wheel's tipsed—"

"What?"

"Loaded. Tipsed means loaded. Don't ask me why. Until the wheel's tipsed, you just alternate between super-slow and stop. Once you've got a full load—which you'll have most of the time, if we have a good season—you go to the normal slow speed. They get four minutes." He pointed to his suitcase radio. "It's my boomie, but the rule is when you run the ride, you control the tunes. Just no real blasting rock and roll—Who, Zep, Stones, stuff like that—until after the sun goes down. Got it?"

"Yeah. What about letting them off?"

"Exactly the same. Super-slow, stop. Super-slow, stop. Always line up the yellow stripe with the Happy Hound, and you'll always have a car right at the ramp. You should be able to get ten spins an hour. If the wheel's loaded each time, that's over seven hundred customers, which comes to almost a d-note."

"Which is what, in English?"

"Five hundred."

I looked at him uncertainly. "I won't really have to do this, will I? I mean, it's your ride."

"It's Brad Easterbrook's ride, kiddo. They all are. I'm just another employee, although I've been here a few years. I'll run the hoister most of the time, but not *all* of the time. And hey, stop sweating. There are carnies where half-drunk bikers covered with tattoos do this, and if they can, you can."

"If you say so."

Lane pointed. "Gates're open and here come the conies, rolling down Joyland Avenue. You're going to stick with me for the first three rides. Later on you teach the rest of your team, and that includes your Hollywood Girl. Okay?"

It wasn't even close to okay—I was supposed to send people a hundred and seventy feet in the air after a five-minute tutorial? It was insane.

He gripped my shoulder. "You can do this, Jonesy. So never mind 'if you say so.' Tell me it's okay."

"It's okay," I said.

"Good boy." He turned on his radio, now hooked to a speaker high on the Spin's frame. The Hollies began to sing "Long Cool Woman in a Black Dress" as Lane took a pair of rawhide gloves from the back pocket of his jeans. "And get you a pair of these—you're going to need them. Also, you better start learning how to pitch." He bent down, grabbed a hand-held mike from the ever-present orange crate, put one foot up, and began to work the crowd.

"Hey folks welcome in, time to take a little spin, hurry hurry, summer won't last forever, take a ride upstairs where the air is rare, this is where the fun begins, step over here and ride the Spin."

He lowered the mike and gave me a wink. "That's my pitch, more or less; give me a drink or three and it gets a lot better. You work out your own."

The first time I ran the Spin by myself, my hands were shaking with terror, but by the end of that first week I was running it like a pro (although Lane said my pitch needed a lot of work). I was also capable of running the Whirly Cups and the Devil Wagons…although ride-jocking the latter came down to little more than pushing the green START button, the red STOP button, and getting the cars untangled when the rubes got them stuck together against the rubber bumpers, which was at least four times during each four-minute ride. Only when you were running the Devil Wagons, you didn't call them rides; each run was a spree.

I learned the Talk; I learned the geography, both above and below ground; I learned how to run a joint, take over a shy, and award plushies to good-looking points. It took a week or so to get most of it down, and it was two weeks before I started getting comfortable. Wearing the fur, however, I understood by twelve-thirty on my first day, and it was just my luck—good or bad—that Bradley Easterbrook happened to be in Wiggle-Waggle Village at the time, sitting on a bench and eating his usual lunch of bean sprouts and tofu—hardly amusement park chow, but let's keep in mind that the man's food-processing system hadn't been new since the days of bathtub gin and flappers.

After my first impromptu performance as Howie the Happy Hound, I wore the fur a lot. Because I was good at it, you see. And Mr. Easterbrook *knew* I was good at it. I was wearing it a month or so later, when I met the little girl in the red hat on Joyland Avenue.

♥

That first day was a madhouse, all right. I ran the Carolina Spin with Lane until ten o'clock, then alone for the next ninety minutes while he rushed around the park putting out opening day fires. By then I no longer believed the wheel was going to malfunction and start running out of control, like the merry-go-round in that old Alfred Hitchcock movie. The most terrifying thing was how *trusting* people were. Not a single dad with kids in tow detoured to my pitch to ask if I knew what I was doing. I didn't get as many spins as I should have—I was concentrating so hard on that damn yellow stripe that I gave myself a headache—but every spin I did get was tipsed.

Erin came by once, pretty as a picture in her green Hollywood Girl dress, and took pictures of some of the family groups waiting to get on. She took one of me, too—I still have it somewhere. When the wheel was turning again, she gripped me by the arm, little beads of sweat standing out on her forehead, her lips parted in a smile, her eyes shining.

"Is this great, or what?" she asked.

"As long as I don't kill anybody, yeah," I said.

"If some little kid falls out of a car, just make sure you catch him." Then, having given me something new to obsess about, she jogged off in search of new photo subjects. There was no shortage of people willing to pose for a gorgeous redhead on a summer morning. And she was right, actually. It was pretty great.

Around eleven-thirty, Lane came back. By that point, I was comfortable enough ride-jocking the Spin to turn the rudimentary controls over to him with some reluctance.

"Who's your team leader, Jonesy? Gary Allen?"

"That's right."

"Well, go on over to his bang-shy and see what he's got for you. If you're lucky, he'll send you down to the boneyard for lunch."

"What's the boneyard?"

"Where the help goes when they've got time off. Most carnies, it's the parking lot or out behind the trucks, but Joyland's lux. There's a nice break-room where the Boulevard and Hound Dog Under connect. Take the stairs between the balloon-pitch and the knife-show. You'll like it, but you only eat if Pop says it's okay. I ain't getting in dutch with that old bastard. His team is his team; I got my own. You got a dinner bucket?"

"Didn't know I was supposed to bring one."

He grinned. "You'll learn. For today, stop at Ernie's joint—the fried chicken place with the big plastic rooster on top. Show him your Joyland ID card and he'll give you the company discount."

I did end up eating fried chicken at Ernie's, but not until two that afternoon. Pop had other plans for me. "Go by the costume shop—it's the trailer between Park Services and the carpentry shop. Tell Dottie Lassen I sent you. Damn woman's busting her girdle."

"Want me to help you reload first?" The Shootin' Gallery was also tipsed, the counter crowded with high school kids anxious to win those elusive plushies. More rubes (so I was already thinking of them) were lined up three deep behind the current shooters. Pop Allen's hands never stopped moving as he talked to me.

"What I want is for you to get on your pony and ride. I was doin this shit long before you were born. Which one are you, anyway, Jonesy or Kennedy? I know you're not the dingbat in the college-boy hat, but beyond that I can't remember."

"I'm Jonesy."

"Well, Jonesy, you're going to spend an edifying hour in the Wiggle-Waggle. It'll be edifying for the kiddies, anyhow. For you, maybe not so much." He bared his yellow fangs in a trademark Pop Allen grin, the one that made him look like an elderly shark. "Enjoy that fur suit."

♥

The costume shop was also a madhouse, filled with women running every whichway. Dottie Lassen, a skinny lady who needed a girdle like I needed elevator shoes, fell on me the second I walked through the door. She hooked her long-nailed fingers into my armpit and dragged me past clown costumes, cowboy costumes, a huge Uncle Sam suit (with stilts leaning beside it against the wall), a couple of princess outfits, a rack of Hollywood Girl dresses, and a rack of old-fashioned Gay Nineties bathing suits…which, I found out, we were condemned to wear when on lifeguard duty. At the very back of her crowded little empire were a dozen deflated dogs. Howies, in fact, complete with the Happy Hound's delighted stupid-and-loving-it grin, his big blue eyes, and his fuzzy cocked ears. Zippers ran down the backs of the suits from the neck to the base of the tail.

"Christ, you're a big one," Dottie said. "Thank God I got the extra-large mended last week. The last kid who wore it ripped it out under both arms. There was a hole under the tail, too. He must have been eating Mexican food." She snatched the XL Howie off the rack and slammed it into my arms. The tail curled around my leg like a python. "You're going to the Wiggle-Waggle, and I mean chop-fucking-chop. Butch Hadley was supposed to take care of that from Team Corgi—or so I thought—but he says his whole team's out with a key to the midway." I had no idea what that meant, and Dottie gave me no time to ask. She rolled her eyes in a way that indicated either good humor or the onset of madness, and continued. "You say 'What's the big deal?' I'll tell you what's the big deal, greenie: Mr. Easterbrook usually eats his lunch there, he *always* eats it there on the first day we're running full-out, and if there's no Howie, he'll be very disappointed."

"Like as in someone will get fired?"

"No, as in very disappointed. Stick around awhile and you'll know that's plenty bad enough. No one wants to disappoint him, because he's a great man. Which is nice, I suppose, but what's more important is he's a good guy. In this business, good guys are scarcer than hen's teeth." She looked at me and made a sound like a small animal with its paw caught in a trap. "Dear *Christ*, you're a big one. And green as grass. But it can't be helped."

I had a billion questions, but my tongue was frozen. All I could do was stare at the deflated Howie. Who stared back at me. Do you know what I felt like just then? James Bond, in the movie where he's tied to some kind of crazy exercise gadget. *Do you expect me to talk?* he asks Goldfinger, and Goldfinger replies, with chilling good humor, *No, Mr. Bond! I expect you to die!* I was tied to a happiness machine instead of an exercise machine, but hey, same idea. No matter how hard I worked to keep up on that first day, the damn thing just kept going faster.

"Take it down to the boneyard, kid. Please tell me you know where that is."

"I do." Thank God Lane had told me.

"Well, that's one for the home team, anyway. When you get there, strip down to your undies. If you wear more than that while you're wearing the fur, you'll roast. And…anybody ever tell you the First Rule of Carny, kid?"

I thought so, but it seemed safer to keep my mouth shut.

"Always know where your wallet is. This park isn't anywhere near as sleazy as some of the places I worked in the flower of my youth—thank God—but that's still the First Rule. Give it to me, I'll keep it for you."

I handed over my wallet without protest.

"Now go. But even before you strip down, drink a lot of water. I mean until your belly feels swollen. And don't eat anything, I don't care how hungry you are. I've had kids get heatstroke and barf in Howie suits, and the results ain't pretty. Suit almost always has to be thrown out. Drink, strip, put on the fur, get someone to zip you up, then hustle down the Boulevard to the Wiggle-Waggle. There's a sign, you can't miss it."

I looked doubtfully at Howie's big blue eyes.

"They're screen mesh," she said. "Don't worry, you'll see fine."

"But what do I *do*?"

She looked at me, at first unsmiling. Then her face—not just her mouth and eyes but her whole face—broke into a grin. The laugh that accompanied it was this weird honk that seemed to come through her nose. "You'll be fine," she said. People kept telling me that. "It's method acting, kiddo. Just find your inner dog."

♥

There were over a dozen new hires and a handful of old-timers having lunch in the boneyard when I arrived. Two of the greenies were Hollywood Girls, but I had no time to be modest. After gulping a bellyful from the drinking fountain, I shucked down to my Jockeys and sneakers. I shook out the Howie costume and stepped in, making sure to get my feet all the way down in the back paws.

"Fur!" one of the old-timers yelled, and slammed a fist down on the table. "Fur! Fur! Fur!"

The others took it up, and the boneyard rang with the chant

as I stood there in my underwear with a deflated Howie puddled around my shins. It was like being in the middle of a prison messhall riot. Rarely have I felt so exquisitely stupid…or so oddly heroic. It was showbiz, after all, and I was stepping into the breach. For a moment it didn't matter that I didn't know what the fuck I was doing.

"*Fur! Fur! FUR! FUR!*"

"*Somebody zip me the hell up!*" I shouted. "*I have to get down to the Wiggle-Waggle posthaste!*"

One of the girls did the honors, and I immediately saw why wearing the fur was such a big deal. The boneyard was air conditioned—all of Joyland Under was—but I was already popping hard sweat.

One of the old-timers came over and gave me a kindly pat on my Howie-head. "I'll give you a ride, son," he said. "Cart's right there. Jump in."

"Thanks." My voice was muffled.

"Woof-woof, Bowser!" someone called, and they all cracked up.

We rolled down the Boulevard with its spooky, stuttering fluorescent lights, a grizzled old guy in janitor's greens with a giant blue-eyed German Shepherd riding co-pilot. As he pulled up at the stairs marked with an arrow and the painted legend WIGWAG on the cinderblocks, he said: "Don't talk. Howie never talks, just gives hugs and pats em on the head. Good luck, and if you start feelin all swimmy, get the hell out. The kids don't want to see Howie flop over with heatstroke."

"I have no idea what I'm supposed to do," I said. "Nobody's told me."

I don't know if that guy was carny-from-carny or not, but he knew something about Joyland. "It don't matter. The kids all love Howie. *They'll* know what to do."

I clambered out of the cart, almost tripped over my tail, then grasped the string in the left front paw and gave it a yank to get the damn thing out of my way. I staggered up the stairs and fumbled with the lever of the door at the top. I could hear music, something vaguely remembered from my early childhood. I finally got the lever to go down. The door opened and bright Junelight flooded through Howie's screen-mesh blue eyes, momentarily dazzling me.

The music was louder now, being piped from overhead speakers, and I could put a name to it: "The Hokey Pokey," that all-time nursery school hit. I saw swings, slides, and teeter-totters, an elaborate jungle gym, and a roundy-round being pushed by a greenie wearing long fuzzy rabbit ears and a powder-puff tail stuck to the seat of his jeans. The Choo-Choo Wiggle, a toy train capable of dazzling speeds approaching four miles an hour, steamed by, loaded with little kids dutifully waving to their camera-toting parents. About a gazillion kids were boiling around, watched over by plenty of summer hires, plus a couple of full-time personnel who probably *did* have child-care licenses. These two, a man and a woman, were wearing sweatshirts that read WE LUV HAPPY KIDS. Dead ahead was the long daycare building called Howie's Howdy House.

I saw Mr. Easterbrook, too. He was sitting on a bench beneath a Joyland umbrella, dressed in his mortician's suit and eating his lunch with chopsticks. He didn't see me at first; he was looking at a crocodile line of children being led toward the Howdy House by a couple of greenies. The kiddies could be parked there (I found this out later) for a maximum of two hours while the parents either took their older kids on the bigger rides or had lunch at Rock Lobster, the park's class-A restaurant.

I also found out later that the eligibility ages for Howdy House ran from three to six. Many of the children now approaching looked pretty mellow, probably because they were daycare vets from families where both parents worked. Others weren't taking it so well. Maybe they'd managed to keep a stiff upper lip at first, hearing mommy and daddy say they'd all be back together in just an hour or two (as if a four-year-old has any real concept of what an hour is), but now they were on their own, in a noisy and confusing place filled with strangers and mommy and daddy nowhere in sight. Some of those were crying. Buried in the Howie costume, looking out through the screen mesh that served as eyeholes and already sweating like a pig, I thought I was witnessing an act of uniquely American child abuse. Why would you bring your kid—your *toddler*, for Christ's sake—to the jangling sprawl of an amusement park only to fob him or her off on a crew of strange babysitters, even for a little while?

The greenies in charge could see the tears spreading (toddler-angst is just another childhood disease, really, like measles), but their faces said they had no idea what to do about it. Why would they? It was Day One, and they had been thrown into the mix with as little preparation as I'd had when Lane Hardy walked away and left me in charge of a gigantic Ferris wheel. *But at least kids under eight can't get on the Spin without an adult*, I thought. *These little buggers are pretty much on their own.*

I didn't know what to do either, but felt I had to try something.

I walked toward the line of kids with my front paws up and wagging my tail like mad (I couldn't see it, but I could feel it). And just as the first two or three saw me and pointed me out, inspiration struck. It was the music. I stopped at the intersection of Jellybean Road and Candy Cane Avenue, which happened to be directly beneath two of the blaring speakers. Standing almost seven feet from paws to furry cocked ears, I'm sure I was quite a presence. I bowed to the kids, who were now all staring with open mouths and wide eyes. As they watched, I began to do the Hokey Pokey.

Sorrow and terror over lost parents were forgotten, at least for the time being. They laughed, some with tears still gleaming on their cheeks. They didn't quite dare approach, not while I was doing my clumsy little dance, but they crowded forward. There was wonder but no fear. They all knew Howie; those from the Carolinas had seen his afternoon TV show, and even those from far-flung exotic locales like St. Louis and Omaha had seen brochures and advertisements on the Saturday morning cartoons. They understood that although Howie was a *big* dog, he was a *good* dog. He'd never bite. He was their friend.

I put my left foot in; I put my left foot out; I put my left foot in and I shook it all about. I did the Hokey Pokey and I turned myself around, because—as almost every little kid in America knows—that's what it's all about. I forgot about being hot and uncomfortable. I didn't think about how my undershorts were sticking in the crack of my ass. Later I would have a bitch of a heat-headache, but just then I felt okay—really good, in fact. And you know what? Wendy Keegan never once crossed my mind.

When the music changed to the *Sesame Street* theme, I quit

dancing, dropped to one padded knee, and held out my arms like Al Jolson.

"*HOWWWIE!*" a little girl screamed, and all these years later I can still hear the perfect note of rapture in her voice. She ran forward, pink skirt swirling around her chubby knees. That did it. The orderly crocodile line dissolved.

The kids will know what to do, the old-timer had said, and how right he was. First they swarmed me, then they knocked me over, then they gathered around me, hugging and laughing. The little girl in the pink skirt kissed my snout repeatedly, shouting "Howie, Howie, Howie!" as she did it.

Some of the parents who had ventured into the Wiggle-Waggle to snap pictures were approaching, equally fascinated. I paddled my paws to get some space, rolled over, and got up before they could crush me with their love. Although just then I was loving them right back. For such a hot day, it was pretty cool.

I didn't notice Mr. Easterbrook reach into the jacket of his mortician's suit, bring out a walkie-talkie, and speak into it briefly. All I knew was that the *Sesame Street* music suddenly cut out and "The Hokey Pokey" started up again. I put my right paw in and my right paw out. The kids got into it right away, their eyes never leaving me, not wanting to miss the next move and be left behind.

Pretty soon we were all doing the Hokey Pokey at the intersection of Jellybean and Candy Cane. The greenie minders joined in. I'll be goddamned if some of the parents didn't join in as well. I even put my long tail in and pulled my long tail out. Laughing madly, the kids turned around and did the same, only with invisible tails.

As the song wound down, I made an extravagant "Come on,

kids!" gesture with my left paw (inadvertently yanking my tail up so stringently I almost tore the troublesome fucker off) and led them toward Howdy House. They followed as willingly as the children of Hamelin followed the pied piper, and not one of them was crying. That actually wasn't the best day of my brilliant (if I do say so myself, and I do) career as Howie the Happy Hound, but it was right up there.

♥

When they were safely inside Howdy House (the little girl in the pink skirt stood in the door long enough to wave me a bye-bye), I turned around and the world seemed to keep right on turning when I stopped. Sweat sheeted into my eyes, doubling Wiggle-Waggle Village and everything in it. I wavered on my back paws. The entire performance, from my first Hokey Pokey moves to the little girl waving bye-bye, had only taken seven minutes—nine, tops—but I was totally fried. I started trudging back the way I had come, not sure what to do next.

"Son," a voice said. "Over here."

It was Mr. Easterbrook. He was holding open a door in the back of the Wishing Well Snack Bar. It might have been the door I'd come through, probably was, but then I'd been too anxious and excited to notice.

He ushered me inside, closed the door behind us, and pulled down the zipper at the back of the costume. Howie's surprisingly heavy head fell off my own, and my damp skin drank up the blessed air conditioning. My skin, still winter-white (it wouldn't stay that way for long), rashed out in goosebumps. I took big deep breaths.

"Sit down on the steps," he said. "I'll call for a ride in a minute, but right now you need to get your wind back. The first few turns as Howie are always difficult, and the performance you just gave was particularly strenuous. It was also extraordinary."

"Thanks." It was all I could manage. Until I was back inside the cool quiet, I hadn't realized how close to my limit I was. "Thanks very much."

"Head down if you feel faint."

"Not faint. Got a headache, though." I snaked one arm out of Howie and wiped my face, which was dripping. "You kinda rescued me."

"Maximum time wearing Howie on a hot day—I'm talking July and August, when the humidity is high and the temperature goes into the nineties—is fifteen minutes," Mr. Easterbrook said. "If someone tries to tell you different, send them directly to me. And you'll be well advised to swallow a couple of salt pills. We want you summer kids to work hard, but we don't want to kill you."

He took out his walkie-talkie and spoke briefly and quietly. Five minutes later, the old-timer showed up again in his cart, with a couple of Anacin and a bottle of blessedly cold water. In the meantime Mr. Easterbrook sat next to me, lowering himself to the top step leading down to the Boulevard with a glassy care that made me a trifle nervous.

"What's your name, son?"

"Devin Jones, sir."

"Do they call you Jonesy?" He didn't wait for me to reply. "Of course they do, it's the carny way, and that's all Joyland is, really—a thinly disguised carny. Places like this won't last much longer. The Disneys and Knott's Berry Farms are going to rule the amusement world, except maybe down here in the mid-south. Tell me, aside from the heat, how did you enjoy your first turn wearing the fur?"

"I liked it."

"Because?"

"Because some of them were crying, I guess."

He smiled. "And?"

"Pretty soon *all* of them would have been crying, but I stopped it."

"Yes. You did the Hokey Pokey. A splinter of genius. How did you know it would work?"

"I didn't." But actually...I did. On some level, I did.

He smiled. "At Joyland, we throw our new hires—our greenies—into the mix without much in the way of preparation, because in some people, some *gifted* people, it encourages a sort of spontaneity that's very special and valuable, both to us and to our patrons. Did you learn something about yourself just now?"

"Jeez, I don't know. Maybe. But...can I say something, sir?"

"Feel free."

I hesitated, then decided to take him at his word. "Sending those kids to daycare—daycare at an amusement park—that seems, I don't know, kind of mean." I added hastily, "Although the Wiggle-Waggle seems really good for little people. Really fun."

"You have to understand something, son. At Joyland, we're in the black this much." He held a thumb and forefinger only a smidge apart. "When parents know there's care for their wee ones—even for just a couple of hours—they bring the whole family. If they needed to hire a babysitter at home, they might not come at all, and our profit margin would disappear. I take your point, but I have a point, too. Most of those little ones have never been to a place like this before. They'll remember it the way they'll remember their first movie, or their first day at school. Because of you, they won't remember crying because they were abandoned by their parents for a little while; they'll remember doing the Hokey Pokey with Howie the Happy Hound, who appeared like magic."

"I guess."

He reached out, not for me but for Howie. He stroked the fur with his gnarled fingers as he spoke. "The Disney parks are scripted, and I hate that. *Hate* it. I think what they're doing down there in Orlando is fun-pimping. I'm a seat-of-the-pants fan, and sometimes I see someone who's a seat-of-the-pants genius. That could be you. Too early to tell for sure, but yes, it could be you." He put his hands to the small of his back and stretched. I heard an alarmingly loud series of cracking noises. "Might I share your cart back to the boneyard? I think I've had enough sun for one day."

"My cart is your cart." Since Joyland was his park, that was literally true.

"I think you'll wear the fur a lot this summer. Most of the young people see that as a burden, or even a punishment. I don't believe that you will. Am I wrong?"

He wasn't. I've done a lot of jobs in the years since then, and my current editorial gig—probably my last gig before retirement seizes me in its claws—is terrific, but I never felt so weirdly happy, so absolutely in-the-right-place, as I did when I was twenty-one, wearing the fur and doing the Hokey Pokey on a hot day in June.

Seat of the pants, baby.

♥

I stayed friends with Tom and Erin after that summer, and I'm friends with Erin still, although these days we're mostly email and Facebook buddies who sometimes get together for lunch in New York. I've never met her second husband. She says he's a nice guy, and I believe her. Why would I not? After being married to Mr. Original Nice Guy for eighteen years and having that yardstick to measure by, she'd hardly pick a loser.

In the spring of 1992, Tom was diagnosed with a brain tumor. He was dead six months later. When he called and told me he was sick, his usual ratchetjaw delivery slowed by the wrecking ball swinging back and forth in his head, I was stunned and depressed, the way almost anyone would be, I suppose, when he hears that a guy who should be in the very prime of life is instead approaching the finish line. You want to ask how a thing like that can be fair. Weren't there supposed to be a few more good things for Tom, like a couple of grandchildren and maybe that long-dreamed-of vacation in Maui?

During my time at Joyland, I once heard Pops Allen talk about burning the lot. In the Talk, that means to blatantly cheat the rubes at what's supposed to be a straight game. I thought of that for the first time in years when Tom called with his bad news.

But the mind defends itself as long as it can. After the first shock of such news dissipates, maybe you think, *Okay, it's bad, I get that, but it's not the final word; there still might be a chance. Even if ninety-five percent of the people who draw this particular card go down, there's still that lucky five percent. Also, doctors misdiagnose shit all the time. Barring those things, there's the occasional miracle.*

You think that, and then you get the follow-up call. The woman who makes the follow-up call was once a beautiful young girl who ran around Joyland in a flippy green dress and a silly Sherwood Forest hat, toting a big old Speed Graphic camera, and the conies she braced hardly ever said no. How could they say no to that blazing red hair and eager smile? How could anyone say no to Erin Cook?

Well, God said no. God burned Tom Kennedy's lot, and He burned hers in the process. When I picked up the phone at five-thirty on a gorgeous October afternoon in Westchester, that girl had become a woman whose voice, blurry with the tears, sounded old and tired to death. "Tom died at two this afternoon. It was very peaceful. He couldn't talk, but he was aware. He...Dev, he squeezed my hand when I said goodbye."

I said, "I wish I could have been there."

"Yes." Her voice wavered, then firmed. "Yes, that would have been good."

You think *Okay, I get it, I'm prepared for the worst*, but you hold out that small hope, see, and that's what fucks you up. That's what kills you.

I talked to her, I told her how much I loved her and how much I had loved Tom, I told her yes, I'd be at the funeral, and if there was anything I could do before then, she should call. Day or night. Then I hung up the phone and lowered my head and bawled my goddam eyes out.

The end of my first love doesn't measure up to the death of one old friend and the bereavement of the other, but it followed the same pattern. Exactly the same. And if it seemed like the end of the world to me—first causing those suicidal ideations (silly and halfhearted though they may have been) and then a seismic shift in the previously unquestioned course of my life—you have to understand I had no scale by which to judge it. That's called being young.

♥

As June wore on, I started to understand that my relationship with Wendy was as sick as William Blake's rose, but I refused to believe it was *mortally* sick, even when the signs became increasingly clear.

Letters, for instance. During my first week at Mrs. Shoplaw's, I wrote Wendy four long ones, even though I was run off my feet at Joyland and came drag-assing into my second-floor room each night with my head full of new information and new experiences, feeling like a kid dropped into a challenging college course (call it The Advanced Physics of Fun) halfway through the semester. What I got in return was a single postcard with Boston Common on the front and a very peculiar collaborative message on the back. At the top, written in a hand I didn't recognize, was this: **Wenny writes the card while Rennie drives the bus!** Below, in a hand I *did* recognize, Wendy—or Wenny, if you like; I hated it, myself—had written breezily: **Whee! We is salesgirls off on a venture to Cape Cod! It's a party! Hoopsie muzik! Don't worry I held the wheel while Ren wrote her part. Hope your good. W.**

Hoopsie muzik? Hope your good? No love, no do you miss me, just *hope your good?* And although, judging by the bumps and jags and inkblots, the card had been written while on the move in Renee's car (Wendy didn't have one), they both sounded either stoned or drunk on their asses. The following week I sent four more letters, plus an Erin-photo of me wearing the fur. From Wendy, nothing in reply.

You start to worry, then you start to get it, then you know. Maybe you don't want to, maybe you think that lovers as well as doctors misdiagnose shit all the time, but in your heart you know.

Twice I tried calling her. The same grumpy girl answered both times. I imagined her wearing harlequin glasses, an ankle-length granny dress, and no lipstick. Not there, she said the first time. Out with Ren. Not there and not likely to be there in the future, Grumpy Girl said the second time. Moved.

"Moved where?" I asked, alarmed. This was in the parlor of *Maison* Shoplaw, where there was a long-distance honor sheet beside the phone. My fingers were holding the big old-fashioned receiver so tightly they had gone numb. Wendy was going to college on a patchwork magic carpet of scholarships, loans, and work-study employment, the same as me. She couldn't afford a place on her own. Not without help, she couldn't.

"I don't know and don't care," Grumpy Girl said. "I got tired of all the drinking and hen-parties at two in the morning. Some of us actually like to get a little sleep. Strange but true."

My heart was beating so hard I could feel it pulsing in my temples. "Did Renee go with her?"

"No, they had a fight. Over that guy. The one who helped Wennie move out." She said *Wennie* with a kind of bright contempt that made me sick to my stomach. Surely it wasn't the guy part that made me feel that way; *I* was her guy. If some friend, someone she'd met at work, had pitched in and helped her move her stuff, what was that to me? Of course she could have guy friends. I had made at least one *girl* friend, hadn't I?

"Is Renee there? Can I talk to her?"

"No, she had a date." Some penny must have finally dropped, because all at once Grumpy Girl got interested in the conversation. "Heyyy, is your name Devin?"

I hung up. It wasn't something I planned, just something I did. I told myself I hadn't heard Grumpy Girl all of a sudden change into *Amused* Grumpy Girl, as if there was some sort of joke going on and I was part of it. Maybe even the butt of it. As I believe I have said, the mind defends itself as long as it can.

♥

Three days later, I got the only letter I received from Wendy Keegan that summer. The last letter. It was written on her stationery, which was deckle-edged and featured happy kittens playing with balls of yarn. It was the stationery of a fifth-grade girl, although that thought didn't occur to me until much later. There were three breathless pages, mostly saying how sorry she was, and how she had fought against the attraction but it was just hopeless, and she knew I would be hurt so I probably shouldn't call her or try to see her for a while, and she hoped we could be good friends after the initial shock wore off, and he was a nice guy, he went to Dartmouth, he played lacrosse, she knew I'd like him, maybe she could introduce him to me when the fall semester started, etc. etc. fucking etc.

That night I plopped myself down on the sand fifty yards or so from Mrs. Shoplaw's Beachside Accommodations, planning to get drunk. At least, I thought, it wouldn't be expensive. In those days, a sixpack was all it took to get me pie-eyed. At some point Tom and Erin joined me, and we watched the waves roll in together: the three Joyland Musketeers.

"What's wrong?" Erin asked.

I shrugged, the way you do when it's small shit but annoying shit, all the same. "Girlfriend broke up with me. Sent me a Dear John letter."

"Which in your case," Tom said, "would be a Dear Dev letter."

"Show a little compassion," Erin told him. "He's sad and hurt and trying not to show it. Are you too much of a dumbass to see that?"

"No," Tom said. He put his arm around my shoulders and briefly hugged me against him. "I'm sorry for your pain, pal. I feel it coming off you like a cold wind from Canada or maybe even the Arctic. Can I have one of your beers?"

"Sure."

We sat there for quite a while, and under Erin's gentle questioning, I spilled some of it, but not all of it. I *was* sad. I *was* hurt. But there was a lot more, and I didn't want them to see it. This was partly because I'd been raised by my parents to believe barfing your feelings on other people was the height of impoliteness, but mostly because I was dismayed by the depth and strength of my jealousy. I didn't want them to even guess at that lively worm (he was from *Dartmouth*, oh God *yes*, he'd probably pledged the best frat and drove a Mustang his folks had given him as a high school graduation present). Nor was jealousy the worst of it. The worst was the horrifying realization—that night it was just starting to sink in—that I had been really and truly rejected for the first time in my life. She was through with me, but I couldn't imagine being through with her.

Erin also took a beer, and raised the can. "Let's toast the next one to come along. I don't know who she'll be, Dev, only that meeting you will be her lucky day."

"Hear-hear!" Tom said, raising his own can. And, because he was Tom, he felt compelled to add "Where-where!" and "There-there!"

I don't think either of them realized, then or all the rest of the summer, how fundamentally the ground under my feet had shifted. How lost I felt. I didn't want them to know. It was more than embarrassing; it seemed shameful. So I made myself smile, raised my own can of suds, and drank.

At least with them to help me drink the six, I didn't have to wake up the next morning hungover as well as heartbroke. That was good, because when we got to Joyland that morning, I found out from Pop Allen that I was down to wear the fur that afternoon on Joyland Avenue—three fifteen-minute shifts at three, four, and five. I bitched for form's sake (everybody was supposed to bitch about wearing the fur) but I was glad. I liked being mobbed by the kids, and for the next few weeks, playing Howie also had a bitter sort of amusement value. As I made my tail-wagging way down Joyland Avenue, followed by crowds of laughing children, I thought it was no wonder Wendy had dumped me. Her new boyfriend went to Dartmouth and played lacrosse. Her old one was spending the summer in a third-tier amusement park. Where he played a dog.

♥

Joyland summer.

I ride-jockeyed. I flashed the shys in the mornings—meaning I restocked them with prizes—and ran some of them in the afternoons. I untangled Devil Wagons by the dozen, learned how to fry dough without burning my fingers off, and worked on my pitch for the Carolina Spin. I danced and sang with the other greenies on the Wiggle-Waggle Village's Story Stage. Several times Fred Dean sent me to scratch the midway, a true sign of trust because it meant picking up the noon or five PM take from the various concessions. I made runs to Heaven's Bay or Wilmington when some piece of machinery broke down and stayed late on Wednesday nights—usually along with Tom, George Preston, and Ronnie Houston—to lube the Whirly Cups and a vicious, neck-snapping ride called the Zipper. Both of those babies drank oil the way camels drink water when they get to the next oasis. And, of course, I wore the fur.

In spite of all this, I wasn't sleeping for shit. Sometimes I'd lie on my bed, clap my elderly, taped-up headphones over my ears, and listen to my Doors records. (I was particularly partial to such cheerful tunes as "Cars Hiss By My Window," "Riders on the Storm," and—of course—"The End.") When Jim Morrison's voice and Ray Manzarek's mystic, chiming organ weren't enough to sedate me, I'd creep down the outside staircase and walk on the beach. Once or twice I *slept* on the beach. At least there were no bad dreams when I did manage to get under for a little while. I don't remember dreaming that summer at all.

I could see bags under my eyes when I shaved in the morning, and sometimes I'd feel lightheaded after a particularly strenuous turn as Howie (birthday parties in the overheated bedlam of Howdy House were the worst), but that was normal; Mr. Easterbrook had told me so. A little rest in the boneyard always put me right again. On the whole, I thought I was *representing*, as they say nowadays. I learned different on the first Monday in July, two days before the Glorious Fourth.

♥

My team—Beagle—reported to Pop Allen's shy first thing, as always, and he gave us our assignments as he laid out the popguns. Usually our early chores involved toting boxes of prizes (MADE IN TAIWAN stamped on most of them) and flashing shys until Early Gate, which was what we called opening. That morning, however, Pop told me that Lane Hardy wanted me. This was a surprise; Lane rarely showed his face outside the boneyard until twenty minutes or so before Early Gate. I started that way, but Pop yelled at me.

"Nah, nah, he's at the simp-hoister." This was a derogatory term for the Ferris wheel he would have known better than to use if Lane had actually been there. "Beat feet, Jonesy. Got a lot to do today."

I beat feet, but saw no one at the Spin, which stood tall, still, and silent, waiting for the day's first customers.

"Over here," a woman called. I turned to my left and saw Rozzie Gold standing outside her star-studded fortune-telling shy, all kitted out in one of her gauzy Madame Fortuna rigs. On her head was an electric blue scarf, the knotted tail of which fell almost to the small of her back. Lane was standing beside her in *his* usual rig: faded straight-leg jeans and a skin-tight strappy tee-shirt perfect for showing off his fully loaded guns. His derby was tilted at the proper wiseguy angle. Looking at him, you'd believe he didn't have a brain in his head, but he had plenty.

Both dressed for show, and both wearing bad-news faces. I ran quickly through the last few days, trying to think of anything I'd done that might account for those faces. It crossed my mind that Lane might have orders to lay me off…or even fire me. But at the height of the summer? And wouldn't that be Fred Dean's or Brenda Rafferty's job? Also, why was Rozzie here?

"Who died, guys?" I asked.

"Just as long as it isn't you," Rozzie said. She was getting into character for the day and sounded funny: half Brooklyn and half Carpathian Mountains.

"Huh?"

"Walk with us, Jonesy," Lane said, and immediately started down the midway, which was largely deserted ninety minutes before Early Gate; no one around but a few members of the janitorial staff—gazoonies, in the Talk, and probably not a green card among them—sweeping up around the concessions: work that should have been done the night before. Rozzie made room for me between them when I caught up. I felt like a crook being escorted to the pokey by a couple of cops.

"What's this about?"

"You'll see," Rozzie/Fortuna said ominously, and pretty soon I did. Next to Horror House—the two connected, actually—was Mysterio's Mirror Mansion. Next to the agent's booth was a regular mirror with a sign over it reading SO YOU WON'T FORGET HOW YOU **REALLY** LOOK. Lane took me by one arm, Rozzie by the other. Now I really did feel like a perp being brought in for booking. They placed me in front of the mirror.

"What do you see?" Lane asked.

"Me," I said, and then, because that didn't seem to be the answer they wanted: "Me needing a haircut."

"Look at your clothes, silly boy," Rozzie said, pronouncing the last two words *seely poy*.

I looked. Above my yellow workboots I saw jeans (with the recommended brand of rawhide gloves sticking out of the back pocket), and above my jeans was a blue chambray workshirt, faded but reasonably clean. On my head was an admirably battered Howie dogtop, the finishing touch that means so much.

"What about them?" I said. I was starting to get a little mad.

"Kinda hangin on ya, aren't they?" Lane said. "Didn't used to. How much weight you lost?"

"Jesus, I don't know. Maybe we ought to go see Fat Wally." Fat Wally ran the guess-your-weight joint.

"Is not funny," Fortuna said. "You can't wear that damn dog costume half the day under the hot summer sun, then swallow two more salt pills and call it a meal. Mourn your lost love all you want, but eat while you do it. *Eat*, dammit!"

"Who's been talking to you? Tom?" No, it wouldn't have been him. "Erin. She had no business—"

"No one has been talking to me," Rozzie said. She drew herself up impressively. "I have the sight."

"I don't know about the sight, but you've got one hell of a nerve."

All at once she reverted to Rozzie. "I'm not talking about psychic sight, kiddo, I'm talking about ordinary woman-sight. You think I don't know a lovestruck Romeo when I see one? After all the years I've been gigging palms and peeping the crystal? *Hah*!" She stepped forward, her considerable breastworks leading the way. "I don't care about your love life; I just don't want to see you taken to the hospital on July Fourth—when it's supposed to hit ninety-five in the shade, by the way—with heat prostration or something worse."

Lane took off his derby, peered into it, and re-set it on his head cocked the other way. "What she won't come right out and say because she has to protect her famous crusty reputation is we all like you, kid. You learn fast, you do what's asked of you,

you're honest, you don't make no trouble, and the kids love you like mad when you're wearing the fur. But you'd have to be blind not to see something's wrong with you. Rozzie thinks girl trouble. Maybe she's right. Maybe she ain't."

Rozzie gave him a haughty dare-you-doubt-me stare.

"Maybe your parents are getting a divorce. Mine did, and it damn near killed me. Maybe your big brother got arrested for selling dope—"

"My mother's dead and I'm an only child," I said sulkily.

"I don't care what you are in the straight world," he said. "This is Joyland. The *show*. And you're one of us. Which means we got a right to care about you, whether you like it or not. So get something to eat."

"Get a *lot* to eat," Rozzie said. "Now, noon, all day. *Every* day. And try to eat something besides fried chicken where, I tell you what, there's a heart attack in every drumstick. Go in Rock Lobster and tell them you want a take-out of fish and salad. Tell them to make it a double. Get your weight up so you don't look like the Human Skeleton in a ten-in-one." She turned her gaze on Lane. "It's a girl, of course it is. Anybody can see that."

"Whatever it is, stop fucking *pining*," Lane said.

"Such language to use around a lady," Rozzie said. She was sounding like Fortuna again. Soon she'd come out with *Ziss is vat za spirits vant*, or something equivalent.

"Ah, blow it out," Lane said, and walked back toward the Spin.

When he was gone, I looked at Rozzie. She really wasn't much in the mother-figure department, but right then she was what I had. "Roz, does *everyone* know?"

She shook her head. "Nah. To most of the old guys, you're just another greenie jack-of-all-trades...although not as green as you were three weeks ago. But many people here like you, and they see something is wrong. Your friend Erin, for one. Your friend Tom for another." She said *friend* like it rhymed with *rent*. "I am another friend, and as a friend I tell you that you can't fix your heart. Only time can do that, but you can fix your body. Eat!"

"You sound like a Jewish mother joke," I said.

"I *am* a Jewish mother, and believe me, it's no joke."

"*I'm* the joke," I said. "I think about her all the time."

"That you can't help, at least for now. But you must turn your back on the other thoughts that sometimes come to you."

I think my mouth dropped open. I'm not sure. I know I stared. People who've been in the business as long as Rozzie Gold had been back then—they are called *mitts* in the Talk, for their palmistry skills—have their ways of picking your brains so that what they say sounds like the result of telepathy, but usually it's just close observation.

Not always, though.

"I don't understand."

"Give those morbid records a rest, do you understand that?" She looked grimly into my face, then laughed at the surprise she saw there. "Rozzie Gold may be just a Jewish mother and grandmother, but Madame Fortuna sees much."

So did my landlady, and I found out later—after seeing Rozzie and Mrs. Shoplaw having lunch together in Heaven's Bay on one of Madame Fortuna's rare days off—that they were close friends who had known each other for years. Mrs. Shoplaw dusted my room and vacuumed the floor once a week; she would have seen my records. As for the rest—those famous suicidal ideations that sometimes came to me—might not a woman who had spent most of her life observing human nature and watching for psychological clues (called *tells* both in the Talk and big-league poker) guess that a sensitive young man, freshly dumped, might entertain thoughts of pills and ropes and riptide undertows?

"I'll eat," I promised. I had a thousand things to do before Early Gate, but mostly I was just anxious to be away from her before she said something totally outrageous like *Her name is Vendy, and you still think of her ven you mess-turbate*.

"Also, drink big glass of milk before you go to bed." She raised an admonitory finger. "No coffee; milk. Vill help you sleep."

"Worth a try," I said.

She went back to Roz again. "The day we met, you asked if I saw a beautiful woman with dark hair in your future. Do you remember that?"

"Yes."

"What did I say?"

"That she was in my past."

Rozzie gave a single nod, hard and imperious. "So she is. And when you want to call her and beg for a second chance—you will, you will—show a little spine. Have a little self-respect. Also remember that the long-distance is expensive."

Tell me something I don't know, I thought. "Listen, I really have to get going, Roz. Lots to do."

"Yes, a busy day for all of us. But before you go, Jonesy—have you met the boy yet? The one with the dog? Or the girl who wears the red hat and carries the doll? I told you about them, too, when we met."

"Roz, I've met a billion kids in the last—"

"You haven't, then. Okay. You will." She stuck out her lower lip and blew, stirring the fringe of hair that stuck out from beneath her scarf. Then she seized my wrist. "I see danger for you, Jonesy. Sorrow and danger."

I thought for a moment she was going to whisper something like *Beware the dark stranger! He rides a unicycle!* Instead, she let go of me and pointed at Horror House. "Which team turns that unpleasant hole? Not yours, is it?"

"No, Team Doberman." The Dobies were also responsible for the adjacent attractions: Mysterio's Mirror Mansion and the Wax Museum. Taken together, these three were Joyland's half-hearted nod to the old carny spook-shows.

"Good. Stay out of it. It's haunted, and a boy with bad thoughts needs to be visiting a haunted house like he needs arsenic in his mouthwash. *Kapish*?"

"Yeah." I looked at my watch.

She got the point and stepped back. "Watch for those kids. And watch your step, boychick. There's a shadow over you."

♥

Lane and Rozzie gave me a pretty good jolt, I'll admit it. I didn't stop listening to my Doors records—not immediately, at least—but I made myself eat more, and started sucking down three milkshakes a day. I could feel fresh energy pouring into my body as if someone had turned on a tap, and I was very grateful for that on the afternoon of July Fourth. Joyland was tipsed and I was down to wear the fur ten times, an all-time record.

Fred Dean himself came down to give me the schedule, and to hand me a note from old Mr. Easterbrook. *If it becomes too much, stop at once and tell your team leader to find a sub.*

"I'll be fine," I said.

"Maybe, but make sure Pop sees this memo."

"Okay."

"Brad likes you, Jonesy. That's rare. He hardly ever notices the greenies unless he sees one of them screw up."

I liked him, too, but didn't say so to Fred. I thought it would have sounded suck-assy.

♥

All my July Fourth shifts were tenners, not bad even though most ten-minute shifts actually turned out to be fifteenies, but the heat was crushing. *Ninety-five in the shade*, Rozzie had said, but by noon that day it was a hundred and two by the thermometer that hung outside the Park Ops trailer. Luckily for me, Dottie Lassen had repaired the other XL Howie suit and I could swap between the two. While I was wearing one, Dottie would have the other turned as inside-out as it would go and hung in front of three fans, drying the sweat-soaked interior.

At least I could remove the fur by myself; by then I'd discovered the secret. Howie's right paw was actually a glove, and when you knew the trick, pulling down the zipper to the neck of the costume was a cinch. Once you had the head off, the rest was cake. This was good, because I could change by myself behind a pull-curtain. No more displaying my sweaty, semi-transparent undershorts to the costume ladies.

As the bunting-draped afternoon of July Fourth wore on, I was excused from all other duties. I'd do my capering, then retreat to Joyland Under and collapse on the ratty old couch in the boneyard for a while, soaking up the air conditioning. When I felt revived, I'd use the alleys to get to the costume shop and swap one fur for the other. Between shifts I guzzled pints of water and quarts of unsweetened iced tea. You won't believe I was having fun, but I was. Even the brats were loving me that day.

So: quarter to four in the afternoon. I'm jiving down Joyland Avenue—our midway—while the overhead speakers blast out Daddy Dewdrop's "Chick-A-Boom, Chick-A-Boom, Don'tcha Just Love It." I'm giving out hugs to the kiddies and Awesome August coupons to the adults, because Joyland's business always dropped off as the summer wound down. I'm posing for pictures (some taken by Hollywood Girls, most by hordes of sweat-soaked, sunburned Parent Paparazzi), and trailing adoring kids after me in cometary splendor. I'm also looking for the nearest door to Joyland Under, because I'm pretty well done up. I have just one more turn as Howie scheduled today, because Howie the Happy Hound never shows his blue eyes and cocked ears after sundown. I don't know why; it was just a show tradition.

Did I notice the little girl in the red hat before she fell down on the baking pavement of Joyland Avenue, writhing and jerking? I think so but can't say for sure, because passing time adds false memories and modifies real ones. I surely wouldn't have noticed the Pup-A-Licious she was waving around, or her bright red Howie dogtop; a kid at an amusement park with a hotdog is hardly a unique sighting, and we must have sold a thousand red Howie hats that day. If I did notice her, it was because of the doll she held curled to her chest in the hand not holding her mustard-smeared Pup. It was a big old Raggedy Ann. Madame Fortuna had suggested I be on the lookout for a little girl with a doll only two days before, so maybe I did notice her. Or maybe I was only thinking of getting off the midway before I fell down in a faint. Anyway, her doll wasn't the problem. The Pup-A-Licious she was eating—*that* was the problem.

I only *think* I remember her running toward me (hey, they all did), but I know what happened next, and why it happened. She had a bite of her Pup in her mouth, and when she drew in breath to scream *HOWWWIE*, she pulled it down her throat. Hot dogs: the perfect choking food. Luckily for her, just enough of Rozzie Gold's Fortuna bullshit had stuck in my head for me to act quickly.

When the little girl's knees buckled, her expression of happy ecstasy turning first to surprise and then terror, I was already reaching behind me and grabbing the zipper with my paw-glove. The Howie-head tumbled off and lolled to the side, revealing the red face and sweat-soaked, clumpy hair of Mr. Devin Jones. The little girl dropped her Raggedy Ann. Her hat fell off. She began clawing at her neck.

"Hallie?" a woman cried. "Hallie, what's *wrong*?"

Here's more Luck in Action: I not only knew what was wrong, I knew what to do. I'm not sure you'll understand how fortunate that was. This is 1973 we're talking about, remember, and Henry Heimlich would not publish the essay that would give the Heimlich Maneuver its name for another full year. Still, it's always been the most commonsense way to deal with choking, and we had learned it during our first and only orientation session before beginning work in the UNH Commons. The teacher was a tough old veteran of the restaurant wars who had lost his Nashua coffee shop a year after a new McDonald's went up nearby.

"Just remember, it won't work if you don't do it hard," he told us. "Don't worry about breaking a rib if you see someone dying in front of you."

I saw the little girl's face turning purple and didn't even think about her ribs. I seized her in a vast, furry embrace, with my tail-pulling left paw jammed against the bony arch in her midsection where her ribs came together. I gave a single hard squeeze, and a yellow-smeared chunk of hotdog almost two inches long came popping out of her mouth like a cork from a champagne bottle. It flew nearly four feet. And no, I didn't break any of her ribs. Kids are flexible, God bless 'em.

I wasn't aware that I and Hallie Stansfield—that was her name—were hemmed in by a growing circle of adults. I certainly wasn't aware that we were being photographed dozens of times, including the shot by Erin Cook that wound up in the Heaven's Bay *Weekly* and several bigger papers, including the Wilmington *Star-News*. I've still got a framed copy of that photo in an attic box somewhere. It shows the little girl dangling in the arms of this weird man/dog hybrid with one of its two heads lolling on its shoulder. The girl is holding out her arms to her mother, perfectly caught by Erin's Speed Graphic just as Mom collapses to her knees in front of us.

All of that is a blur to me, but I remember the mother sweeping the little girl up into her own arms and the father saying *Kid, I think you saved her life*. And I remember—this is as clear as crystal—the girl looking at me with her big blue eyes and saying, "Oh poor Howie, your head fell off."

♥

The all-time classic newspaper headline, as everyone knows, is MAN BITES DOG. The *Star-News* couldn't equal that, but the one over Erin's picture gave it a run for its money: DOG SAVES GIRL AT AMUSEMENT PARK.

Want to know my first snarky urge? To clip the article and send it to Wendy Keegan. I might even have done it, had I not looked so much like a drowned muskrat in Erin's photo. I did send it to my father, who called to say how proud of me he was. I could tell by the tremble in his voice that he was close to tears.

"God put you in the right place at the right time, Dev," he said.

Maybe God. Maybe Rozzie Gold, aka Madame Fortuna. Maybe a little of both.

The next day I was summoned to Mr. Easterbrook's office, a pine-paneled room raucous with old carny posters and photographs. I was particularly taken by a photo that showed a straw-hatted agent with a dapper mustache standing next to a test-your-strength shy. The sleeves of his white shirt were rolled up, and he was leaning on a sledgehammer like it was a cane: a total dude. At the top of the ding-post, next to the bell, was a sign reading KISS HIM, LADY, HE'S A HE-MAN!

"Is that guy you?" I asked.

"It is indeed, although I only ran the ding-show for a season. It wasn't to my taste. Gaff jobs never have been. I like my games straight. Sit down, Jonesy. You want a Coke or anything?"

"No, sir. I'm fine." I was, in fact, sloshing with that morning's milkshake.

"I'll be perfectly blunt. You gave this show twenty thousand dollars' worth of good publicity yesterday afternoon, and I still can't afford to give you a bonus. If you knew...but never mind." He leaned forward. "What I *can* do is owe you a favor. If you need one, ask. I'll grant it if it's in my power. Will that do?"

"Sure."

"Good. And would you be willing to make one more appearance—as Howie—with the little girl? Her parents want to thank you in private, but a public appearance would be an excellent thing for Joyland. Entirely your call, of course."

"When?"

"Saturday, after the noon parade. We'd put up a platform at the intersection of Joyland and Hound Dog Way. Invite the press."

"Happy to," I said. I liked the idea of being in the newspapers again, I will admit. It had been a tough summer on my ego and self-image, and I'd take all the turnaround I could get.

He rose to his feet in his glassy, unsure way, and offered me his hand. "Thank you again. On behalf of that little girl, but also on behalf of Joyland. The accountants who run my damn life will be very happy about this."

♥

When I stepped out of the office building, which was located with the other administrative buildings in what we called the backyard, my entire team was there. Even Pop Allen had come. Erin, dressed for success in Hollywood Girl green, stepped forward with a shiny metal crown of laurels made from Campbell's Soup cans. She dropped to one knee. "For you, my hero."

I would have guessed I was too sunburned to flush, but that turned out not to be true. "Oh Jesus, get up."

"Savior of little girls," Tom Kennedy said. "Not to mention savior of our place of employment getting its ass sued off and possibly having to shut its doors."

Erin bounced to her feet, stuck the ludicrous soup-can crown on my head, then gave me a big old smackaroonie. Everyone on Team Beagle cheered.

"Okay," Pop said when it died down. "We can all agree that you're a knight in shining ah-mah, Jonesy. You are also not the first guy to save a rube from popping off on the midway. Could we maybe all get back to work?"

I was good with that. Being famous was fun, but the don't-get-a-swelled-head message of the tin laurels wasn't lost on me.

♥

I was wearing the fur that Saturday, on the makeshift platform at the center of our midway. I was happy to take Hallie in my arms, and she was clearly happy to be there. I'd guess there were roughly nine miles of film burned as she proclaimed her love for her favorite doggy and kissed him again and again for the cameras.

Erin was in the front row with her camera for a while, but the news photogs were bigger and all male. Soon they shunted her away to a less favorable position, and what did they all want? What Erin had already gotten, a picture of me with my Howie-head off. That was one thing I wouldn't do, although I'm sure none of Fred, Lane, or Mr. Easterbrook himself would have penalized me for it. I wouldn't do it because it would have flown in the face of park tradition: Howie *never* took off the fur in public; to do so would have been like outing the Tooth Fairy. I'd done it when Hallie Stansfield was choking, but that was the necessary exception. I would not deliberately break the rule. So I guess I was carny after all (although not carny-from-carny, never that).

Later, dressed in my own duds again, I met with Hallie and her parents in the Joyland Customer Service Center. Close-up, I could see that Mom was pregnant with number two, although she probably had three or four months of eating pickles and ice cream still ahead of her. She hugged me and wept some more. Hallie didn't seem overly concerned. She sat in one of the plastic chairs, swinging her feet and looking at old copies of *Screen Time*, speaking the names of the various celebrities in the declamatory voice of a court page announcing visiting royalty. I patted Mom's back and said there-there. Dad didn't cry, but the tears were standing in his eyes as he approached me and held out a check in the amount of five hundred dollars, made out to me. When I asked what he did for a living, he said he had started his own contracting firm the year before—just now little, but gettin on our feet pretty good, he told me. I considered that, factored in one kid here plus another on the way, and tore up the check. I told him I couldn't take money for something that was just part of the job.

You have to remember I was only twenty-one.

♥

There were no weekends *per se* for Joyland summer help; we got a day and a half every nine, which meant they were never the same days. There was a sign-up sheet, so Tom, Erin, and I almost always managed to get the same downtime. That was why we were together on a Wednesday night in early August, sitting around a campfire on the beach and having the sort of meal that can only nourish the very young: beer, burgers, barbecue-flavored potato chips, and coleslaw. For dessert we had s'mores that Erin cooked over the fire, using a grill she borrowed from Pirate Pete's Ice Cream Waffle joint. It worked pretty well.

We could see other fires—great leaping bonfires as well as

cooking fires—all the way down the beach to the twinkling metropolis of Joyland. They made a lovely chain of burning jewelry. Such fires are probably illegal in the twenty-first century; the powers that be have a way of outlawing many beautiful things made by ordinary people. I don't know why that should be, I only know it is.

While we ate, I told them about Madame Fortuna's prediction that I would meet a boy with a dog and a little girl in a red hat who carried a doll. I finished by saying, "One down and one to go."

"Wow," Erin said. "Maybe she really *is* psychic. A lot of people have told me that, but I didn't really—"

"Like who?" Tom demanded.

"Well...Dottie Lassen in the costume shop, for one. Tina Ackerley, for another. You know, the librarian Dev creeps down the hall to visit at night?"

I flipped her the bird. She giggled.

"Two is not a lot," Tom said, speaking in his Hot Shit Professor voice.

"Lane Hardy makes three," I said. "He says she's told people stuff that rocked them back on their heels." In the interest of total disclosure, I felt compelled to add: "Of course he also said that ninety percent of her predictions are total crap."

"Probably closer to ninety-five," said the Hot Shit Professor. "Fortune telling's a con game, boys and girls. An Ikey Heyman, in the Talk. Take the hat thing. Joyland dogtops only come in three colors—red, blue, and yellow. Red's by far the most popular. As for the doll, c'mon. How many little kids bring some sort of toy to the amusement park? It's a strange place, and a favorite toy is a comfort thing. If she hadn't choked on her hotdog right in front of you, if she'd just given Howie a big old hug and passed on, you would have seen some other little girl wearing a red dogtop and carrying a doll and said, 'Aha! Madame Fortuna really *can* see the future, I must cross her palm with silver so she will tell me more.' "

"You're such a cynic," Erin said, giving him an elbow. "Rozzie Gold would never try taking money from someone in the show."

"She didn't ask for money," I said, but I thought what Tom said made a lot of sense. It was true she had known (or *seemed* to know) that my dark-haired girl was in my past, not my future, but that could have been no more than a guess based on percentages—or the look on my face when I asked.

"Course not," Tom said, helping himself to another s'more. "She was just practicing on you. Staying sharp. I bet she's told a lot of other greenies stuff, too."

"Would you be one of them?" I asked.

"Well…no. But that means nothing."

I looked at Erin, who shook her head.

"She also thinks Horror House is haunted," I said.

"I've heard that one, too," Erin said. "By a girl who got murdered in there."

"Bullshit!" Tom cried. "Next you'll be telling me it was the Hook, and he still lurks behind the Screaming Skull!"

"There really was a murder," I said. "A girl named Linda Gray. She was from Florence, South Carolina. There are pictures of her and the guy who killed her at the shooting gallery and standing in line at the Whirly Cups. No hook, but there was a tattoo of a bird on his hand. A hawk or an eagle."

That silenced him, at least for the time being.

"Lane Hardy said that Roz only *thinks* Horror House is

haunted, because she won't go inside and find out for sure. She won't even go near it, if she can help it. Lane thinks that's ironic, because he says it really *is* haunted."

Erin made her eyes big and round and scooted a little closer to the fire—partly for effect, mostly I think so that Tom would put his arm around her. "He's *seen*—?"

"I don't know. He said to ask Mrs. Shoplaw, and she gave me the whole story." I ran it down for them. It was a good story to tell at night, under the stars, with the surf rolling and a beach-fire just starting to burn down to coals. Even Tom seemed fascinated.

"Does *she* claim to have seen Linda Gray?" he asked when I finally ran down. "La Shoplaw?"

I mentally replayed her story as told to me on the day I rented the room on the second floor. "I don't think so. She would have said."

He nodded, satisfied. "A perfect lesson in how these things work. Everyone *knows* someone who's seen a UFO, and everyone *knows* someone who's seen a ghost. Hearsay evidence, inadmissible in court. Me, I'm a Doubting Thomas. Geddit? Tom Kennedy, Doubting Thomas?"

Erin threw him a much sharper elbow. "We get it." She looked thoughtfully into the fire. "You know what? Summer's two-thirds gone, and I've never been in the Joyland scream-shy a single time, not even the baby part up front. It's a no-photo zone. Brenda Rafferty told us it's because lots of couples go in there to make out." She peered at me. "What are you grinning about?"

"Nothing." I was thinking of La Shoplaw's late husband going through the place after Late Gate and picking up cast-off panties.

"Have either of you guys been in?"

We both shook our heads. "HH is Dobie Team's job," Tom said.

"Let's do it tomorrow. All three of us in one car. Maybe we'll see her."

"Go to Joyland on our day off when we could spend it on the beach?" Tom asked. "That's masochism at its very finest."

This time in spite of giving him an elbow, she poked him in the ribs. I didn't know if they were sleeping together yet, but it seemed likely; the relationship had certainly become very physical. "Poop on that! As employees we get in free, and what does the ride take? Five minutes?"

"I think a little longer," I said. "Nine or ten. Plus some time in the baby part. Say fifteen minutes, all told."

Tom put his chin on her head and looked at me through the fine cloud of her hair. "Poop on that, she says. You can tell that here is a young woman with a fine college education. Before she started hanging out with sorority girls, she would have said *shitsky* and left it at that."

"The day I start hanging out with that bunch of half-starved mix-n-match sluts will be the day I crawl up my own ass and die!" For some reason, this vulgarity pleased me to no end. Possibly because Wendy was a veteran mix-n-matcher. "You, Thomas Patrick Kennedy, are just afraid we *will* see her, and you'll have to take back all those things you said about Madame Fortuna and ghosts and UFOs and—"

Tom raised his hands. "I give up. We'll get in the line with the rest of the rubes—the conies, I mean—and take the Horror House tour. I only insist it be in the afternoon. I need my beauty rest."

"You certainly do," I said.

"Coming from someone who looks like you, that's pretty funny. Give me a beer, Jonesy."

I gave him a beer.

"Tell us how it went with the Stansfields," Erin said. "Did they blubber all over you and call you their hero?"

That was pretty close, but I didn't want to say so. "The parents were okay. The kid sat in the corner, reading *Screen Time* and saying she spied Dean Martin with her little eye."

"Forget the local color and cut to the chase," Tom said. "Did you get any money out of it?"

I was preoccupied with thoughts of how the little girl announcing the celebrities with such reverence could have been in a flatline coma instead. Or in a casket. Thus distracted, I answered honestly. "The guy offered me five hundred dollars, but I wouldn't take it."

Tom goggled. "Say *what*?"

I looked down at the remains of the s'more I was holding. Marshmallow was drooling onto my fingers, so I tossed it into the fire. I was full, anyway. I was also embarrassed, and pissed off to be feeling that way. "The man's trying to get a little business up and running, and based on the way he talked about it, it's at the point where it could go either way. He's also got a wife and a kid and another kid coming soon. I didn't think he could afford to be giving money away."

"*He* couldn't? What about *you*?"

I blinked. "What about me?"

To this day I don't know if Tom was genuinely angry or faking it. I think he might have started out faking, then gathered steam as full understanding of what I'd done struck him. I have no idea exactly what his home situation was, but I know he was living from paycheck to paycheck, and had no car. When he wanted to take Erin out, he borrowed mine…and was careful —punctilious, I should say—about paying for the gas he used. Money mattered to him. I never got the sense it completely owned him, but yes, it mattered to him a great deal.

"You're going to school on a wing and a prayer, same as Erin and me, and working at Joyland isn't going to land any of us in a limousine. What's wrong with you? Did your mother drop you on your head when you were a baby?"

"Take it easy," Erin said.

He paid no attention. "Do you *want* to spend the fall semester next year getting up early so you can pull dirty breakfast dishes off a Commons conveyor belt? You must, because five hundred a semester is about what it pays at Rutgers. I know, because I checked before lucking into a tutoring gig. You know how I made it through freshman year? Writing papers for rich frat-boys majoring in Advanced Beerology. If I'd been caught, I could have been suspended for a semester or tossed completely. I'll tell you what your grand gesture amounted to: giving away twenty hours a week you could have spent studying." He heard himself ranting, stopped, and raised a grin. "Or chatting up lissome females."

"*I'll* give you lissome," Erin said, and pounced on him. They went rolling across the sand, Erin tickling and Tom yelling (with a notable lack of conviction) for her to get off. That was fine with me, because I did not care to pursue the issues Tom had raised. I had already made up my mind about some things, it seemed, and all that remained was for my conscious mind to get the news.

♥

The next day, at quarter past three, we were in line at Horror House. A kid named Brady Waterman was agenting the shy. I remember him because he was also good at playing Howie. (But not as good as I was, I feel compelled to add…strictly in the cause of honesty.) Although quite stout at the beginning of the summer, Brady was now slim and trim. As a diet program, wearing the fur had Weight Watchers beat six ways to Tulsa.

"What are you guys doing here?" he asked. "Isn't it your day off?"

"We had to see Joyland's one and only dark ride," Tom said, "and I'm already feeling a satisfying sense of dramatic unity—Brad Waterman and Horror House. It's the perfect match."

He scowled. "You're all gonna try to cram into one car, aren'tcha?"

"We have to," Erin told him. Then she leaned close to one of Brad's juggy ears and whispered, "It's a Truth or Dare thing."

As Brad considered this, he touched the tip of his tongue to the middle of his upper lip. I could see him calculating the possibilities.

The guy behind us spoke up. "Kids, could you move the line along? I understand there's air conditioning inside, and I could use some."

"Go on," Brad told us. "Put an egg in your shoe and beat it." Coming from Brad, this was Rabelaisian wit.

"Any ghosts in there?" I asked.

"Hundreds, and I hope they all fly right up your ass."

♥

We started with Mysterio's Mirror Mansion, pausing briefly to regard ourselves drawn tall or smashed squat. With that minor giggle accomplished, we followed the tiny red dots on the bottoms of certain mirrors. These led us directly to the Wax Museum. Given this secret roadmap, we arrived well ahead of the rest of the current group, who wandered around, laughing and bumping into the various angled panes of glass.

To Tom's disappointment, there were no murderers in the Wax Museum, only pols and celebs. A smiling John F. Kennedy and a jumpsuited Elvis Presley flanked the doorway. Ignoring the PLEASE DO NOT TOUCH sign, Erin gave Elvis's guitar a strum. "Out of tu—" she began, then recoiled as Elvis jerked to life and began singing "Can't Help Falling in Love with You."

"Gotcha!" Tom said gleefully, and gave her a hug.

Beyond the Wax Museum was a doorway leading to the Barrel and Bridge Room, which rumbled with machinery that sounded dangerous (it wasn't) and stuttered with strobe lights of conflicting colors. Erin crossed to the other side on the shaking, tilting Billy Goat's Bridge while the macho men accompanying her dared the Barrel. I stumbled my way through, reeling like a drunk but only falling once. Tom stopped in the middle, stuck out his hands and feet so he looked like a paperdoll, and made a complete three-sixty that way.

"Stop it, you goof, you'll break your neck!" Erin called.

"He won't even if he falls," I said. "It's padded."

Tom rejoined us, grinning and flushed to the roots of his hair. "That woke up brain cells that have been asleep since I was three."

"Yeah, but what about all the ones it killed?" Erin asked.

Next came the Tilted Room and beyond that was an arcade filled with teenagers playing pinball and Skee-Ball. Erin watched the Skee-Ball for a while, with her arms folded beneath her breasts and a disapproving look on her face. "Don't they know that's a complete butcher's game?"

"People come here to be butched," I said. "It's part of the attraction."

Erin sighed. "And I thought *Tom* was a cynic."

On the far side of the arcade, beneath a glowing green skull, was a sign reading: HORROR HOUSE LIES BEYOND! BEWARE! PREGNANT WOMEN AND THOSE WITH SMALL CHILDREN MAY EXIT LEFT.

We walked into an antechamber filled with echoing recorded cackles and screams. Pulsing red light illuminated a single steel track and a black tunnel entrance beyond. From deep within it came rumbles, flashing lights, and more screams. These were not recorded. From a distance, they didn't sound particularly happy, but probably they were. Some, at least.

Eddie Parks, proprietor of Horror House and boss of Team Doberman, walked over to us. He was wearing rawhide gloves and a dogtop so old it was faded to no color at all (although it turned blood red each time the lights pulsed). He gave us a dismissive sniff. "Must have been a damn boring day off."

"Just wanted to see how the other half lives," Tom said.

Erin gave Eddie her most radiant smile. It was not returned.

"Three to a car, I guess. That what you want?"

"Yes," I said.

"Fine with me. Just remember that the rules apply to you, same as anyone else. Keep your fuckin hands inside."

"Yessir," Tom said, and gave a little salute. Eddie looked at him the way a man might look at a new species of bug and walked back to his controls, which consisted of three shifter-knobs sticking out of a waist-high podium. There were also a few buttons illuminated by a Tensor lamp bent low to minimize its less-than-ghostly white light.

"Charming guy," Tom muttered.

Erin hooked an arm into Tom's right elbow and my left, drawing us close. "Does anyone like him?" she murmured.

"No," Tom said. "Not even his own team. He's already fired two of them."

The rest of our group started to catch up just as a train filled with laughing conies (plus a few crying kids whose parents probably should have heeded the warning and exited from the arcade) arrived. Erin asked one of the girls if it was scary.

"The scary part was trying to keep *his* hands where they belong," she said, then squealed happily as her boyfriend first kissed her neck and then pulled her toward the arcade.

We climbed aboard. Three of us in a car designed for two made for an extremely tight fit, and I was very aware of Erin's thigh pressing against mine, and the brush of her breast against my arm. I felt a sudden and far from unpleasant southward tingle. I would argue that—fantasies aside—the majority of men are monogamous from the chin up. Below the belt-buckle, however, there's a wahoo stampeder who just doesn't give a shit.

"Hands inside the *caaa*!" Eddie Parks was yelling in a bored-to-death monotone that was the complete antithesis of a cheerful Lane Hardy pitch. "Hands inside the *caaa*! You got a kid under three feet, put im in your lap or get out of the *caaa*! Hold still and watch for the *baaa*!"

The safety bars came down with a clank, and a few girls tuned up with preparatory screams. Clearing their vocal cords for dark-ride arias to come, you might say.

There was a jerk, and we rode into Horror House.

♥

Nine minutes later we got out and exited through the arcade with the rest of the tip. Behind us, we could hear Eddie exhorting his next bunch to keep their hands inside the *caaa* and watch for the *baaa*. He never gave us a look.

"The dungeon part wasn't scary, because all the prisoners were Dobies," Erin said. "The one in the pirate outfit was Billy Ruggerio." Her color was high, her hair was mussed from the blowers, and I thought she had never looked so pretty. "But the Screaming Skull really got me, and the Torture Chamber…my God!"

"Pretty gross," I agreed. I'd seen a lot of horror movies during my high school years, and thought of myself as inured, but seeing an eye-bulging head come rolling down an inclined trough from the guillotine had jumped the shit out of me. I mean, the mouth was still moving.

Out on Joyland Avenue again, we spotted Cam Jorgensen from Team Foxhound selling lemonade. "Who wants one?" Erin asked. She was still bubbling over. "I'm buying!"

"Sure," I said.

"Tom?"

He shrugged his assent. Erin gave him a quizzical look, then ran to get the drinks. I glanced at Tom, but he was watching the Rocket go around and around. Or maybe looking through it.

Erin came back with three tall paper cups, half a lemon bobbing on top of each. We took them to the benches in Joyland Park, just down from the Wiggle-Waggle, and sat in the shade. Erin was talking about the bats at the end of the ride, how she knew they were just wind-up toys on wires, but bats had always scared the hell out of her and—

There she broke off. "Tom, are you okay? You haven't said a

word. Not sick to your stomach from turning in the Barrel, are you?"

"My stomach's fine." He took a sip of his lemonade, as if to prove it. "What was she wearing, Dev? Do you know?"

"Huh?"

"The girl who got murdered. Laurie Gray."

"*Linda* Gray."

"Laurie, Larkin, Linda, whatever. What was she wearing? Was it a full skirt—a long one, down to her shins—and a sleeveless blouse?"

I looked at him closely. We both did, initially thinking it was just another Tom Kennedy goof. Only he didn't look like he was goofing. Now that I really examined him, what he looked like was scared half to death.

"Tom?" Erin touched his shoulder. "Did you see her? Don't joke, now."

He put his hand over hers but didn't look at her. He was looking at me. "Yeah," he said, "long skirt and sleeveless blouse. You know, because La Shoplaw told you."

"What color?" I asked.

"Hard to tell with the lights changing all the time, but I think blue. Blouse and skirt both."

Then Erin got it. "Holy shit," she said in a kind of sigh. The high color was leaving her cheeks in a hurry.

There was something else. Something the police had held back for a long time, according to Mrs. Shoplaw.

"What about her hair, Tom? Ponytail, right?"

He shook his head. Took a small sip of his lemonade. Patted his mouth with the back of his hand. His hair hadn't gone gray, he wasn't all starey-eyed, his hands weren't shaking, but he still didn't look like the same guy who'd joked his way through the Mirror Mansion and the Barrel and Bridge Room. He looked like a guy who'd just gotten a reality enema, one that had flushed all the junior-year-summer-job bullshit out of his system.

"Not a ponytail. Her hair long, all right, but she had a thing across the top of her head to keep it out of her face. I've seen a billion of em, but I can't remember what girls call it."

"An Alice band," Erin said.

"Yeah. I think that was blue, too. She was holding out her hands." He held his out in the exact same way Emmalina Shoplaw had held hers out on the day she told me the story. "Like she was asking for help."

"You already know this stuff from Mrs. Shoplaw," I said. "Isn't that right? Tell us, we won't be mad. Will we, Erin?"

"No, uh-uh."

But Tom shook his head. "I'm just telling you what I saw. Neither of you saw her?"

We had not, and said so.

"Why me?" Tom asked plaintively. "Once we were inside, I wasn't even thinking of her. I was just having fun. So *why me*?"

♥

Erin tried to get more details while I drove us back to Heaven's Bay in my heap. Tom answered the first two or three of her questions, then said he didn't want to talk about it anymore in an abrupt tone I'd never heard him use with Erin before. I don't think she had, either, because she was quiet as a mouse for the rest of the ride. Maybe they talked about it some more between themselves, but I can tell you that he never spoke of it again to me until about a month before he died, and then only briefly. It was near the end of a phone conversation that had been painful because of his halting, nasal voice and the way he sometimes got confused.

"At least...I know...there's *something*," he said. "I saw...for myself...that summer. In the Hasty Hut." I didn't bother to correct him; I knew what he meant. "Do you...remember?"

"I remember," I said.

"But I don't know...the *something*...if it's good...or bad." His dying voice filled with horror. "The way she...Dev, *the way she held out her hands...*"

Yes.

The way she held out her hands.

♥

The next time I had a full day off, it was nearly the middle of August, and the tide of conies was ebbing. I no longer had to jink and juke my way up Joyland Avenue to the Carolina Spin ...and to Madame Fortuna's shy, which stood in its revolving shadow.

Lane and Fortuna—she was all Fortuna today, in full gypsy kit—were talking together by the Spin's control station. Lane saw me and tipped his derby widdershins, which was his way of acknowledging me.

"Look what the cat drug in," he said. "How ya be, Jonesy?"

"Fine," I said, although this wasn't strictly true. The sleepless nights had come back now that I was only wearing the fur four or five times a day. I lay in my bed waiting for the small hours to get bigger, window open so I could hear the incoming surf, thinking about Wendy and her new boyfriend. Also thinking about the girl Tom had seen standing beside the tracks in Horror

House, in the fake brick tunnel between the Dungeon and the Chamber of Torture.

I turned to Fortuna. "Can I talk to you?"

She didn't ask why, just led me to her shy, swept aside the purple curtain that hung in the doorway, and ushered me in. There was a round table covered with a rose-pink cloth. On it was Fortuna's crystal, now draped. Two simple folding chairs were positioned so that seer and supplicant faced each other over the crystal (which, I happened to know, was underlit by a small bulb Madame Fortuna could operate with her foot). On the back wall was a giant silk-screened hand, fingers spread and palm out. On it, neatly labeled, were the Seven: lifeline, heartline, headline, loveline (also known as the Girdle of Venus), sunline, fateline, healthline.

Madame Fortuna gathered her skirts and seated herself. She motioned for me to do the same. She did not undrape her crystal, nor did she invite me to cross her palm with silver so that I might know the future.

"Ask what you came to ask," she said.

"I want to know if the little girl was just an informed guess or if you really knew something. Saw something."

She looked at me, long and steadily. In Madame Fortuna's place of business, there was a faint smell of incense instead of popcorn and fried dough. The walls were flimsy, but the music, the chatter of the conies, and the rumble of the rides all seemed very far away. I wanted to look down, but managed not to.

"Actually, you want to know if I'm a fraud. Isn't that so?"

"I...ma'am, I honestly don't know *what* I want."

At that she smiled. It was a good one—as if I had passed

some sort of test. "You're a sweet boy, Jonesy, but like so many sweet boys, you're a punk liar."

I started to reply; she hushed me with a wave of her ring-heavy right hand. She reached beneath her table and brought out her cashbox. Madame Fortuna's readings were free—all part of your admission fee, ladies and gentlemen, boys and girls—but tips were encouraged. And legal under North Carolina law. When she opened the box, I saw a sheaf of crumpled bills, mostly ones, something that looked suspiciously like a punch-board (*not* legal under North Carolina law), and a single small envelope. Printed on the front was my name. She held it out. I hesitated, then took it.

"You didn't come to Joyland today just to ask me that," she said.

"Well..."

She waved me off again. "You know *exactly* what you want. In the short term, at least. And since the short term is all any of us have, who is Fortuna—or Rozzie Gold, for that matter—to argue with you? Go now. Do what you came here to do. When it's done, open that and read what I've written." She smiled. "No charge to employees. Especially not good kids like you."

"I don't—"

She rose in a swirl of skirts and a rattle of jewelry. "Go, Jonesy. We're finished here."

♥

I left her tight little booth in a daze. Music from two dozen shys and rides seemed to hit me like conflicting winds, and the sun was a hammer. I went directly to the administration building (actually a doublewide trailer), gave a courtesy knock, went in, and said hello to Brenda Rafferty, who was going back and forth between an open account book and her faithful adding machine.

"Hello, Devin," she said. "Are you taking care of your Hollywood Girl?"

"Yes, ma'am, we all watch out for her."

"Dana Elkhart, isn't it?"

"Erin Cook, ma'am."

"Erin, of course. Team Beagle. The redhead. What can I do for you?"

"I wonder if I could speak to Mr. Easterbrook."

"He's resting, and I hate to disturb him. He had an awful lot of phone calls to make earlier, and we still have to go over some numbers, much as I hate to bother him with them. He tires very easily these days."

"I wouldn't be long."

She sighed. "I suppose I could see if he's awake. Can you tell me what it's about?"

"A favor," I said. "He'll understand."

♥

He did, and only asked me two questions. The first was if I was sure. I said I was. The second…

"Have you told your parents yet, Jonesy?"

"It's just me and my dad, Mr. Easterbrook, and I'll do that tonight."

"Very well, then. Put Brenda in the picture before you leave. She'll have all the necessary paperwork, and you can fill it out…" Before he could finish, his mouth opened and he displayed his horsey teeth in a vast, gaping yawn. "Excuse me, son. It's been a tiring day. A tiring *summer*."

"Thank you, Mr. Easterbrook."

He waved his hand. "Very welcome. I'm sure you'll be a great addition, but if you do this without your father's consent, I shall be disappointed in you. Close the door on your way out, please."

I tried not to see Brenda's frown as she searched her file cabinets and hunted out the various forms Joyland, Inc. required for full-time employment. It didn't matter, because I felt her disapproval anyway. I folded the paperwork, stuck it in the back pocket of my jeans, and left.

Beyond the line of donnikers at the far end of the backyard was a little grove of blackgum trees. I went in there, sat down with my back against one, and opened the envelope Madame Fortuna had given me. The note was brief and to the point.

> *You're going to Mr. Easterbrook to ask if you can stay on at the park after Labor Day. You know he will not refuse your request.*

She was right, I wanted to know if she was a fraud. Here was her answer. And yes, I had made up my mind about what came next in the life of Devin Jones. She had been right about that, too.

But there was one more line.

> *You saved the little girl, but dear boy! You can't save everyone.*

♥

After I told my dad I wasn't going back to UNH—that I needed a year off from college and planned to spend it at Joyland—there was a long silence at the southern Maine end of the line. I thought he might yell at me, but he didn't. He only sounded tired. "It's that girl, isn't it?"

I'd told him almost two months earlier that Wendy and I were "taking some time off," but Dad saw right through that. Since then, he hadn't spoken her name a single time in our weekly phone conversations. Now she was just *that girl*. After the first couple of times he said it I tried a joke, asking if he thought I'd been going out with Marlo Thomas. He wasn't amused. I didn't try again.

"Wendy's part of it," I admitted, "but not all of it. I just need some time off. A breather. And I've gotten to like it here."

He sighed. "Maybe you do need a break. At least you'll be working instead of hitchhiking around Europe, like Dewey Michaud's girl. Fourteen months in youth hostels! Fourteen and counting! Ye gods! She's apt to come back with ringworm and a bun in the oven."

"Well," I said, "I think I can avoid both of those. If I'm careful."

"Just make sure you avoid the hurricanes. It's supposed to be a bad season for them."

"Are you really all right with this, Dad?"

"Why? Did you want me to argue? Try to talk you out of it? If that's what you want, I'm willing to give it a shot, but I know what your mother would say—if he's old enough to buy a legal drink, he's old enough to start making decisions about his life."

I smiled. "Yeah. That sounds like her."

"As for me, I guess I don't want you going back to college if you're going to spend all your time mooning over that girl and letting your grades go to hell. If painting rides and fixing up concessions will help get her out of your system, probably that's a good thing. But what about your scholarship and loan package, if you want to go back in the fall of '74?"

"It won't be a problem. I've got a 3.2 cume, which is pretty persuasive."

"That girl," he said in tones of infinite disgust, and then we moved on to other topics.

♥

I was still sad and depressed about how things had ended with Wendy, he was right about that, but I had begun the difficult trip (*the journey*, as they say in the self-help groups these days) from denial to acceptance. Anything like true serenity was still over the horizon, but I no longer believed—as I had in the long, painful days and nights of June—that serenity was out of the question.

Staying had to do with other things that I couldn't even begin to sort out, because they were piled helter-skelter in an untidy stack and bound with the rough twine of intuition. Hallie Stansfield was there. So was Bradley Easterbrook, way back at the beginning of the summer, saying *we sell fun*. The sound of the ocean at night was there, and the way a strong onshore breeze would make a little song when it blew through the struts of the Carolina Spin. The cool tunnels under the park were there. So was the Talk, that secret language the other greenies would have forgotten by the time Christmas break rolled around. I didn't want to forget it; it was too rich. I felt that Joyland had something more to give me. I didn't know what, just…s'more.

But mostly—this is weird, I have examined and re-examined my memories of those days to make sure it's a true memory, and it seems to be—it was because it had been our Doubting Thomas to see the ghost of Linda Gray. It had changed him in small but fundamental ways. I don't think Tom *wanted* to change—I think he was happy just as he was—but *I* did.

I wanted to see her, too.

♥

During the second half of August, several of the old-timers—Pop Allen for one, Dottie Lassen for another—told me to pray for rain on Labor Day weekend. There was no rain, and by Saturday afternoon I understood what they meant. The conies came back in force for one final grand hurrah, and Joyland was tipsed to the gills. What made it worse was that half of the summer help was gone by then, headed back to their various schools. The ones who were left worked like dogs.

Some of us didn't just work *like* dogs, but *as* dogs—one dog in particular. I saw most of that holiday weekend through the mesh eyes of Howie the Happy Hound. On Sunday I climbed into that damned fur suit a dozen times. After my second-to-last turn of the day, I was three-quarters of the way down the Boulevard beneath Joyland Avenue when the world started to swim away from me in shades of gray. *Shades of* Linda *Gray*, I remember thinking.

I was driving one of the little electric service-carts with the fur pushed down to my waist so I could feel the air conditioning on my sweaty chest, and when I realized I was losing it, I had the good sense to pull over to the wall and take my foot off the rubber button that served as the accelerator. Fat Wally Schmidt, who ran the guess-your-weight shy, happened to be taking a break in the boneyard at the time. He saw me parked askew and slumped over the cart's steering bar. He got a pitcher of icewater out of the fridge, waddled down to me, and lifted my chin with one chubby hand.

"Hey greenie. You got another suit, or is that the only one that fits ya?"

"Theresh another one," I said. I sounded drunk. "Cossume shop. Ex'ra large."

"Oh hey, that's good," he said, and dumped the pitcher over my head. My scream of surprise echoed up and down the Boulevard and brought several people running.

"What the *fuck*, Fat Wally?"

He grinned. "Wakes ya up, don't it? Damn right it does. Labor Day weekend, greenie. That means ya labor. No sleepin on the job. Thank yer lucky stars n bars it ain't a hunnert and ten out there."

If it *had* been a hunnert and ten, I wouldn't be telling this story; I would have died of a baked brain halfway through a Happy Howie Dance on the Wiggle-Waggle Story Stage. But Labor Day itself was actually cloudy, and featured a nice sea-breeze. I got through it somehow.

Around four o'clock that Monday, as I was climbing into the spare fur for my final show of the summer, Tom Kennedy strolled into the costume shop. His dogtop and filthy sneakers were gone. He was wearing crisply pressed chinos (*wherever were you keeping them*, I wondered), a neatly tucked-in Ivy League shirt, and Bass Weejuns. Rosy-cheeked son of a bitch had even gotten a haircut. He looked every inch the up-and-coming college boy with his eye on the business world. You never would have guessed that he'd been dressed in filthy Levis only two days before, displaying at least an inch of ass-cleavage as he crawled under the Zipper with an oil-bucket and cursing Pop Allen, our fearless Team Beagle leader, every time he bumped his head on a strut.

"You on your way?" I asked.

"That's a big ten-four, good buddy. I'm taking the train to Philly at eight tomorrow morning. I've got a week at home, then it's back to the grind."

"Good for you."

"Erin's got some stuff to finish up, but then she's meeting me in Wilmington tonight. I booked us a room at a nice little bed and breakfast."

I felt a dull throb of jealousy at that. "Good deal."

"She's the real thing," he said.

"I know."

"So are you, Dev. We'll stay in touch. People say that and don't mean it, but I do. We *will* stay in touch." He held out his hand.

I took it and shook it. "That's right, we will. You're okay, Tom, and Erin's the total package. You take care of her."

"No problem there." He grinned. "Come spring semester, she's transferring to Rutgers. I already taught her the Scarlet Knights fight song. You know, 'Upstream, Redteam, Redteam, Upstream—' "

"Sounds complex," I said.

He shook his finger at me. "Sarcasm will get you nowhere in this world, boy. Unless you're angling for a writing job at *Mad* magazine, that is."

Dottie Lassen called, "Maybe you could shorten up the farewells and keep the tears to a minimum? You've got a show to do, Jonesy."

Tom turned to her and held out his arms. "Dottie, how I love you! How I'll *miss* you!"

She slapped her bottom to show just how much this moved her and turned away to a costume in need of repair.

Tom handed me a scrap of paper. "My home address, school address, phone numbers for both. I expect you to use them."

"I will."

"You're really going to give up a year you could spend drinking beer and getting laid to scrape paint here at Joyland?"

"Yep."

"Are you crazy?"

I considered this. "Probably. A little. But getting better."

I was sweaty and his clothes were clean, but he gave me a brief hug just the same. Then he headed for the door, pausing to give Dottie a kiss on one wrinkled cheek. She couldn't cuss at him—her mouth was full of pins at the time—but she shooed him away with a flap of her hand.

At the door, he turned back to me. "You want some advice, Dev? Stay away from..." He finished with a head-jerk, and I knew well enough what he meant: Horror House. Then he was gone, probably thinking about his visit home, and Erin, the car he hoped to buy, and Erin, the upcoming school year, and Erin. Upstream, Redteam, Redteam, Upstream. Come spring semester, they could chant it together. Hell, they could chant it that very night, if they wanted to. In Wilmington. In bed. Together.

♥

There was no punch-clock at the park; our comings and goings were supervised by our team leaders. After my final turn as Howie on that first Monday in September, Pop Allen told me to bring him my time-card.

"I've got another hour," I said.

"Nah, someone's waiting at the gate to walk you back." I knew who the someone had to be. It was hard to believe there was a soft spot in Pop's shriveled-up raisin of a heart for anyone, but there was, and that summer Miss Erin Cook owned it.

"You know the deal tomorrow?"

"Seven-thirty to six," I said. And no fur. What a blessing.

"I'll be running you for the first couple of weeks, then I'm off to sunny Florida. After that, you're Lane Hardy's responsibility. And Freddy Dean, I guess, if he happens to notice you're still around."

"Got it."

"Good. I'll sign your card and then you're ten-forty-two." Which meant the same thing in the Talk as it did on the CBs that were so popular then: *End of tour*. "And Jonesy? Tell that girl to send me a postcard once in a while. I'll miss her."

He wasn't the only one.

♥

Erin had also begun making the transition back from Joyland Life to Real Life. Gone were the faded jeans and tee-shirt with the sassy rolled-to-the-shoulder sleeves; ditto the green Hollywood Girl dress and Sherwood Forest hat. The girl standing in the scarlet shower of neon just outside the gate was wearing a silky blue sleeveless blouse tucked into a belted A-line skirt. Her hair was pinned back and she looked gorgeous.

"Walk me up the beach," she said. "I'll just have time to catch the bus to Wilmington. I'm meeting Tom."

"He told me. But never mind the bus. I'll drive you."

"Would you do that?"

"Sure."

We walked along the fine white sand. A half-moon had risen in the sky, and it beat a track across the water. Halfway to Heaven's Beach—it was, in fact, not far from the big green Victorian that played such a part in my life that fall—she took my hand, and we walked that way. We didn't say much until we reached the steps leading up to the beach parking lot. There she turned to me.

"You'll get over her." Her eyes were on mine. She wasn't wearing makeup that night, and didn't need any. The moonlight was her makeup.

"Yes," I said. I knew it was true, and part of me was sorry. It's hard to let go. Even when what you're holding onto is full of thorns, it's hard to let go. Maybe especially then.

"And for now this is the right place for you. I feel that."

"Does Tom feel it?"

"No, but he never felt about Joyland the way you do…and the way I did this summer. And after what happened that day in the funhouse…what he saw…"

"Do the two of you ever talk about that?"

"I tried. Now I leave it alone. It doesn't fit into his philosophy of how the world works, so he's trying to make it gone. But I think he worries about you."

"Do *you* worry about me?"

"About you and the ghost of Linda Gray, no. About you and the ghost of that Wendy, a little."

I grinned. "My father no longer speaks her name. Just calls her 'that girl.' Erin, would you do me a favor when you get back to school? If you have time, that is?"

"Sure. What is it?"

I told her.

♥

She asked if I would drop her at the Wilmington bus station instead of taking her directly to the B&B Tom had booked. She said she'd rather take a taxi there. I started to protest that it was a waste of money, then didn't. She looked flustered, a trifle embarrassed, and I guessed it had something to do with not wanting to climb out of my car just so she could drop her clothes and climb into the sack with Tom Kennedy two minutes later.

When I pulled up opposite the taxi stand, she put her hands on the sides of my face and kissed my mouth. It was a long and thoroughly thorough kiss.

"If Tom hadn't been there, *I* would have made you forget that stupid girl," she said.

"But he was," I said.

"Yes. He was. Stay in touch, Dev."

"Remember what I asked you to do. If you get a chance, that is."

"I'll remember. You're a sweet man."

I don't know why, but that made me feel like crying. I smiled instead. "Also, admit it, I made one hell of a Howie."

"That you did. Devin Jones, savior of little girls."

For a moment I thought she was going to kiss me again, but she didn't. She slid out of my car and ran across the street to the taxis, skirt flying. I sat there until I saw her climb into the back of a Yellow and drive away. Then I drove away myself, back to Heaven's Beach, and Mrs. Shoplaw's, and my autumn at Joyland—both the best and worst autumn of my life.

♥

Were Annie and Mike Ross sitting at the end of the green Victorian's boardwalk when I headed down the beach to the park on that Tuesday after Labor Day? I remember the warm croissants I ate as I walked, and the circling gulls, but of them I can't be completely sure. They became such an important part of the scenery—such a landmark—that it's impossible to pinpoint the first time I actually noticed their presence. Nothing screws with memory like repetition.

Ten years after the events I'm telling you about, I was (for my sins, maybe) a staff writer on *Cleveland* magazine. I used to do most of my first-draft writing on yellow legal pads in a coffee shop on West Third Street, near Lakefront Stadium, which was the Indians' stomping grounds back then. Every day at ten, this young woman would come in and get four or five coffees, then take them back to the real estate office next door. I couldn't tell you the first time I saw her, either. All I know is that one day I *saw* her, and realized that she sometimes glanced at me as she went out. The day came when I returned that glance, and when she smiled, I did, too. Eight months later we were married.

Annie and Mike were like that; one day they just became a real part of my world. I always waved, the kid in the wheelchair always waved back, and the dog sat watching me with his ears cocked and the wind ruffling his fur. The woman was blonde and beautiful—high cheekbones, wide-set blue eyes, and full lips, the kind that always look a little bruised. The boy in the wheelchair wore a White Sox cap that came down over his ears. He looked very sick. His smile was healthy enough, though. Whether I was going or coming, he always flashed it. Once or twice he even flashed me the peace sign, and I sent it right back. I had become part of his landscape, just as he had become part of mine. I think even Milo, the Jack Russell, came to recognize me as part of the landscape. Only Mom held herself apart. Often when I passed, she never even looked up from whatever book she was reading. When she did she didn't wave, and she certainly never flashed the peace sign.

♥

I had plenty to occupy my time at Joyland, and if the work wasn't as interesting and varied as it had been during the summer, it was steadier and less exhausting. I even got a chance to reprise my award-winning role as Howie, and to sing a few more choruses of "Happy Birthday to You" in the Wiggle-Waggle Village, because Joyland was open to the public for the first three weekends in September. Attendance was way down, though, and I didn't jock a single tipsed ride. Not even the Carolina Spin, which was second only to the merry-go-round as our most popular attraction.

"Up north in New England, most parks stay open weekends until Halloween," Fred Dean told me one day. We were sitting on a bench and eating a nourishing, vitamin-rich lunch of chili burgers and pork rinds. "Down south in Florida, they run year-round. We're in a kind of gray zone. Mr. Easterbrook tried pushing for a fall season back in the sixties—spent a bundle on a big advertising blitz—but it didn't work very well. By the time the nights start getting nippy, people around here start thinking about county fairs and such. Also, a lot of our vets head south or out west for the winter." He looked down the empty expanse of Hound Dog Way and sighed. "This place gets kind of lonely this time of year."

"I like it," I said, and I did. That was my year to embrace loneliness. I sometimes went to the movies in Lumberton or Myrtle Beach with Mrs. Shoplaw and Tina Ackerley, the librarian with the goo-goo-googly eyes, but I spent most evenings in my room, re-reading *The Lord of the Rings* and writing letters to Erin, Tom, and my dad. I also wrote a fair amount of poetry, which I am now embarrassed even to think about. Thank God I burned it. I added a new and satisfyingly grim record to my small collection—*The Dark Side of the Moon*. In the Book of Proverbs we are advised that "as a dog returns to its vomit, so a fool repeats his folly." That autumn I returned to *Dark Side* again and again, only giving Floyd the occasional rest so I could listen to Jim Morrison once more intone, "This is the end, beautiful friend." Such a really bad case of the twenty-ones—I know, I know.

At least there was plenty at Joyland to occupy my days. The first couple of weeks, while the park was still running part-time, were devoted to fall cleaning. Fred Dean put me in charge of a small crew of gazoonies, and by the time the CLOSED FOR THE SEASON sign went up out front, we had raked and cut every lawn, prepared every flowerbed for winter, and scrubbed down every joint and shy. We slapped together a prefab corrugated metal shed in the backyard and stored the food carts (called grub-rollers in the Talk) there for the winter, each popcorn wagon, Sno-Cone wagon, and Pup-a-Licious wagon snugged under its own green tarp.

When the gazoonies headed north to pick apples, I started the winterizing process with Lane Hardy and Eddie Parks, the ill-tempered vet who ran Horror House (and Team Doberman) during the season. We drained the fountain at the intersection of Joyland Avenue and Hound Dog Way, and had moved on to Captain Nemo's Splash & Crash—a much bigger job—when Bradley Easterbrook, dressed for traveling in his black suit, came by.

"I'm off to Sarasota this evening," he told us. "Brenda Rafferty will be with me, as usual." He smiled, showing those horse teeth of his. "I'm touring the park and saying my thank-yous. To those who are left, that is."

"Have a wonderful winter, Mr. Easterbrook," Lane said.

Eddie muttered something that sounded to me like *eat a wooden ship*, but was probably *have a good trip*.

"Thanks for everything," I said.

He shook hands with the three of us, coming to me last. "I hope to see you again next year, Jonesy. I think you're a young man with more than a little carny in his soul."

But he didn't see me the following year, and nobody saw him. Mr. Easterbrook died on New Year's Day, in a condo on John Ringling Boulevard, less than half a mile from where the famous circus winters.

"Crazy old bastid," Parks said, watching Easterbrook walk to his car, where Brenda was waiting to receive him and help him in.

Lane gave him a long, steady look, then said: "Shut it, Eddie."

Eddie did. Which was probably wise.

♥

One morning, as I walked to Joyland with my croissants, the Jack Russell finally trotted down the beach to investigate me.

"Milo, come back!" the woman called.

Milo turned to look at her, then looked back at me with his bright black eyes. On impulse, I tore a piece from one of my pastries, squatted, and held it out to him. Milo came like a shot.

"Don't you feed him!" the woman called sharply.

"Aw, Mom, get over it," the boy said.

Milo heard her and didn't take the shred of croissant…but he did sit up before me with his front paws held out. I gave him the bite.

"I won't do it again," I said, getting up, "but I couldn't let a good trick go to waste."

The woman snorted and went back to her book, which was thick and looked arduous. The boy called, "We feed him all the time. He never puts on weight, just runs it off."

Without looking up from her book, Mom said: "What do we know about talking to strangers, Mike-O?"

"He's not exactly a stranger when we see him every day," the boy pointed out. Reasonably enough, at least from my point of view.

"I'm Devin Jones," I said. "From down the beach. I work at Joyland."

"Then you won't want to be late." Still not looking up.

The boy shrugged at me—*whattaya gonna do*, it said. He was pale and as bent-over as an old man, but I thought there was a lively sense of humor in that shrug and the look that went with it. I returned the shrug and walked on. The next morning I took care to finish my croissants before I got to the big green Victorian so Milo wouldn't be tempted, but I waved. The kid, Mike, waved back. The woman was in her usual place under the green umbrella, and she had no book, but—as per usual—she didn't wave to me. Her lovely face was closed. *There is nothing here for you*, it said. *Go on down to your trumpery amusement park and leave us alone.*

So that was what I did. But I continued to wave, and the kid waved back. Morning and night, the kid waved back.

♥

The Monday after Gary "Pop" Allen left for Florida—bound for Alston's All-Star Carnival in Jacksonville, where he had a job waiting as shy-boss—I arrived at Joyland and found Eddie Parks, my least favorite old-timer, sitting in front of Horror

House on an apple-box. Smoking was *verboten* in the park, but with Mr. Easterbrook gone and Fred Dean nowhere in evidence, Eddie seemed to feel it safe to flout the rule. He was smoking with his gloves on, which would have struck me as strange if he ever took them off, but he never seemed to.

"There you are, kiddo, and only five minutes late." Everyone else called me either Dev or Jonesy, but to Eddie I was just *kiddo*, and always would be.

"I've got seven-thirty on the nose," I said, tapping my watch.

"Then you're slow. Why don't you drive from town, like everybody else? You could be here in five minutes."

"I like the beach."

"I don't give a tin shit what you like, kiddo, just get here on time. This isn't like one of your college classes, when you can duck in and out anytime you want to. This is a *job*, and now that the Head Beagle is gone, you're gonna work like it's a job."

I could have pointed out that Pop had told me Lane Hardy would be in charge of my schedule after he, Pop, was gone, but kept my lip zipped. No sense making a bad situation worse. As to why Eddie had taken a dislike to me, that was obvious. Eddie was an equal-opportunity disliker. I'd go to Lane if life with Eddie got too hard, but only as a last resort. My father had taught me—mostly by example—that if a man wanted to be in charge of his life, he had to be in charge of his problems.

"What have you got for me, Mr. Parks?"

"Plenty. I want you to get a tub of Turtle Wax from the supply shed to start with, and don't be lingerin down there to shoot the shit with any of your pals, either. Then I want you to go on in Horra and wax all them cars." Except, of course, he said it *caaas*. "You know we wax em once the season's over, don't you?"

"Actually I didn't."

"Jesus Christ, you kids." He stomped on his cigarette butt, then lifted the apple-box he was sitting on enough to toss it under. As if that would make it gone. "You want to really put some elbow-grease into it, kiddo, or I'll send you back in to do it again. You got that?"

"I got it."

"Good for you." He stuck another cigarette in his gob, then fumbled in his pants pocket for his lighter. With the gloves on, it took him awhile. He finally got it, flicked back the lid, then stopped. "What are you looking at?"

"Nothing," I said.

"Then get going. Flip on the house lights so you can see what the fuck you're doing. You know where the switches are, don't you?"

I didn't, but I'd find them without his help. "Sure."

He eyed me sourly. "Ain't you the smart one." *Smaaat*.

♥

I found a metal box marked LTS on the wall between the Wax Museum and the Barrel and Bridge Room. I opened it and flipped up all the switches with the heel of my hand. Horror House should have lost all of its cheesy/sinister mystique with all the house lights on, but somehow didn't. There were still shadows in the corners, and I could hear the wind—quite strong that morning—blowing outside the joint's thin wooden walls and rattling a loose board somewhere. I made a mental note to track it down and fix it.

I had a wire basket swinging from one hand. It was filled with clean rags and a giant economy-size can of Turtle Wax. I carried it through the Tilted Room—now frozen on a starboard slant—and into the arcade. I looked at the Skee-Ball machines and remembered Erin's disapproval: *Don't they know that's a complete butcher's game*? I smiled at the memory, but my heart was beating hard. I knew what I was going to do when I'd finished my chore, you see.

The cars, twenty in all, were lined up at the loading point. Ahead, the tunnel leading into the bowels of Horror House was lit by a pair of bright white work lights instead of flashing strobes. It looked a lot more prosaic that way.

I was pretty sure Eddie hadn't so much as swiped the little cars with a damp rag all summer long, and that meant I had to start by washing them down. Which also meant fetching soap powder from the supply shed and carrying buckets of water from the nearest working tap. By the time I had all twenty cars washed and rinsed off, it was break-time, but I decided to work right through instead of going out to the backyard or down to the boneyard for coffee. I might meet Eddie at either place, and I'd listened to enough of his grouchy bullshit for one morning. I set to work polishing instead, laying the Turtle Wax on thick and then buffing it off, moving from car to car, making them shine in the overhead lights until they looked new again. Not that the next crowd of thrill-seekers would notice as they crowded in for their nine-minute ride. My own gloves were ruined by the time I was finished. I'd have to buy a new pair at the hardware store in town, and good ones didn't come cheap. I amused myself briefly by imagining how Eddie would react if I asked him to pay for them.

I stashed my basket of dirty rags and Turtle Wax (the can now mostly empty) by the exit door in the arcade. It was ten past noon, but right then food wasn't what I was hungry for. I tried to stretch the ache out of my arms and legs, then went back to the loading-point. I paused to admire the cars gleaming mellowly beneath the lights, then walked slowly along the track and into Horror House proper.

I had to duck my head when I passed beneath the Screaming Skull, even though it was now pulled up and locked in its home position. Beyond it was the Dungeon, where the live talent from Eddie's Team Doberman had tried (and mostly succeeded) in scaring the crap out of children of all ages with their moans and howls. Here I could straighten up again, because it was a tall room. My footfalls echoed on a wooden floor painted to look like stone. I could hear my breathing. It sounded harsh and dry. I was scared, okay? Tom had told me to stay away from this place, but Tom didn't run my life any more than Eddie Parks did. I had the Doors, and I had Pink Floyd, but I wanted more. I wanted Linda Gray.

Between the Dungeon and the Torture Chamber, the track descended and described a double-S curve where the cars picked up speed and whipped the riders back and forth. Horror House was a dark ride, but when it was in operation, this stretch was the only completely dark part. It had to be where the girl's killer had cut her throat and dumped her body. How quick he must have been, and how certain of exactly what he was going to do! Beyond the last curve, riders were dazzled by a mix of stuttering, multi-colored strobes. Although Tom had never said it in so many words, I was positive it was where he had seen what he'd seen.

I walked slowly down the double-S, thinking it would not be beyond Eddie to hear me and shut off the overhead work-lights as a joke. To leave me in here to feel my way past the murder site with only the sound of the wind and that one slapping board to keep me company. And suppose…just suppose…a young girl's hand reached out in that darkness and took mine, the way Erin had taken my hand that last night on the beach?

The lights stayed on. No bloody shirt and gloves appeared beside the track, glowing spectrally. And when I came to what I felt sure was the right spot, just before the entrance to the Torture Chamber, there was no ghost-girl holding her hands out to me.

Yet something was there. I knew it then and I know it now. The air was colder. Not cold enough to see my breath, but yes, definitely colder. My arms and legs and groin all prickled with gooseflesh, and the hair at the nape of my neck stiffened.

"Let me see you," I whispered, feeling foolish and terrified. Wanting it to happen, hoping it wouldn't.

There was a sound. A long, slow sigh. Not a human sigh, not in the least. It was as if someone had opened an invisible steam-valve. Then it was gone. There was no more. Not that day.

♥

"Took you long enough," Eddie said when I finally reappeared at quarter to one. He was seated on the same apple-box, now with the remains of a BLT in one hand and a Styrofoam cup of coffee in the other. I was filthy from the neck down. Eddie, on the other hand, looked fresh as a daisy.

"The cars were pretty dirty. I had to wash them before I could wax them."

Eddie hawked back phlegm, twisted his head, and spat. "If you want a medal, I'm fresh out. Go find Hardy. He says it's time to drain the irry-gation system. That should keep a lag-ass like you busy until quittin time. If it don't, come see me and I'll find something else for you to do. I got a whole list, believe me."

"Okay." I started off, glad to be going.

"Kiddo!"

I turned back reluctantly.

"Did you see her in there?"

"Huh?"

He grinned unpleasantly. "Don't 'huh' me. I know what you were doin. You weren't the first, and you won't be the last. Did you see her?"

"Have *you* ever seen her?"

"Nope." He looked at me, sly little gimlet eyes peering out of a narrow sunburned face. How old was he? Thirty? Sixty? It was impossible to tell, just as it was impossible to tell if he was speaking the truth. I didn't care. I just wanted to be away from him. He gave me the creeps.

Eddie raised his gloved hands. "The guy who did it wore a pair of these. Did you know that?"

I nodded. "Also an extra shirt."

"That's right." His grin widened. "To keep the blood off. And it worked, didn't it? They never caught him. Now get out of here."

♥

When I got to the Spin, only Lane's shadow was there to greet me. The man it belonged to was halfway up the wheel, climbing the struts. He tested each steel crosspiece before he put his weight on it. A leather toolkit hung on one hip, and every now and then he reached into it for a socket wrench. Joyland only had a single dark ride, but almost a dozen so-called high rides, including the Spin, the Zipper, the Thunderball, and the Delirium Shaker. There was a three-man maintenance crew that checked them each day before Early Gate during the season, and of course there were visits (both announced and unannounced) from the North Carolina State Inspector of Amusements, but Lane said a ride-jock who didn't check his ride himself was both lazy and irresponsible. Which made me wonder when Eddie Parks had last ridden in one of his own *caaas* and safety-checked the *baaas*.

Lane looked down, saw me, and shouted: "Did that ugly sonofabitch ever give you a lunch break?"

"I worked through it," I called back. "Lost track of time." But now I *was* hungry.

"There's some tuna-and-macaroni salad in my doghouse, if you want it. I made up way too much last night."

I went into the little control shack, found a good-sized Tupperware container, and popped it open. By the time Lane was back on the ground, the tuna-and-macaroni was in my stomach and I was tamping it down with a couple of leftover Fig Newtons.

"Thanks, Lane. That was tasty."

"Yeah, I'll make some guy a good wife someday. Gimme some of those Newtons before they all go down your throat."

I handed over the box. "How's the ride?"

"The Spin is tight and the Spin is right. Want to help me work on the engine for a while after you've digested a little?"

"Sure."

He took off his derby and spun it on his finger. His hair was pulled back in a tight little ponytail, and I noticed a few threads of white in the black. They hadn't been there at the start of the summer—I was quite sure of it. "Listen, Jonesy, Eddie Parks is carny-from-carny, but that doesn't change the fact that he's one mean-ass sonofabitch. In his eyes, you got two strikes against you: you're young and you've been educated beyond the eighth grade. When you get tired of taking his shit, tell me and I'll get him to back off."

"Thanks, but I'm okay for now."

"I know you are. I've been watching how you handle yourself, and I'm impressed. But Eddie's not your average bear."

"He's a bully," I said.

"Yeah, but here's the good news: like with most bullies, you scratch the surface and find pure chickenshit underneath. Usually not very far underneath, either. There are people on the show he's afraid of, and I happen to be one of them. I've whacked his nose before and I don't mind whacking it again. All I'm saying is that if the day comes when you want a little breathing room, I'll see that you get it."

"Can I ask you a question about him?"

"Shoot."

"Why does he always wear those gloves?"

Lane laughed, stuck his derby on his head, and gave it the correct tilt. "Psoriasis. His hands are scaly with it, or so he says—I can't tell you the last time I actually saw them. He says without the gloves, he scratches them until they bleed."

"Maybe that's what makes him so bad-tempered."

"I think it's more likely the other way around—the bad temper made the bad skin." He tapped his temple. "Head controls body, that's what I believe. Come on, Jonesy, let's get to work."

♥

We finished putting the Spin right for its long winter's nap, then moved on to the irrigation system. By the time the pipes were blown out with compressed air and the drains had swallowed several gallons of antifreeze, the sun was lowering toward the trees west of the park and the shadows were lengthening.

"That's enough for today," Lane said. "More than enough. Bring me your card and I'll sign it."

I tapped my watch, showing him it was only quarter past five.

He shook his head, smiling. "I've got no problem writing six on the card. You did twelve hours' worth today, kiddo. Twelve easy."

"Okay," I said, "but don't call me kiddo. That's what *he* calls me." I jerked my head toward Horror House.

"I'll make a note of it. Now bring me your card and buzz off."

♥

The wind had died a little during the afternoon, but it was still warm and breezy when I set off down the beach. On many of those walks back to town I liked to watch my long shadow on the waves, but that evening I mostly watched my feet. I was tired out. What I wanted was a ham and cheese sandwich from Betty's Bakery and a couple of beers from the 7-Eleven next door. I'd go back to my room, settle into my chair by the window, and read me some Tolkien as I ate. I was deep into *The Two Towers*.

What made me look up was the boy's voice. The breeze was in my favor, and I could hear him clearly. "*Faster, Mom! You've almost g*—" He was temporarily stopped by a coughing fit. Then: "*You've almost got it*!"

Mike's mother was on the beach tonight instead of beneath

her umbrella. She was running toward me but didn't see me, because she was looking at the kite she was holding over her head. The string ran back to the boy, seated in his wheelchair at the end of the boardwalk.

Wrong direction, Mom, I thought.

She released the kite. It rose a foot or two, wagged naughtily from side to side, then took a dive into the sand. The breeze kicked up and it went skittering. She had to chase it down.

"*Once more!*" Mike called. "*That time—*" Cough-cough-cough, harsh and bronchial. "*That time you almost had it!*"

"No, I didn't." She sounded tired and pissed off. "Goddamned thing hates me. Let's go in and get some sup—"

Milo was sitting beside Mike's wheelchair, watching the evening's activities with bright eyes. When he saw me, he was off like a shot, barking. As I watched him come, I remembered Madame Fortuna's pronouncement on the day I first met her: *In your future is a little girl and a little boy. The boy has a dog.*

"Milo, come back!" Mom shouted. Her hair had probably started that evening tied up, but after several experiments in aviation, it hung around her face in strings. She pushed it away wearily with the backs of her hands.

Milo paid no attention. He skidded to a stop in front of me with his front paws spraying sand, and did his sitting-up thing. I laughed and patted his head. "That's all you get, pal—no croissants tonight."

He barked at me once, then trotted back to Mom, who was standing ankle-deep in the sand, breathing hard and eyeing me with mistrust. The captured kite hung down by her leg.

"See?" she said. "That's why I didn't want you to feed him.

He's a terrible beggar, and he thinks anybody who gives him a scrap is his friend."

"Well, I'm a friendly sort of guy."

"Good to know," she said. "Just don't feed our dog anymore." She was wearing pedal pushers and an old blue tee-shirt with faded printing on the front. Judging from the sweat-stains on it, she had been trying to get the kite airborne for quite some time. Trying hard, and why not? If I had a kid stuck in a wheelchair, I'd probably want to give him something that would fly, too.

"You're going the wrong way with that thing," I said. "And you don't need to run with it, anyway. I don't know why everybody thinks that."

"I'm sure you're quite the expert," she said, "but it's late and I have to get Mike his supper."

"Mom, let him try," Mike said. "Please?"

She stood for a few more seconds with her head lowered and escaped locks of her hair—also sweaty—clumped against her neck. Then she sighed and held the kite out to me. Now I could read the printing on her shirt: CAMP PERRY MATCH COMPETITION (PRONE) 1959. The front of the kite was a lot better, and I had to laugh. It was the face of Jesus.

"Private joke," she said. "Don't ask."

"Okay."

"You get one try, Mr. Joyland, and then I'm taking him in for his supper. He can't get chilled. He was sick last year, and he still hasn't gotten over it. He thinks he has, but he hasn't."

It was still at least seventy-five on the beach, but I didn't point this out; Mom was clearly not in the mood for further contradictions. Instead I told her again that my name was Devin

Jones. She raised her hands and then let them flop: *Whatever you say, bub.*

I looked at the boy. "Mike?"

"Yes?"

"Reel in the string. I'll tell you when to stop."

He did as I asked. I followed, and when I was even with where he sat, I looked at Jesus. "Are you going to fly this time, Mr. Christ?"

Mike laughed. Mom didn't, but I thought I saw her lips twitch.

"He says he is," I told Mike.

"Good, because—" Cough. Cough-cough-cough. She was right, he wasn't over it. Whatever *it* was. "Because so far he hasn't done anything but eat sand."

I held the kite over my head, but facing Heaven's Bay. I could feel the wind tug at it right away. The plastic rippled. "I'm going to let go, Mike. When I do, start reeling in the string again."

"But it'll just—"

"No, it won't just. But you have to be quick and careful." I was making it sound harder than it was, because I wanted him to feel cool and capable when the kite went up. It would, too, as long as the breeze didn't die on us. I really hoped that wouldn't happen, because I thought Mom had meant what she said about me getting only one chance. "The kite will rise. When it does, start paying out the twine again. Just keep it taut, okay? That means if it starts to dip, you—"

"I pull it in some more. I get it. God's sake."

"Okay. Ready?"

"Yeah!"

Milo sat between Mom and me, looking up at the kite.

"Okay, then. Three…two…one…lift-off."

The kid was hunched over in his chair and the legs beneath his shorts were wasted, but there was nothing wrong with his hands and he knew how to follow orders. He started reeling in, and the kite rose at once. He began to pay the string out—at first too much, and the kite sagged, but he corrected and it started going up again. He laughed. "I can feel it! I can feel it in my hands!"

"That's the wind you feel," I said. "Keep going, Mike. Once it gets up a little higher, the wind will own it. Then all you have to do is not let go."

He let out the twine and the kite climbed, first over the beach and then above the ocean, riding higher and higher into that September day's late blue. I watched it awhile, then chanced looking at the woman. She didn't bristle at my gaze, because she didn't see it. All her attention was focused on her son. I don't think I ever saw such love and such happiness on a person's face. Because *he* was happy. His eyes were shining and the coughing had stopped.

"Mommy, it feels like it's *alive*!"

It is, I thought, remembering how my father had taught me to fly a kite in the town park. I had been Mike's age, but with good legs to stand on. *As long as it's up there, where it was made to be, it really is.*

"Come and feel it!"

She walked up the little slope of beach to the boardwalk and stood beside him. She was looking at the kite, but her hand was stroking his cap of dark brown hair. "Are you sure, honey? It's your kite."

"Yeah, but you have to try it. It's incredible!"

She took the reel, which had thinned considerably as the twine paid out and the kite rose (it was now just a black diamond, the face of Jesus no longer visible) and held it in front of her. For a moment she looked apprehensive. Then she smiled. When a gust tugged the kite, making it wag first to port and then to starboard above the incoming waves, the smile widened into a grin.

After she'd flown it for a while, Mike said: "Let *him*."

"No, that's okay," I said.

But she held out the reel. "We insist, Mr. Jones. You're the flightmaster, after all."

So I took the twine, and felt the old familiar thrill. It tugged the way a fishing-line does when a fair-sized trout has taken the hook, but the nice thing about kite-flying is nothing gets killed.

"How high will it go?" Mike asked.

"I don't know, but maybe it shouldn't go much higher tonight. The wind up there is stronger, and might rip it. Also, you guys need to eat."

"Can Mr. Jones eat supper with us, Mom?"

She looked startled at the idea, and not in a good way. Still, I saw she was going to agree because I'd gotten the kite up.

"That's okay," I said. "I appreciate the invitation, but it was quite a day at the park. We're battening down the hatches for winter, and I'm dirt from head to toe."

"You can wash up in the house," Mike said. "We've got, like, seventy bathrooms."

"Michael Ross, we do not!"

"Maybe seventy-five, with a Jacuzzi in each one." He started laughing. It was a lovely, infectious sound, at least until it turned to coughing. The coughing became whooping. Then, just as Mom was starting to look really concerned (I was already there), he got it under control.

"Another time," I said, and handed him the reel of twine. "I love your Christ-kite. Your dog ain't bad, either." I bent and patted Milo's head.

"Oh...okay. Another time. But don't wait too long, because—"

Mom interposed hastily. "Can you go to work a little earlier tomorrow, Mr. Jones?"

"Sure, I guess."

"We could have fruit smoothies right here, if the weather's nice. I make a mean fruit smoothie."

I bet she did. And that way, she wouldn't have to have a strange man in the house.

"Will you?" Mike asked. "That'd be cool."

"I'd love to. I'll bring a bag of pastries from Betty's."

"Oh, you don't have to—" she began.

"My pleasure, ma'am."

"Oh!" She looked startled. "I never introduced myself, did I? I'm Ann Ross." She held out her hand.

"I'd shake it, Mrs. Ross, but I really am filthy." I showed her my hands. "It's probably on the kite, too."

"You should have given Jesus a mustache!" Mike shouted, and then laughed himself into another coughing fit.

"You're getting a little loose with the twine there, Mike," I said. "Better reel it in." And, as he started doing it, I gave Milo a farewell pat and started back down the beach.

"Mr. Jones," she called.

I turned back. She was standing straight, with her chin raised. Sweat had molded the shirt to her, and she had great breasts.

"It's *Miss* Ross. But since I guess we've now been properly introduced, why don't you call me Annie?"

"I can do that." I pointed at her shirt. "What's a match competition? And why is it prone?"

"That's when you shoot lying down," Mike said.

"Haven't done it in ages," she said, in a curt tone that suggested she wanted the subject closed.

Fine with me. I tipped Mike a wave and he sent one right back. He was grinning. Kid had a great grin.

Forty or fifty yards down the beach, I turned around for another look. The kite was descending, but for the time being the wind still owned it. They were looking up at it, the woman with her hand on her son's shoulder.

Miss, I thought. *Miss, not Mrs. And is there a mister with them in the big old Victorian with the seventy bathrooms?* Just because I'd never seen one with them didn't mean there wasn't one, but I didn't think so. I thought it was just the two of them. On their own.

♥

I got no clarification from Annie Ross the next morning, but plenty of dish from Mike. I also got one hell of a nice fruit smoothie. She said she made the yogurt herself, and it was layered with fresh strawberries from God knows where. I brought croissants and blueberry muffins from Betty's Bakery. Mike skipped the pastries, but finished his smoothie and asked for another. From the way his mother's mouth dropped open, I gathered that this was an astounding development. But not, I guessed, in a bad way.

"Are you sure you can eat another one?"

"Maybe just half," he said. "What's the deal, Mom? You're the one who says fresh yogurt helps me move my bowels."

"I don't think we need to discuss your bowels at seven in the morning, Mike." She got up, then cast a doubtful glance my way.

"Don't worry," Mike said brightly, "if he tries to kiddie-fiddle me, I'll tell Milo to sic 'im."

Color bloomed in her cheeks. "*Michael Everett Ross!*"

"Sorry," he said. He didn't look sorry. His eyes were sparkling.

"Don't apologize to me, apologize to Mr. Jones."

"Accepted, accepted."

"Will you keep an eye on him, Mr. Jones? I won't be long."

"I will if you'll call me Devin."

"Then I'll do that." She hurried up the boardwalk, pausing once to look over her shoulder. I think she had more than half a mind to come back, but in the end, the prospect of stuffing a few more healthy calories into her painfully thin boy was too much for her to resist, and she went on.

Mike watched her climb the steps to the back patio and sighed. "Now I'll have to eat it."

"Well...yeah. You asked for it, right?"

"Only so I could talk to you without her butting in. I mean, I love her and all, but she's always butting in. Like what's wrong with me is this big shameful secret we have to keep." He shrugged. "I've got muscular dystrophy, that's all. That's why I'm in the wheelchair. I *can* walk, you know, but the braces and crutches are a pain in the butt."

"I'm sorry," I said. "That stinks, Mike."

"I guess, but I can't remember *not* having it, so what the hell. Only it's a special kind of MD. Duchenne's muscular dystrophy, it's called. Most kids who have it croak in their teens or early twenties."

So, you tell me—what do you say to a ten-year-old kid who's just told you he's living under a death sentence?

"*But.*" He raised a teacherly finger. "Remember her talking about how I was sick last year?"

"Mike, you don't have to tell me all this if you don't want to."

"Yeah, except I do." He was looking at me with clear intensity. Maybe even urgency. "Because you want to know. Maybe you even need to know."

I was thinking of Fortuna again. Two children, she had told me, a girl in a red hat and a boy with a dog. She said one of them had the sight, but she didn't know which. I thought that now I did.

"Mom said I think I got over it. Do I sound like I got over it?"

"Nasty cough," I ventured, "but otherwise..." I couldn't think how to finish. *Otherwise your legs are nothing but sticks? Otherwise you look like your mom and I could tie a string to the back of your shirt and fly* you *like a kite? Otherwise if I had to bet on whether you or Milo would live longer, I'd put my money on the dog?*

"I came down with pneumonia just after Thanksgiving, okay? When I didn't improve after a couple of weeks in the hospital, the doctor told my mom I was probably going to die and she ought to, you know, get ready for that."

But he didn't tell her in your hearing, I thought. *They'd never have a conversation like that in your hearing.*

"I hung in, though." He said this with some pride. "My grandfather called my mom—I think it was the first time they'd talked in a long time. I don't know who told him what was going on, but he has people everywhere. It could have been any of them."

People everywhere sounded kind of paranoid, but I kept my mouth shut. Later I found out it wasn't paranoid at all. Mike's grandfather *did* have them everywhere, and they all saluted Jesus, the flag, and the NRA, although possibly not in that order.

"Grampa said I got over the pneumonia because of God's will. Mom said he was full of bullshit, just like when he said me having DMD in the first place was God's punishment. She said I was just one tough little sonofabitch, and God had nothing to do with it. Then she hung up on him."

Mike might have heard her end of that conversation, but not Grampa's, and I doubted like hell if his mother had told him. I didn't think he was making it up, though. I found myself hoping Annie wouldn't hurry back. This wasn't like listening to Madame Fortuna. What she had, I believed (and still do, all these years later), was some small bit of authentic psychic ability amped up by a shrewd understanding of human nature and then packaged in glittering carny bullshit. Mike's thing was clearer. Simpler. *Purer*. It wasn't like seeing the ghost of Linda Gray, but it was akin to that, okay? It was touching another world.

"Mom said she'd never come back here, but here we are. Because I wanted to come to the beach and because I wanted to fly a kite and because I'm never going to make twelve, let alone my early twenties. It was the pneumonia, see? I get steroids, and they help, but the pneumonia combined with the Duchenne's MD fucked up my lungs and heart permanently."

He looked at me with a child's defiance, watching for how I'd react to what is now so coyly referred to as "the f-bomb." I didn't react, of course. I was too busy processing the sense to worry about his choice of words.

"So," I said. "I guess what you're saying is an extra fruit smoothie won't help."

He threw back his head and laughed. The laughter turned into the worst coughing fit yet. Alarmed, I went to him and pounded his back…but gently. It felt as if there were nothing under there but chicken bones. Milo barked once and put his paws up on one of Mike's wasted legs.

There were two pitchers on the table, water in one and fresh-squeezed orange juice in the other. Mike pointed to the water and I poured him half a glass. When I tried to hold it for him, he gave me an impatient look—even with the coughing fit still wracking him—and took it himself. He spilled some on his shirt, but most of it went down his throat, and the coughing eased.

"That was a bad one," he said, patting his chest. "My heart's going like a bastard. Don't tell my mother."

"Jesus, kid! Like she doesn't know?"

"She knows too much, that's what I think," Mike said. "She knows I might have three more good months and then four or five really bad ones. Like, in bed all the time, not able to do anything but suck oxygen and watch *MASH* and *Fat Albert*. The only question is whether or not she'll let Grammy and Grampa Ross come to the funeral." He'd coughed hard enough to make his eyes water, but I didn't mistake that for tears. He was bleak, but in control. Last evening, when the kite went up and he felt it tugging the twine, he had been younger than his age. Now I was watching him struggle to be a lot older. The scary thing was how well he was succeeding. His eyes met mine, dead-on. "She knows. She just doesn't know that *I* know."

The back door banged. We looked and saw Annie crossing the patio, heading for the boardwalk.

"Why would *I* need to know, Mike?"

He shook his head. "I don't have any idea. But you can't talk about it to Mom, okay? It just upsets her. I'm all she's got." He said this last not with pride but a kind of gloomy realism.

"All right."

"Oh, one other thing. I almost forgot." He shot a glance at her, saw she was only halfway down the boardwalk, and turned back to me. "It's not white."

"What's not white?"

Mike Ross looked mystified. "No idea. When I woke up this morning, I remembered you were coming for smoothies, and that came into my head. I thought *you'd* know."

Annie arrived. She had poured a mini-smoothie into a juice glass. On top was a single strawberry.

"Yum!" Mike said. "Thanks, Mom!"

"You're very welcome, hon."

She eyed his wet shirt but didn't mention it. When she asked me if I wanted some more juice, Mike winked at me. I said more juice would be great. While she poured, Mike fed Milo two heaping spoonfuls of his smoothie.

She turned back to him, and looked at the smoothie glass, now half empty. "Wow, you really *were* hungry."

"Told you."

"What were you and Mr. Jones—Devin—talking about?"

"Nothing much," Mike said. "He's been sad, but he's better now."

I said nothing, but I could feel heat rising in my cheeks. When I dared a look at Annie, she was smiling.

"Welcome to Mike's world, Devin," she said, and I must have looked like I'd swallowed a goldfish, because she burst out laughing. It was a nice sound.

♥

That evening when I walked back from Joyland, she was standing at the end of the boardwalk, waiting for me. It was the first time I'd seen her in a blouse and skirt. And she was alone. That was a first, too.

"Devin? Got a second?"

"Sure," I said, angling up the sandy slope to her. "Where's Mike?"

"He has physical therapy three times a week. Usually Janice—she's his therapist—comes in the morning, but I arranged for her to come this evening instead, because I wanted to speak to you alone."

"Does Mike know that?"

Annie smiled ruefully. "Probably. Mike knows far more than he should. I won't ask what you two talked about after he got rid of me this morning, but I'm guessing that his…insights…come as no surprise to you."

"He told me why he's in a wheelchair, that's all. And he mentioned he had pneumonia last Thanksgiving."

"I wanted to thank you for the kite, Dev. My son has very restless nights. He's not in pain, exactly, but he has trouble breathing when he's asleep. It's like apnea. He has to sleep in a semi-sitting position, and that doesn't help. Sometimes he stops breathing completely, and when he does, an alarm goes off and wakes him up. Only last night—after the kite—he slept right through. I even went in once, around two AM, to make sure the monitor wasn't malfunctioning. He was sleeping like a baby. No restless tossing and turning, no nightmares—he's prone to them—and no moaning. It was the kite. It satisfied him in a way nothing else possibly could. Except maybe going to that damned amusement park of yours, which is completely out of the question." She stopped, then smiled. "Oh, shit. I'm making a speech."

"It's all right," I said.

"It's just that I've had so few people to talk to. I have house-keeping help—a very nice woman from Heaven's Bay—and of course there's Janice, but it's not the same." She took a deep breath. "Here's the other part. I was rude to you on several occasions, and with no cause. I'm sorry."

"Mrs.... Miss..." Shit. "Annie, you don't have anything to apologize for."

"Yes. I do. You could have just walked on when you saw me struggling with the kite, and then Mike wouldn't have gotten that good night's rest. All I can say is that I have problems trusting people."

This is where she invites me in for supper, I thought. But she didn't. Maybe because of what I said next.

"You know, he *could* come to the park. It'd be easy to arrange, and with it closed and all, he could have the run of the place."

Her face closed up hard, like a hand into a fist. "Oh, no. Absolutely not. If you think that, he didn't tell you as much about his condition as I thought he did. Please don't mention it to him. In fact, I have to insist."

"All right," I said. "But if you change your mind..."

I trailed off. She wasn't going to change her mind. She looked at her watch, and a new smile lit her face. It was so brilliant you could almost overlook how it never reached her eyes. "Oh boy, look how late it's getting. Mike will be hungry after his PE, and I haven't done a thing about supper. Will you excuse me?"

"Sure."

I stood there watching her hurry back down the boardwalk to the green Victorian—the one I was probably never going to see the inside of, thanks to my big mouth. But the idea of taking Mike through Joyland had seemed so right. During the summer, we had groups of kids with all sorts of problems and disabilities—crippled kids, blind kids, cancer kids, kids who were mentally challenged (what we called *retarded* back in the unenlightened 70s). It wasn't as though I expected to stick Mike in the front car of the Delirium Shaker and then blast him off. Even if the Shaker hadn't been buttoned up for the winter, I'm not a total idiot.

But the merry-go-round was still operational, and surely he could ride that. Ditto the train that ran through the Wiggle-Waggle Village. I was sure Fred Dean wouldn't mind me touring the kid through Mysterio's Mirror Mansion, either. But no. No. He was her delicate hothouse flower, and she intended to keep it that way. The thing with the kite had just been an aberration, and the apology a bitter pill she felt she had to swallow.

Still, I couldn't help admiring how quick and lithe she was, moving with a grace her son would never know. I watched her bare legs under the hem of her skirt and thought about Wendy Keegan not at all.

♥

I had the weekend free, and you know what happened. I guess the idea that it always rains on the weekends must be an illusion, but it sure doesn't *seem* like one; ask any working stiff who ever planned to go camping or fishing on his days off.

Well, there was always Tolkien. I was sitting in my chair by the window on Saturday afternoon, moving ever deeper into the mountains of Mordor with Frodo and Sam, when Mrs. Shoplaw knocked on the door and asked if I'd like to come down to the parlor and play Scrabble with her and Tina Ackerley. I am not at all crazy about Scrabble, having suffered many humiliations at the hands of my aunts Tansy and Naomi, who each have a huge mental vocabulary of what I still think of as "Scrabble shit-words"—stuff like *suq*, *tranq*, and *bhoot* (an Indian ghost, should you wonder). Nevertheless, I said I'd love to play. Mrs. Shoplaw was my landlady, after all, and diplomacy takes many forms.

On our way downstairs, she confided, "We're helping Tina bone up. She's quite the Scrabble-shark. She's entered in some sort of tournament in Atlantic City next weekend. I believe there is a cash prize."

It didn't take long—maybe four turns—to discover that our resident librarian could have given my aunts all the game they could handle, and more. By the time Miss Ackerley laid down *nubility* (with the apologetic smile all Scrabble-sharks seem to have; I think they must practice it in front of their mirrors), Emmalina Shoplaw was eighty points behind. As for me...well, never mind.

"I don't suppose either of you know anything about Annie and Mike Ross, do you?" I asked during a break in the action (both women seemed to feel a need to study the board a *looong* time before laying down so much as a single tile). "They live on Beach Row in the big green Victorian?"

Miss Ackerley paused with her hand still inside the little brown bag of letters. Her eyes were big, and her thick lenses made them even bigger. "Have *you* met them?"

"Uh-huh. They were trying to fly a kite...well, *she* was...and

I helped out a little. They're very nice. I just wondered...the two of them all alone in that big house, and him pretty sick..."

The look they exchanged was pure incredulity, and I started to wish I hadn't raised the subject.

"She *talks* to you?" Mrs. Shoplaw asked. "The Ice Queen actually *talks* to you?"

Not only talked to me, but gave me a fruit smoothie. Thanked me. Even apologized to me. But I said none of that. Not because Annie really had iced up when I presumed too much, but because to do so would have seemed disloyal, somehow.

"Well, a little. I got the kite up for them, that's all." I turned the board. It was Tina's, the pro kind with its own little built-in spindle. "Come on, Mrs. S. Your turn. Maybe you'll even make a word that's in my puny vocabulary."

"Given the correct positioning, *puny* can be worth seventy points," Tina Ackerley said. "Even more, if a *y*-word is connected to *pun*."

Mrs. Shoplaw ignored both the board and the advice. "You know who her father is, of course."

"Can't say I do." Although I *did* know she was on the outs with him, and big-time.

"Buddy Ross? As in *The Buddy Ross Hour of Power*? Ring any bells?"

It did, vaguely. I thought I might have heard some preacher named Ross on the radio in the costume shop. It kind of made sense. During one of my quick-change transformations into Howie, Dottie Lassen had asked me—pretty much out of a clear blue sky—if I had found Jesus. My first impulse had been to tell her that I didn't know He was lost, but I restrained it.

"One of those Bible-shouters, right?"

"Next to Oral Roberts and that Jimmy Swaggart fellow, he's just about the biggest of them," Mrs. S. said. "He broadcasts from this gigantic church—God's Citadel, he calls it—in Atlanta. His radio show goes out all over the country, and now he's getting more and more into TV. I don't know if the stations give him the time free, or if he has to buy it. I'm sure he can afford it, especially late at night. That's when the old folks are up with their aches and pains. His shows are half miracle healings and half pleas for more love-offerings."

"Guess he didn't have any luck healing his grandson," I said.

Tina withdrew her hand from the letter-bag with nothing in it. She had forgotten about Scrabble for the time being, which was a good thing for her hapless victims. Her eyes were sparkling. "You don't know any of this story, do you? Ordinarily I don't believe in gossip, but..." She dropped her voice to a confidential tone pitched just above a whisper. "...but since you've *met* them, I could tell you."

"Yes, please," I said. I thought one of my questions—how Annie and Mike came to be living in a huge house on one of North Carolina's ritziest beaches—had already been answered. It was Grampa Buddy's summer retreat, bought and paid for with love-offerings.

"He's got two sons," Tina said. "They're both high in his church—deacons or assistant pastors, I don't know what they call them exactly, because I don't go for that holy rolling stuff. The daughter, though, *she* was different. A sporty type. Horseback riding, tennis, archery, deer hunting with her father, quite a bit of competition shooting. All that got in the papers after her trouble started."

Now the CAMP PERRY shirt made sense.

"Around the time she turned eighteen, it all went to hell—quite literally, as he saw it. She went to what they call 'a secular-humanist college,' and by all accounts she was quite the wild child. Giving up the shooting competitions and tennis tournaments was one thing; giving up the church-going for parties and liquor and men was quite another. Also…" Tina lowered her voice. "*Pot-smoking.*"

"Gosh," I said, "not that!"

Mrs. Shoplaw gave me a look, but Tina didn't notice. "Yes! *That!* She got into the newspapers, too, those tabloids, because she was pretty and rich, but mostly because of her father. And being fallen-away. That's what they call it. She was a scandal to that church of his, wearing mini-skirts and going braless and all. Well, you know what those fundamentalists preach is straight out of the Old Testament, all that about the righteous being rewarded and sinners being punished even unto the seventh generation. And she did more than hit the party circuit down there in Green Witch Village." Tina's eyes were now so huge they looked on the verge of tumbling from their sockets and rolling down her cheeks. "*She quit the NRA and joined the American Atheist Society*!"

"Ah. And did *that* get in the papers?"

"Did it ever! Then she got pregnant, no surprise there, and when the baby turned out to have some sort of problem…cerebral palsy, I think—"

"Muscular dystrophy."

"Whatever it is, her father was asked about it on one of his crusade things, and do you know what he said?"

I shook my head, but thought I could make a pretty good guess.

"He said that God punishes the unbeliever and the sinner. He said his daughter was no different, and maybe her son's affliction would bring her back to God."

"I don't think it's happened yet," I said. I was thinking of the Jesus-kite.

"I can't understand why people use religion to hurt each other when there's already so much pain in the world," Mrs. Shoplaw said. "Religion is supposed to *comfort*."

"He's just a self-righteous old prig," Tina said. "No matter how many men she might have been with or how many joints of pot she might have smoked, she's still his daughter. And the child is still his grandson. I've seen that boy in town once or twice, either in a wheelchair or tottering along in those cruel braces he has to wear if he wants to walk. He seems like a perfectly nice boy, and she was sober. Also wearing a bra." She paused for further recollection. "I think."

"Her father might change," Mrs. Shoplaw said, "but I doubt it. Young women and young men grow up, but old women and old men just grow older and surer they've got the right on their side. Especially if they know scripture."

I remembered something my mother used to say. "The devil can quote scripture."

"And in a pleasing voice," Mrs. Shoplaw agreed moodily. Then she brightened. "Still, if the Reverend Ross is letting them use his place on Beach Row, maybe he's willing to let bygones be bygones. It *might* have crossed his mind by now that she was only a young girl, maybe not even old enough to vote. Dev, isn't it your turn?"

It was. I made *tear*. It netted me four points.

♥

My drubbing wasn't merciful, but once Tina Ackerley really got rocking, it was relatively quick. I returned to my room, sat in my chair by the window, and tried to rejoin Frodo and Sam on the road to Mount Doom. I couldn't do it. I closed the book and stared out through the rain-wavery glass at the empty beach and the gray ocean beyond. It was a lonely prospect, and at times like that, my thoughts had a way of turning back to Wendy—wondering where she was, what she was doing, and who she was with. Thinking about her smile, the way her hair fell against her cheek, the soft rise of her breasts in one of her seemingly endless supply of cardigan sweaters.

Not today. Instead of Wendy, I found myself thinking of Annie Ross and realizing I'd developed a small but powerful crush on her. The fact that nothing could come of it—she had to be ten years older than me, maybe twelve—only seemed to make things worse. Or maybe I mean better, because unrequited love *does* have its attractions for young men.

Mrs. S. had suggested that Annie's holier-than-thou father might be willing to let bygones be bygones, and I thought she might have something there. I'd heard that grandchildren had a way of softening stiff necks, and he might want to get to know the boy while there was still time. He could have found out (from the people he had everywhere) that Mike was smart as well as crippled. It was even possible he'd heard rumors that Mike had what Madame Fortuna called "the sight." Or maybe all that was too rosy. Maybe Mr. Fire-and-Brimstone had given her the use of the house in exchange for a promise that she'd keep her mouth shut and not brew up any fresh pot-and-miniskirt scandals while he was making the crucial transition from radio to television.

I could speculate until the cloud-masked sun went down, and not be sure of anything on Buddy Ross's account, but I thought I could be sure about one thing on Annie's: she was *not* ready to let bygones be bygones.

I got up and trotted downstairs to the parlor, fishing a scrap of paper with a phone number on it out of my wallet as I went. I could hear Tina and Mrs. S. in the kitchen, chattering away happily. I called Erin Cook's dorm, not expecting to get her on a Saturday afternoon; she was probably down in New Jersey with Tom, watching Rutgers football and singing the Scarlet Knights' fight song.

But the girl on phone duty said she'd get her, and three minutes later, her voice was in my ear.

"Dev, I was going to call you. In fact, I want to come down and see you, if I can get Tom to go along. I think I can, but it wouldn't be next weekend. Probably the one after."

I checked the calendar hanging on the wall and saw that would be the first weekend in October. "Have you actually found something out?"

"I don't know. Maybe. I love to do research, and I really got into this. I've piled up lots of background stuff for sure, but it's not like I solved the murder of Linda Gray in the college library, or anything. Still…there are things I want to show you. Things that trouble me."

"Trouble you why? Trouble you how?"

"I don't want to try explaining over the phone. If I can't persuade Tom to come down, I'll put everything in a big manila envelope and send it to you. But I think I can. He wants to see you, he just doesn't want anything to do with my little investigation. He wouldn't even look at the photos."

I thought she was being awfully mysterious, but decided to

let it go. "Listen, have you heard of an evangelist named Buddy Ross?"

"Buddy—" She burst into giggles. "*The Buddy Ross Hour of Power*! My gramma listens to that old faker all the time! He pretends to pull goat stomachs out of people and claims they're tumors! Do you know what Pop Allen would say?"

"Carny-from-carny," I said, grinning.

"Right you are. What do you want to know about him? And why can't you find out for yourself? Did your mother get scared by a card catalogue while she was carrying you?"

"Not that I know of, but by the time I get off work, the Heaven's Bay library is closed. I doubt if they've got *Who's Who*, anyway. I mean, it's only one room. It's not about him, anyway. It's about his two sons. I want to know if they have any kids."

"Why?"

"Because his daughter has one. He's a great kid, but he's dying."

A pause. Then: "What are you into down there now, Dev?"

"Meeting new people. Come on down. I'd love to see you guys again. Tell Tom we'll stay out of the funhouse."

I thought that might make her laugh, but it didn't. "Oh, he will. You couldn't get him within thirty yards of the place."

We said our goodbyes, I wrote the length of my call on the honor sheet, then went back upstairs and sat by the window. I was feeling that strange dull jealousy again. Why had Tom Kennedy been the one to see Linda Gray? Why him and not me?

♥

The Heaven's Bay weekly paper came out on Thursdays, and the headline on the October fourth edition read JOYLAND EMPLOYEE SAVES SECOND LIFE. I thought that was an exaggeration. I'll take full credit for Hallie Stansfield, but only part of it for the unpleasant Eddie Parks. The rest—not neglecting a tip of the old Howie-hat to Lane Hardy—belongs to Wendy Keegan, because if she hadn't broken up with me in June, I would have been in Durham, New Hampshire that fall, seven hundred miles from Joyland.

I certainly had no idea that more life-saving was on the agenda; premonitions like that were strictly for folks like Rozzie Gold and Mike Ross. I was thinking of nothing but Erin and Tom's upcoming visit when I arrived at the park on October first, after another rainy weekend. It was still cloudy, but in honor of Monday, the rain had stopped. Eddie was seated on his apple-box throne in front of Horror House, and smoking his usual morning cigarette. I raised my hand to him. He didn't bother to raise his in return, just stomped on his butt and leaned over to raise the apple-box and toss it under. I'd seen it all fifty times or more (and sometimes wondered how many butts were piled up beneath that box), but this time, instead of lifting the apple-box, he just went right on leaning.

Was there a look of surprise on his face? I can't say. By the time I realized something was wrong, all I could see was his faded and grease-smeared dogtop as his head dropped between his knees. He kept going forward, and ended up doing a complete somersault, landing on his back with his legs splayed out and his face up to the cloudy sky. And by then the only thing on it was a knotted grimace of pain.

I dropped my lunchsack, ran to him, and fell on my knees beside him. "Eddie? What is it?"

"Ticka," he managed.

For a moment I thought he was talking about some obscure

disease engendered by tick-bites, but then I saw the way he was clutching the left side of his chest with his gloved right hand.

The pre-Joyland version of Dev Jones would simply have yelled for help, but after four months of talking the Talk, *help* never even crossed my mind. I filled my lungs, lifted my head, and screamed "*HEY, RUBE!*" into the damp morning air as loud as I could. The only person close enough to hear was Lane Hardy, and he came fast.

The summer employees Fred Dean hired didn't have to know CPR when they signed on, but they had to learn. Thanks to the life-saving class I'd taken as a teenager, I already knew. The half-dozen of us in that class had learned beside the YMCA pool, working on a dummy with the unlikely name of Herkimer Saltfish. Now I had a chance to put theory into practice for the first time, and do you know what? It wasn't really that much different from the clean-and-jerk I'd used to pop the hotdog out of the little Stansfield girl's throat. I wasn't wearing the fur, and there was no hugging involved, but it was still mostly a matter of applying hard force. I cracked four of the old bastard's ribs and broke one. I can't say I'm sorry, either.

By the time Lane arrived, I was kneeling alongside Eddie and doing closed chest compressions, first rocking forward with my weight on the heels of my hands, then rocking back and listening to see if he'd draw in a breath.

"Christ," Lane said. "Heart attack?"

"Yeah, I'm pretty sure. Call an ambulance."

The closest phone was in the little shack beside Pop Allen's Shootin' Gallery—his doghouse, in the Talk. It was locked, but Lane had the Keys to the Kingdom: three masters that opened everything in the park. He ran. I went on doing CPR, rocking back and forth, my thighs aching now, my knees barking about their long contact with the rough pavement of Joyland Avenue. After each five compressions I'd slow-count to three, listening for Eddie to inhale, but there was nothing. No joy in Joyland, not for Eddie. Not after the first five, not after the second five, not after half a dozen fives. He just lay there with his gloved hands at his sides and his mouth open. Eddie fucking Parks. I stared down at him as Lane came sprinting back, shouting that the ambulance was on its way.

I'm not doing it, I thought. *I'll be damned if I'll do it*.

Then I leaned forward, doing another compression on the way, and pressed my mouth to his. It wasn't as bad as I feared; it was worse. His lips were bitter with the taste of cigarettes, and there was the stink of something else in his mouth—God help me, I think it was jalapeno peppers, maybe from a breakfast omelet. I got a good seal, though, pinched his nostrils shut, and breathed down his throat.

I did that five or six times before he started breathing on his own again. I stopped the compressions to see what would happen, and he kept going. Hell must have been full that day, that's all I can figure. I rolled him onto his side in case he vomited. Lane stood beside me with a hand on my shoulder. Shortly after that, we heard the wail of an approaching siren.

Lane hurried to meet them at the gate and direct them. Once he was gone, I found myself looking at the snarling green monster-faces decorating the façade of Horror House. COME IN IF YOU DARE was written above the faces in drippy green letters. I found myself thinking again of Linda Gray, who had gone in alive and had been carried out hours later, cold and dead. I think my mind went that way because Erin was coming with information. Information that *troubled* her. I also thought of the girl's killer.

Could have been you, Mrs. Shoplaw had said. *Except you're dark-haired instead of blond and don't have a bird's head tattooed on one of your hands. This guy did. An eagle or maybe a hawk*.

Eddie's hair was the premature gray of the lifelong heavy smoker, but it could have been blond four years ago. And he always wore gloves. Surely he was too old to have been the man who had accompanied Linda Gray on her last dark ride, *surely*, but...

The ambulance was very close but not quite here, although I could see Lane at the gate, waving his hands over his head, making hurry-up gestures. Thinking what the hell, I stripped off Eddie's gloves. His fingers were lacy with dead skin, the backs of his hands red beneath a thick layer of some sort of white cream. There were no tattoos.

Just psoriasis.

♥

As soon as he was loaded up and the ambulance was heading back to the tiny Heaven's Bay hospital, I went into the nearest donniker and rinsed my mouth again and again. It was a long time before I got rid of the taste of those damn jalapeno peppers, and I have never touched one since.

When I came out, Lane Hardy was standing by the door. "That was something," he said. "You brought him back."

"He won't be out of the woods for a while, and there might be brain damage."

"Maybe yes, maybe no, but if you hadn't been there, he'd have been in the woods permanently. First the little girl, now the dirty old man. I may start calling you Jesus instead of Jonesy, because you sure are the savior."

"You do that, and I'm DS." That was Talk for *down south*, which in turn meant turning in your time-card for good.

"Okay, but you did all right, Jonesy. In fact, I gotta say you rocked the house."

"The *taste* of him," I said. "God!"

"Yeah, I bet, but look on the bright side. With him gone, you're free at last, free at last, thank God Almighty, you're free at last. I think you'll like it better that way, don't you?"

I certainly did.

From his back pocket, Lane drew out a pair of rawhide gloves. Eddie's gloves. "Found these laying on the ground. Why'd you take em off him?"

"Uh…I wanted to let his hands breathe." That sounded primo stupid, but the truth would have sounded even stupider. I couldn't believe I'd entertained the notion of Eddie Parks being Linda Gray's killer for even a moment. "When I took my life-saving course, they told us that heart attack victims need all the free skin they can get. It helps, somehow." I shrugged. "It's supposed to, at least."

"Huh. You learn a new thing every day." He flapped the gloves. "I don't think Eddie's gonna be back for a long time—if at all—so you might as well stick these in his doghouse, yeah?"

"Okay," I said, and that's what I did. But later that day I went and got them again. Something else, too.

♥

I didn't like him, we're straight on that, right? He'd given me no reason to like him. He had, so far as I knew, given not one single Joyland employee a reason to like him. Even old-timers like Rozzie Gold and Pop Allen gave him a wide berth. Nevertheless, I found myself entering the Heaven's Bay Community Hospital that afternoon at four o'clock, and asking if Edward Parks could have a visitor. I had his gloves in one hand, along with the something else.

The blue-haired volunteer receptionist went through her paperwork twice, shaking her head, and I was starting to think Eddie had died after all when she said, "Ah! It's Edwin, not Edward. He's in Room 315. That's ICU, so you'll have to check at the nurse's station first."

I thanked her and went to the elevator—one of those huge ones big enough to admit a gurney. It was slower than old cold death, which gave me plenty of time to wonder what I was doing here. If Eddie needed a visit from a park employee, it should have been Fred Dean, not me, because Fred was the guy in charge that fall. Yet here I was. They probably wouldn't let me see him, anyway.

But after checking his chart, the head nurse gave me the okay. "He may be sleeping, though."

"Any idea about his—?" I tapped my head.

"Mental function? Well...he was able to give us his name."

That sounded hopeful.

He was indeed asleep. With his eyes shut and that day's late-arriving sun shining on his face, the idea that he might have been Linda Gray's date a mere four years ago was even more ludicrous. He looked at least a hundred, maybe a hundred and twenty. I saw I needn't have brought his gloves, either. Someone had bandaged his hands, probably after treating the psoriasis with something a little more powerful than whatever OTC cream he'd been using on them. Looking at those bulky white mittens made me feel a queer, reluctant pity.

I crossed the room as quietly as I could, and put the gloves in the closet with the clothes he'd been wearing when he was brought in. That left me with the other thing—a photograph that had been pinned to the wall of his cluttered, tobacco-smelling little shack next to a yellowing calendar that was two years out of date. The photo showed Eddie and a plain-faced woman standing in the weedy front yard of an anonymous tract house. Eddie looked about twenty-five. He had his arm around the woman. She was smiling at him. And—wonder of wonders—he was smiling back.

There was a rolling table beside his bed with a plastic pitcher and a glass on it. This I thought rather stupid; with his hands bandaged the way they were, he wasn't going to be pouring anything for a while. Still, the pitcher could serve one useful purpose. I propped the photo against it so he'd see it when he woke up. With that done, I started for the door.

I was almost there when he spoke in a whispery voice that was a long way from his usual ill-tempered rasp. "Kiddo."

I returned—not eagerly—to his bedside. There was a chair in the corner, but I had no intention of pulling it over and sitting down. "How you feeling, Eddie?"

"Can't really say. Hard to breathe. They got me all taped up."

"I brought you your gloves, but I see they already…" I nodded at his bandaged hands.

"Yeah." He sucked in air. "If anything good comes out of this, maybe they'll fix em up. Fuckin itch all the time, they do." He looked at the picture. "Why'd you bring that? And what were you doin in my doghouse?"

"Lane told me to put your gloves in there. I did, but then I thought you might want them. And you might want the picture. Maybe she's someone you'd want Fred Dean to call?"

"Corinne?" He snorted. "She's been dead for twenty years. Pour me some water, kiddo. I'm as dry as ten-year dogshit."

I poured, and held the glass for him, and even wiped the corner of his mouth with the sheet when he dribbled. It was all a lot more intimate than I wanted, but didn't seem so bad when I remembered that I'd been soul-kissing the miserable bastard only hours before.

He didn't thank me, but when had he ever? What he said was, "Hold that picture up." I did as he asked. He looked at it fixedly for several seconds, then sighed. "Miserable scolding backbiting cunt. Walking out on her for Royal American Shows was the smartest thing I ever did." A tear trembled at the corner of his left eye, hesitated, then rolled down his cheek.

"Want me to take it back and pin it up in your doghouse, Eddie?"

"No, might as well leave it. We had a kid, you know. A little girl."

"Yeah?"

"Yeah. She got hit by a car. Three years old she was, and died like a dog in the street. That miserable cunt was yakking on the phone instead of watching her." He turned his head aside and closed his eyes. "Go on, get outta here. Hurts to talk, and I'm tired. Got a elephant sitting on my chest."

"Okay. Take care of yourself."

He grimaced without opening his eyes. "That's a laugh. How e'zacly am I s'posed to do that? You got any ideas? Because I haven't. I got no relatives, no friends, no savings, no *in*-surance. What am I gonna do now?"

"It'll work out," I said lamely.

"Sure, in the movies it always does. Go on, get lost."

This time I was all the way out the door before he spoke again.

"You shoulda let me die, kiddo." He said it without melodrama, just as a passing observation. "I coulda been with my little girl."

♥

When I walked back into the hospital lobby I stopped dead, at first not sure I was seeing who I thought I was seeing. But it was her, all right, with one of her endless series of arduous novels open in front of her. This one was called *The Dissertation*.

"Annie?"

She looked up, at first wary, then smiling as she recognized me. "Dev! What are you doing here?"

"Visiting a guy from the park. He had a heart attack today."

"Oh, my God, I'm so sorry. Is he going to be all right?"

She didn't invite me to sit down next to her, but I did, anyway. My visit to Eddie had upset me in ways I didn't understand, and my nerves were jangling. It wasn't unhappiness and it wasn't sorrow. It was a queer, unfocused anger that had something to do with the foul taste of jalapeno peppers that still seemed to linger in my mouth. And with Wendy, God knew why. It was wearying to know I wasn't over her, even yet. A broken arm would have healed quicker. "I don't know. I didn't talk to a doctor. Is *Mike* all right?"

"Yes, it's just a regularly scheduled appointment. A chest X-ray and a complete blood count. Because of the pneumonia, you know. Thank God he's over it now. Except for that lingering cough, Mike's fine." She was still holding her book open, which probably meant she wanted me to go, and that made me angrier. You have to remember that was the year *everyone* wanted me to go, even the guy whose life I'd saved.

Which is probably why I said, "*Mike* doesn't think he's fine. So who am I supposed to believe here, Annie?"

Her eyes widened with surprise, then grew distant. "I'm sure I don't care who or what you believe, Devin. It's really not any of your business."

"Yes it is." That came from behind us. Mike had rolled up in his chair. It wasn't the motorized kind, which meant he'd been turning the wheels with his hands. Strong boy, cough or no cough. He'd buttoned his shirt wrong, though.

Annie turned to him, surprised. "What are you doing here? You were supposed to let the nurse—"

"I told her I could do it on my own and she said okay. It's just a left and two rights from radiology, you know. I'm not blind, just dy—"

"Mr. Jones was visiting a friend of his, Mike." So now I had been demoted back to Mr. Jones. She closed her book with a snap and stood up. "He's probably anxious to get home, and I'm sure you must be ti—"

"I want him to take us to the park." Mike spoke calmly enough, but his voice was loud enough to make people look around. "*Us*."

"Mike, you know that's not—"

"To Joyland. To *Joy*...Land." Still calm, but louder still. Now everyone was looking. Annie's cheeks were flaming. "I want you both to take me." His voice rose louder still. "*I want you to take me to Joyland before I die.*"

Her hand covered her mouth. Her eyes were huge. Her words, when they came, were muffled but understandable. "Mike...you're not going to *die*, who told you..." She turned on me. "Do I have you to thank for putting that idea in his head?"

"Of course not." I was very conscious that our audience was growing—it now included a couple of nurses and a doctor in blue scrubs and booties—but I didn't care. I was still angry. "*He* told *me*. Why would that surprise you, when you know all about his intuitions?"

That was my afternoon for provoking tears. First Eddie, now Annie. Mike was dry-eyed, though, and he looked every bit as furious as I felt. But he said nothing as she grabbed the handles of his wheelchair, spun it around, and drove it at the door. I thought she was going to crash into them, but the magic eye got them open just in time.

Let them go, I thought, but I was tired of letting women go. I was tired of just letting things happen to me and then feeling bad about them.

A nurse approached me. "Is everything all right?"

"No," I said, and followed them out.

♥

Annie had parked in the lot adjacent to the hospital, where a sign announced THESE TWO ROWS RESERVED FOR THE HANDICAPPED. She had a van, I saw, with plenty of room for the folded-up wheelchair in back. She had gotten the passenger door open, but Mike was refusing to get out of the chair. He was gripping the handles with all his strength, his hands dead white.

"Get in!" she shouted at him.

Mike shook his head, not looking at her.

"*Get in, dammit!*"

This time he didn't even bother to shake his head.

She grabbed him and yanked. The wheelchair had its brake on and tipped forward. I grabbed it just in time to keep it from going over and spilling them both into the open door of the van.

Annie's hair had fallen into her face, and the eyes peering through it were wild: the eyes, almost, of a skittish horse in a thunderstorm. "*Let go! This is all your fault! I never should have—*"

"Stop," I said. I took hold of her shoulders. The hollows there were deep, the bones close to the surface. I thought, *She's been too busy stuffing calories into him to worry about herself.*

"*LET ME G—*"

"I don't want to take him away from you," I said. "Annie, that's the last thing I want."

She stopped struggling. Warily, I let go of her. The novel she'd been reading had fallen to the pavement in the struggle. I bent down, picked it up, and put it into the pocket on the back of the wheelchair.

"Mom." Mike took her hand. "It doesn't have to be the last good time."

Then I understood. Even before her shoulders slumped and the sobs started, I understood. It wasn't the fear that I'd stick him on some crazy-fast ride and the burst of adrenaline would kill him. It wasn't fear that a stranger would steal the damaged heart she loved so well. It was a kind of atavistic belief—a *mother's* belief—that if they never started doing certain last things, life would go on as it had: morning smoothies at the end of the boardwalk, evenings with the kite at the end of the boardwalk, all of it in a kind of endless summer. Only it was October now and the beach was deserted. The happy screams of teenagers on the Thunderball and little kids shooting down the Splash & Crash water slide had ceased, there was a nip in the air as the days drew down. No summer is endless.

She put her hands over her face and sat down on the passenger seat of the van. It was too high for her, and she almost slid off. I caught her and steadied her. I don't think she noticed.

"Go on, take him," she said. "I don't give a fuck. Take him parachute-jumping, if you want. Just don't expect me to be a part of your…your *boys' adventure*."

Mike said, "I can't go without you."

That got her to drop her hands and look at him. "Michael, you're all I've got. Do you understand that?"

"Yes," he said. He took one of her hands in both of his. "And you're all *I've* got."

I could see by her face that the idea had never crossed her mind, not really.

"Help me get in," Mike said. "Both of you, please."

When he was settled (I don't remember fastening his seatbelt, so maybe this was before they were a big deal), I closed the door and walked around the nose of the van with her.

"His chair," she said distractedly. "I have to get his chair."

"I'll put it in. You sit behind the wheel and get yourself ready to drive. Take a few deep breaths."

She let me help her in. I had her above the elbow, and I

could close my whole hand around her upper arm. I thought of telling her she couldn't live on arduous novels alone, and thought better of it. She had been told enough this afternoon.

I folded the wheelchair and stowed it in the cargo compartment, taking longer with the job than I needed to, giving her time to compose herself. When I went back to the driver's side, I half-expected to find the window rolled up, but it was still down. She had wiped her eyes and nose, and pushed her hair into some semblance of order.

I said, "He can't go without you, and neither can I."

She spoke to me as if Mike weren't there and listening. "I'm so afraid for him, all the time. He sees so much, and so much of it hurts him. That's what the nightmares are about, I know it. He's such a great kid. Why can't he just get well? Why this? Why *this*?"

"I don't know," I said.

She turned to kiss Mike's cheek. Then she turned back to me. Drew in a deep, shaky breath and let it out. "So when do we go?" she asked.

♥

The Return of the King was surely not as arduous as *The Dissertation*, but that night I couldn't have read *The Cat in the Hat*. After eating some canned spaghetti for supper (and largely ignoring Mrs. Shoplaw's pointed observations about how some young people seem determined to mistreat their bodies), I went up to my room and sat by the window, staring out at the dark and listening to the steady beat-and-retreat of the surf.

I was on the verge of dozing when Mrs. S. knocked lightly on my door and said, "You've got a call, Dev. It's a little boy."

I went down to the parlor in a hurry, because I could think of only one little boy who might call me.

"Mike?"

He spoke in a low voice. "My mom is sleeping. She said she was tired."

"I bet she was," I said, thinking of how we'd ganged up on her.

"I know we did," Mike said, as if I had spoken the thought aloud. "We had to."

"Mike...can you read minds? Are you reading mine?"

"I don't really know," he said. "Sometimes I see things and hear things, that's all. And sometimes I get ideas. It was my idea to come to Grampa's house. Mom said he'd never let us, but I knew he would. Whatever I have, the special thing, I think it came from him. He heals people, you know. I mean, sometimes he fakes it, but sometimes he really does."

"Why did you call, Mike?"

He grew animated. "About Joyland! Can we really ride the merry-go-round and the Ferris wheel?"

"I'm pretty sure."

"Shoot in the shooting gallery?"

"Maybe. If your mother says so. All this stuff is contingent on your mother's approval. That means—"

"I know what it means." Sounding impatient. Then the child's excitement broke through again. "That is so awesome!"

"None of the fast rides," I said. "Are we straight on that? For one thing, they're buttoned up for the winter." The Carolina Spin was, too, but with Lane Hardy's help, it wouldn't take forty minutes to get it running again. "For another—"

"Yeah, I know, my heart. The Ferris wheel would be enough for me. We can see it from the end of the boardwalk, you know. From the top, it must be like seeing the world from my kite."

I smiled. "It is like that, sort of. But remember, only if your mom says you can. She's the boss."

"We're *going* for her. She'll know when we get there." He sounded eerily sure of himself. "And it's for you, Dev. But mostly it's for the girl. She's been there too long. She wants to leave."

My mouth dropped open, but there was no danger of drooling; my mouth had gone entirely dry. "How—" Just a croak. I swallowed again. "How do you know about her?"

"I don't know, but I think she's why I came. Did I tell you it's not white?"

"You did, but you said you didn't know what that meant. Do you now?"

"Nope." He began to cough. I waited it out. When it cleared, he said, "I have to go. My mom's getting up from her nap. Now she'll be up half the night, reading."

"Yeah?"

"Yeah. I really hope she lets me go on the Ferris wheel."

"It's called the Carolina Spin, but people who work there just call it the hoister." Some of them—Eddie, for instance—actually called it the chump-hoister, but I didn't tell him that. "Joyland folks have this kind of secret talk. That's part of it."

"The hoister. I'll remember. Bye, Dev."

The phone clicked in my ear.

♥

This time it was Fred Dean who had the heart attack.

He lay on the ramp leading to the Carolina Spin, his face blue and contorted. I knelt beside him and started chest compressions.

When there was no result from that, I leaned forward, pinched his nostrils shut, and jammed my lips over his. Something tickled across my teeth and onto my tongue. I pulled back and saw a black tide of baby spiders pouring from his mouth.

I woke up half out of bed, the covers pulled loose and wound around me in a kind of shroud, heart pumping, clawing at my own mouth. It took several seconds for me to realize there was nothing in there. Nonetheless, I got up, went to the bathroom, and drank two glasses of water. I may have had worse dreams than the one that woke me at three o'clock on that Tuesday morning, but if so, I can't remember them. I re-made my bed and laid back down, convinced there would be no more sleep for me that night. Yet I had almost dozed off again when it occurred to me that the big emotional scene the three of us had played out at the hospital yesterday might have been for nothing.

Sure, Joyland was happy to make special arrangements for the lame, the halt, and the blind—what are now called "special needs children"—during the season, but the season was over. Would the park's undoubtedly expensive insurance policy still provide coverage if something happened to Mike Ross in October? I could see Fred Dean shaking his head when I made my request and saying he was very sorry, but—

♥

It was chilly that morning, with a strong breeze, so I took my car, parking beside Lane's pickup. I was early, and ours were the only vehicles in Lot A, which was big enough to hold five hundred cars. Fallen leaves tumbled across the pavement, making an insectile sound that reminded me of the spiders in my dream.

Lane was sitting in a lawn chair outside Madame Fortuna's shy (which would soon be disassembled and stored for the winter), eating a bagel generously smeared with cream cheese. His derby was tilted at its usual insouciant angle, and there was a cigarette parked behind one ear. The only new thing was the denim jacket he was wearing. Another sign, had I needed one, that our Indian summer was over.

"Jonesy, Jonesy, lookin lonely. Want a bagel? I got extra."

"Sure," I said. "Can I talk to you about something while I eat it?"

"Come to confess your sins, have you? Take a seat, my son." He pointed to the side of the fortune-telling booth, where another couple of folded lawn chairs were leaning.

"Nothing sinful," I said, opening one of the chairs. I sat down and took the brown bag he was offering. "But I made a promise and now I'm afraid I might not be able to keep it."

I told him about Mike, and how I had convinced his mother to let him come to the park—no easy task, given her fragile emotional state. I finished with how I'd woken up in the middle of the night, convinced Fred Dean would never allow it. The only thing I didn't mention was the dream that had awakened me.

"So," Lane said when I'd finished. "Is she a fox? The mommy?"

"Well...yeah. Actually she is. But that isn't the reason—"

He patted my shoulder and gave me a patronizing smile I could have done without. "Say nummore, Jonesy, say nummore."

"Lane, she's ten years older than I am!"

"Okay, and if I had a dollar for every babe I ever took out who was ten years *younger*, I could buy me a steak dinner at Hanratty's in the Bay. Age is just a number, my son."

"Terrific. Thanks for the arithmetic lesson. Now tell me if I stepped in shit when I told the kid he could come to the park and ride the Spin and the merry-go-round."

"You stepped in shit," he said, and my heart sank. Then he raised a finger. "*But.*"

"But?"

"Have you set a date for this little field trip yet?"

"Not exactly. I was thinking maybe Thursday." Before Erin and Tom showed up, in other words.

"Thursday's no good. Friday, either. Will the kid and his foxy mommy still be here next week?"

"I guess so, but—"

"Then plan on Monday or Tuesday."

"Why wait?"

"For the paper." Looking at me as if I were the world's biggest idiot.

"Paper…?"

"The local rag. It comes out on Thursday. When your latest lifesaving feat hits the front page, you're going to be Freddy Dean's fair-haired boy." Lane tossed the remains of his bagel into the nearest litter barrel—two points—and then raised his hands in the air, as if framing a newspaper headline. " 'Come to Joyland! We not only sell fun, we save lives!' " He smiled and tilted his derby the other way. "Priceless publicity. Fred's gonna owe you another one. Take it to the bank and say thanks."

"How would the paper even find out? I can't see Eddie Parks telling them." Although if he did, he'd probably want them to make sure the part about how I'd practically crushed his ribcage made Paragraph One.

He rolled his eyes. "I keep forgetting what a Jonesy-come-lately you are to this part of the world. The only articles anybody actually reads in that catbox-liner are the Police Beat and the Ambulance Calls. But ambulance calls are pretty dry. As a special favor to you, Jonesy, I'll toddle on down to the *Banner* office on my lunch break and tell the rubes all about your heroism. They'll send someone out to interview you pronto."

"I don't really want—"

"Oh gosh, a Boy Scout with a merit badge in modesty. Save it. You want the kid to get a tour of the park, right?"

"Yes."

"Then do the interview. Also smile pretty for the camera."

Which—if I may jump ahead—is pretty much what I did.

As I was folding up my chair, he said: "Our Freddy Dean might have said fuck the insurance and risked it anyway, you know. He doesn't look it, but he's carny-from-carny himself. His father was a low-pitch jack-jaw on the corn circuit. Freddy told me once his pop carried a Michigan bankroll big enough to choke a horse."

I knew low-pitch, jack-jaw, and corn circuit, but not Michigan bankroll. Lane laughed when I asked him. "Two twenties on the outside, the rest either singles or cut-up green paper. A great gag when you want to attract a tip. But when it comes to Freddy himself, that ain't the point." He re-set his derby yet again.

"What is?"

"Carnies have a weakness for good-looking points in tight skirts and kids down on their luck. They also have a strong allergy to rube rules. Which includes all the bean-counter bullshit."

"So maybe I wouldn't have to—"

He raised his hands to stop me. "Better not to have to find out. Do the interview."

♥

The *Banner*'s photographer posed me in front of the Thunderball. The picture made me wince when I saw it. I was squinting and thought I looked like the village idiot, but it did the job; the paper was on Fred's desk when I came in to see him on Friday morning. He hemmed and hawed, then okayed my request, as long as Lane promised to stick with us while the kid and his mother were in the park.

Lane said okay to that with no hemming or hawing. He said he wanted to see my girlfriend, then burst out laughing when I started to fulminate.

Later that day, I told Annie Ross I'd set up a tour of the park the following Tuesday morning, if the weather was good—Wednesday or Thursday if it wasn't. Then I held my breath.

There was a long pause, followed by a sigh.

Then she said okay.

♥

That was a busy Friday. I left the park early, drove to Wilmington, and was waiting when Tom and Erin stepped off the train. Erin ran the length of the platform, threw herself into my arms, and kissed me on both cheeks and the tip of my nose. She made a lovely armful, but it's impossible to mistake sisterly kisses for anything other than what they are. I let her go and allowed Tom to pull me into an enthusiastic back-thumping manhug. It was as if we hadn't seen each other in five years instead of five weeks. I was a working stiff now, and although I had put on my best chinos and a sport-shirt, I looked it. Even with my grease-spotted jeans and sun-faded dogtop back in the closet of my room at Mrs. S.'s, I looked it.

"It's so great to see you!" Erin said. "My God, what a tan!"

I shrugged. "What can I say? I'm working in the northernmost province of the Redneck Riviera."

"You made the right call," Tom said. "I never would have believed it when you said you weren't going back to school, but you made the right call. Maybe *I* should have stayed at Joyland."

He smiled—that I-French-kissed-the-Blarney-Stone smile of his that could charm the birdies down from the trees—but it didn't quite dispel the shadow that crossed his face. He could never have stayed at Joyland, not after our dark ride.

They stayed the weekend at Mrs. Shoplaw's Beachside Accommodations (Mrs. S. was delighted to have them, and Tina Ackerley was delighted to see them) and all five of us had a hilarious half-drunk picnic supper on the beach, with a roaring bonfire to provide warmth. But on Saturday afternoon, when it came time for Erin to share her troubling information with me, Tom declared his intention to whip Tina and Mrs. S. at Scrabble and sent us off alone. I thought that if Annie and Mike were at the end of their boardwalk, I'd introduce Erin to them. But the day was chilly, the wind off the ocean was downright cold, and the picnic table at the end of the boardwalk was deserted. Even the umbrella was gone, taken in and stored for the winter.

At Joyland, all four parking lots were empty save for the little fleet of service trucks. Erin—dressed in a heavy turtleneck sweater and wool pants, carrying a slim and very businesslike briefcase with her initials embossed on it—raised her eyebrows when I produced my keyring and used the biggest key to open the gate.

"So," she said. "You're one of them now."

That embarrassed me—aren't we all embarrassed (even if we don't know why) when someone says we're one of *them*?

"Not really. I carry a gate-key in case I get here before anyone else, or if I'm the last to leave, but only Fred and Lane have all the Keys to the Kingdom."

She laughed as if I'd said something silly. "The key to the gate *is* the key to the kingdom, that's what I think." Then she sobered and gave me a long, measuring stare. "You look older, Devin. I thought so even before we got off the train, when I saw you waiting on the platform. Now I know why. You went to work and we went back to Never Never Land to play with the Lost Boys and Girls. The ones who will eventually turn up in suits from Brooks Brothers and with MBAs in their pockets."

I pointed to the briefcase. "That would go with a suit from Brooks Brothers…if they really make suits for women, that is."

She sighed. "It was a gift from my parents. My father wants me to be a lawyer, like him. So far I haven't gotten up the nerve to tell him I want to be a freelance photographer. He'll blow his stack."

We walked up Joyland Avenue in silence—except for the bonelike rattle of the fallen leaves. She looked at the covered rides, the dry fountain, the frozen horses on the merry-go-round, the empty Story Stage in the deserted Wiggle-Waggle Village.

"Kind of sad, seeing it this way. It makes me think mortal thoughts." She looked at me appraisingly. "We saw the paper. Mrs. Shoplaw made sure to leave it in our room. You did it again."

"Eddie? I just happened to be there." We had reached Madame Fortuna's shy. The lawn chairs were still leaning against it. I unfolded two and gestured for Erin to sit down. I sat beside her, then pulled a pint bottle of Old Log Cabin from the pocket of my jacket. "Cheap whiskey, but it takes the chill off."

Looking amused, she took a small nip. I took one of my own, screwed on the cap, and stowed the bottle in my pocket. Fifty yards down Joyland Avenue—our midway—I could see the tall false front of Horror House and read the drippy green letters: COME IN IF YOU DARE.

Her small hand gripped my shoulder with surprising strength. "You saved the old bastard. You did. Give yourself some credit, you."

I smiled, thinking of Lane saying I had a merit badge in modesty. Maybe; giving myself credit for stuff wasn't one of my strong points in those days.

"Will he live?"

"Probably. Freddy Dean talked to some doctors who said blah-blah-blah, patient must give up smoking, blah-blah-blah, patient must give up eating French fries, blah-blah-blah, patient must begin a regular exercise regimen."

"I can just see Eddie Parks jogging," Erin said.

"Uh-huh, with a cigarette in his mouth and a bag of pork rinds in his hand."

She giggled. The wind gusted and blew her hair around her face. In her heavy sweater and businesslike dark gray pants, she didn't look much like the flushed American beauty who'd run around Joyland in a little green dress, smiling her pretty Erin smile and coaxing people to let her take their picture with her old-fashioned camera.

"What have you got for me? What did you find out?"

She opened her briefcase and took out a folder. "Are you absolutely sure you want to get into this? Because I don't think you're going to listen, say 'Elementary, my dear Erin,' and spit out the killer's name like Sherlock Holmes."

If I needed evidence that Sherlock Holmes I wasn't, my wild idea that Eddie Parks might have been the so-called Funhouse Killer was it. I thought of telling her that I was more interested in putting the victim to rest than I was in catching the killer, but it would have sounded crazy, even factoring in Tom's experience. "I'm not expecting that, either."

"And by the way, you owe me almost forty dollars for interlibrary loan fees."

"I'm good for it."

She poked me in the ribs. "You better be. I'm not working my way through school for the fun of it."

She settled her briefcase between her ankles and opened the folder. I saw Xeroxes, two or three pages of typewritten notes, and some glossy photographs that looked like the kind the conies got when they bought the Hollywood Girls' pitch. "Okay, here we go. I started with the Charleston *News and Courier* article you told me about." She handed me one of the Xeroxes. "It's a Sunday piece, five thousand words of speculation and maybe eight hundred words of actual info. Read it later if you want, I'll summarize the salient points.

"Four girls. Five if you count *her*." She pointed down the midway at Horror House. "The first was Delight Mowbray, DeeDee to her friends. From Waycross, Georgia. White, twenty-one years old. Two or three days before she was killed, she told her good friend Jasmine Withers that she had a new boyfriend, older and very handsome. She was found beside a trail on the edge of the Okefenokee Swamp on August 31st, 1961, nine days after she disappeared. If the guy had taken her into the swamp, even a little way, she might not have been found for a much longer time."

"If ever," I said. "A body left in there would have been gatorbait in twenty minutes."

"Gross but true." She handed me another Xerox. "This is the story from the Waycross *Journal-Herald*." There was a photo. It showed a somber cop holding up a plaster cast of tire tracks. "The theory is that he dumped her where he cut her throat. The tire tracks were made by a truck, the story says."

"Dumped her like garbage," I said.

"Also gross but true." She handed me another Xeroxed newspaper clipping. "Here's number two. Claudine Sharp, from Rocky Mount, right here in NC. White, twenty-three years old. Found dead in a local theater. August second, 1963. The movie being shown was *Lawrence of Arabia*, which happens to be very long and very loud. The guy who wrote the story quotes 'an unnamed police source' as saying the guy probably cut her throat during one of the battle scenes. Pure speculation, of course. He left a bloody shirt and gloves, then must have walked out in the shirt he was wearing underneath."

"That just about has to be the guy who killed Linda Gray," I said. "Don't you think so?"

"It sure sounds like it. The cops questioned all her friends, but Claudine hadn't said anything about a new boyfriend."

"Or who she was going to the movies with that night? Not even to her parents?"

Erin gave me a patient look. "She was twenty-three, Dev, not fourteen. She lived all the way across town from her parents. Worked in a drugstore and had a little apartment above it."

"You got all that from the newspaper story?"

"Of course not. I also made some calls. Practically dialed my fingers off, if you want to know the truth. You owe me for the long-distance, too. More about Claudine Sharp later. For now, let's move on. Victim number three—according to the *News and Courier* story—was a girl from Santee, South Carolina. Now we're up to 1965. Eva Longbottom, age nineteen. Black. Disappeared on July fourth. Her body was found nine days later by a couple of fishermen, lying on the north bank of the Santee River. Raped and stabbed in the heart. The others were neither black nor raped. You can put her in the Funhouse Killer column if you want to, but I'm doubtful, myself. Last victim—before Linda Gray—was her."

She handed me what had to be a high school yearbook photo of a beautiful golden-haired girl. The kind who's the head cheerleader, the Homecoming Queen, dates the football quarterback...and is *still* liked by everyone.

"Darlene Stamnacher. Probably would have changed her last name if she'd gotten into the movie biz, which was her stated goal. White, nineteen. From Maxton, North Carolina. Disappeared on June 29th, 1967. Found two days later, after a massive search, inside a roadside lean-to in the sugar-pine williwags south of Elrod. Throat cut."

"Christ, she's beautiful. Didn't she have a steady boyfriend?"

"A girl this good-looking, why do you even ask? And that's where the police went first, only he wasn't around. He and three of his buddies had gone camping in the Blue Ridge, and they could all vouch for him. Unless he flapped his arms and flew back, it wasn't him."

"Then came Linda Gray," I said. "Number five. If they were all murdered by the same guy, that is."

Erin raised a teacherly finger. "And only five if all the guy's victims have been found. There could have been others in '62, '64, '66...you get it."

The wind gusted and moaned through the struts of the Spin.

"Now for the things that trouble me," Erin said...as if five dead girls weren't troubling enough. From her folder she took another Xerox. It was a flier—a shout, in the Talk—advertising something called *Manly Wellman's Show of 1000 Wonders*. It showed a couple of clowns holding up a parchment listing some of the wonders, one of which was AMERICA'S FINEST COLLECTION OF **FREAKS**! AND **ODDITIES**! There were also rides, games, fun for the kiddies, and THE WORLD'S SCARIEST FUNHOUSE!

Come in if you dare, I thought.

"You got this from interlibrary loan?" I asked.

"Yes. I've decided you can get anything by way of interlibrary loan, if you're willing to dig. Or maybe I should say cock an ear, because it's really the world's biggest jungle telegraph. This ad appeared in the Waycross *Journal-Herald*. It ran during the first week of August, 1961."

"The Wellman carny was in Waycross when the first girl disappeared?"

"Her name was DeeDee Mowbray, and no—it had moved on by then. But it was there when DeeDee told her girlfriend that she had a new boyfriend. Now look at this. It's from the Rocky Mount *Telegram*. Ran for a week in mid-July of 1963. Standard advance advertising. I probably don't even need to tell you that."

It was another full-pager shouting *Manly Wellman's Show of 1000 Wonders*. Same two clowns holding up the same parchment, but two years after the stop in Waycross, they were also promising a ten thousand dollar cover-all Beano game, and the word *freaks* was nowhere to be seen.

"Was the show in town when the Sharp girl was killed in the movie theater?"

"Left the day before." She tapped the bottom of the sheet. "All you have to do is look at the dates, Dev."

I wasn't as familiar with the timeline as she was, but I didn't bother defending myself. "The third girl? Longbottom?"

"I didn't find anything about a carny in the Santee area, and I sure wouldn't have found anything about the Wellman show, because it went bust in the fall of 1964. I found that in *Outdoor Trade and Industry*. So far as I or any of my many librarian helpers could discover, it's the only trade magazine that covers the carny and amusement park biz."

"Jesus, Erin, you should forget photography and find yourself a rich writer or movie producer. Hire on as his research assistant."

"I'd rather take pictures. Research is too much like work. But don't lose the thread here, Devin. There was no carny in the Santee area, true, but the Eva Longbottom murder doesn't look like the other four, anyway. Not to me. No rape in the others, remember?"

"That you know of. Newspapers are coy about that stuff."

"That's right, they say molested or sexually assaulted instead of raped, but they get the point across, believe me."

"What about Darlene Shoemaker? Was there—"

"*Stamnacher*. These girls were murdered, Dev, the least you can do is get their names right."

"I will. Give me time."

She put a hand over mine. "Sorry. I'm throwing this at you all at once, aren't I? I've had weeks to brood over it."

"Have you been?"

"Sort of. It's pretty awful."

She was right. If you read a whodunit or see a mystery movie, you can whistle gaily past whole heaps of corpses, only interested in finding out if it was the butler or the evil stepmother. But these had been real young women. Crows had probably ripped their flesh; maggots would have infested their eyes and squirmed up their noses and into the gray meat of their brains.

"Was there a carny in the Maxton area when the Stamnacher girl was killed?"

"No, but there was a county fair about to start in Lumberton—that's the nearest town of any size. Here."

She handed me another Xerox, this one advertising the Robeson County Summer Fair. Once again, Erin tapped the sheet. This time she was calling my attention to a line reading 50 **SAFE** RIDES PROVIDED BY SOUTHERN STAR AMUSEMENTS.

"I also looked Southern Star up in *Outdoor Trade and Industry*. The company's been around since after World War II. They're based in Birmingham and travel all over the south, putting up rides. Nothing so grand as the Thunderball or the Delirium Shaker, but they've got plenty of chump-shoots, and the jocks to run them."

I had to grin at that. She hadn't forgotten all the Talk, it seemed. Chump-shoots were rides that could be easily put up or taken down. If you've ever ridden the Krazy Kups or the Wild Mouse, you've been on on a chump-shoot.

"I called the ride-boss at Southern Star. Said I'd worked at Joyland this summer, and was doing a term paper on the amusement industry for my sociology class. Which I just might do, you know. After all this, it would be a slam-dunk. He told me what I'd already guessed, that there's a big turnover in their line of work. He couldn't tell me offhand if they'd picked anyone up from the Wellman show, but he said it was likely—a couple of roughies here, a couple of jocks there, maybe a ride-monkey or two. So the guy who killed DeeDee and Claudine could have been at that fair, and Darlene Stamnacher could have met him. The fair wasn't officially open for business yet, but lots of townies gravitate to the local fairgrounds to watch the ride-monkeys and the local gazoonies do the setup." She looked at me levelly. "And I think that's just what happened."

"Erin, is the carny link in the story the *News and Courier* published after Linda Gray was killed? Or maybe I should call it the amusement link."

"Nope. Can I have another nip from your bottle? I'm cold."

"We can go inside—"

"No, it's this murder stuff that makes me cold. Every time I go over it."

I gave her the bottle, and after she'd taken her nip, I took one of my own. "Maybe *you're* Sherlock Holmes," I said. "What about the cops? Do you think they missed it?"

"I don't know for sure, but I think...they did. If this was a detective show on TV, there'd be one smart old cop—a Lieutenant Columbo type—who'd look at the big picture and put it together, but I guess there aren't many guys like that in real life. Besides, the big picture is hard to see because it's scattered across three states and eight years. One thing you can be sure of is that if he ever worked at Joyland, he's long gone. I'm sure the turnover at an amusement park isn't as fast as it is in a road company like

Southern Star Amusements, but there are still plenty of people leaving and coming in."

I knew that for myself. Ride-jocks and concession shouters aren't exactly the most grounded people, and gazoonies went in and out like the tide.

"Now here's the other thing that troubles me," she said, and handed me her little pile of eight-by-ten photos. Printed on the white border at the bottom of each was PHOTO TAKEN BY YOUR JOYLAND "HOLLYWOOD GIRL."

I shuffled through them, and felt in need of another nip when I realized what they were: the photos showing Linda Gray and the man who had killed her. "Jesus God, Erin, these aren't newspaper pix. Where'd you get them?"

"Brenda Rafferty. I had to butter her up a little, tell her what a good mom she'd been to all us Hollywood Girls, but in the end she came through. These are fresh prints made from negatives she had in her personal files and loaned to me. Here's something interesting, Dev. You see the headband the Gray girl's wearing?"

"Yes." An Alice band, Mrs. Shoplaw had called it. A *blue* Alice band.

"Brenda said they fuzzed that out in the shots they gave to the newspapers. They thought it would help them nail the guy, but it never did."

"So what troubles you?"

God knew all of the pictures troubled me, even the ones where Gray and the man she was with were just passing in the background, only recognizable by her sleeveless blouse and Alice band and his baseball cap and dark glasses. In only two of them were Linda Gray and her killer sharp and clear. The first showed them at the Whirly Cups, his hand resting casually on the swell of Gray's bottom. In the other—the best of the lot—they were at the Annie Oakley Shootin' Gallery. Yet in neither was the man's face really visible. I could have passed him on the street and not known him.

Erin plucked up the Whirly Cups photo. "Look at his hand."

"Yeah, the tattoo. I see it, and I heard about it from Mrs. S. What do you make it to be? A hawk or an eagle?"

"I think an eagle, but it doesn't matter."

"Really?"

"Really. Remember I said I'd come back to Claudine Sharp? A young woman getting her throat cut in the local movie theater—during *Lawrence of Arabia*, no less—was big news in a little town like Rocky Mount. The *Telegram* ran with it for almost a month. The cops turned up exactly one lead, Dev. A girl Claudine went to high school with saw her at the snackbar and said hello. Claudine said hi right back. The girl said there was a man in sunglasses and a baseball cap next to her, but she never thought the guy was with Claudine, because he was a lot older. The only reason she noticed him at all was because he was wearing sunglasses in a movieshow…and because he had a tattoo on his hand."

"The bird."

"No, Dev. It was a Coptic cross. Like this." She took out another Xerox sheet and showed me. "She told the cops she thought at first it was some kind of Nazi symbol."

I looked at the cross. It was elegant, but looked nothing at all like a bird. "Two tats, one on each hand," I said at last. "The bird on one, the cross on the other."

She shook her head and gave me the Whirly Cups photo again. "Which hand's got the bird on it?"

He was standing on Linda Gray's left, encircling her waist. The hand resting on her bottom…

"The right."

"Yes. But the girl who saw him in the movie theater said the *cross* was on his right."

I considered this. "She made a mistake, that's all. Witnesses do it all the time."

"Sure they do. My father could talk all day on that subject. But look, Dev."

Erin handed me the Shootin' Gallery photo, the best of the bunch because they weren't just passing in the background. A roving Hollywood Girl had seen them, noted the cute pose, and snapped them, hoping for a sale. Only the guy had given her the brushoff. A *hard* brushoff, according to Mrs. Shoplaw. That made me remember how she had described the photo: *Him snuggled up to her hip to hip, showing her how to hold the rifle, the way guys always do*. The version Mrs. S. saw would have been a fuzzy newspaper reproduction, made up of little dots. This was the original, so sharp and clear I almost felt I could step into it and warn the Gray girl. He *was* snuggled up to her, his hand over hers on the barrel of the beebee-shooting .22, helping her aim.

It was his *left* hand. And there was no tattoo on it.

Erin said, "You see it, don't you?"

"There's nothing to see."

"That's the point, Dev. That's exactly the point."

"Are you saying that it was two different guys? That one with a cross on his hand killed Claudine Sharp and *another* one—a guy with a bird on his hand—killed Linda Gray? That doesn't seem very likely."

"I couldn't agree more."

"Then what are you saying?"

"I thought I saw something in one of the photos, but I wasn't sure, so I took the print and the negative to a grad student named Phil Hendron. He's a darkroom genius, practically lives in the Bard Photography Department. You know those clunky Speed Graphics we carried?"

"Sure."

"They were mostly for effect—cute girls toting old-fashioned cameras—but Phil says they're actually pretty terrific. You can do a lot with the negs. For example..."

She handed me a blow-up of the Whirly Cups pic. The Hollywood Girl's target had been a young couple with a toddler between them, but in this enlarged version they were hardly there. Now Linda Gray and her murderous date were at the center of the image.

"Look at his hand, Dev. Look at the tattoo!"

I did, frowning. "It's a little hard to see," I complained. "The hand's blurrier than the rest."

"I don't think so."

This time I held the photo close to my eyes. "It's...Jesus, Erin. Is it the ink? Is it running? Just a little?"

She gave me a triumphant smile. "July of 1969. A hot night in Dixie. Almost everybody was sweating buckets. If you don't believe me, look at some of the other pictures and note the perspiration rings. Plus, he had something else to be sweaty about, didn't he? He had murder on his mind. An audacious one, at that."

I said, "Oh, shit. Pirate Pete's."

She pointed a forefinger at me. "Bingo."

Pirate Pete's was the souvenir shop outside the Splash & Crash, proudly flying a Jolly Roger from its roof. Inside you could get the usual stuff—tee-shirts, coffee mugs, beach towels, even a pair of swim-trunks if your kid forgot his, everything imprinted with the Joyland logo. There was also a counter where you could get a wide assortment of fake tattoos. They came on decals. If you didn't feel capable of applying it yourself, Pirate Pete (or one of his greenie minions) would do it for a small surcharge.

Erin was nodding. "I doubt he got it there—that would have been dumb, and this guy isn't dumb—but I'm sure it's not a real tattoo, any more than the Coptic cross the girl saw in that Rocky Mount movie theater was a real tattoo." She leaned forward and gripped my arm. "You know what I think? I think he does it because it draws attention. People notice the tattoo and everything else just..." She tapped the indistinct shapes that had been the actual subject of this photo before her friend at Bard blew it up.

I said, "Everything else about him fades into the background."

"Yup. Later he just washes it off."

"Do the cops know?"

"I have no idea. You could tell them—not me, I'm going back to school—but I'm not sure they'd care at this late date."

I shuffled through the photos again. I had no doubt that Erin had actually discovered something, although I *did* doubt it would, by itself, be responsible for the capture of the Funhouse Killer. But there was something else about the photos. *Something*. You know how sometimes a word gets stuck on the tip of your tongue and just won't come off? It was like that.

"Have there been any murders like these five—or these four, if we leave out Eva Longbottom—since Linda Gray? Did you check?"

"I tried," she said. "The short answer is I don't think so, but I can't say for sure. I've read about fifty murders of young girls and women—fifty at least—and haven't found any that fit the parameters." She ticked them off. "Always in summer. Always as a result of a dating situation with an unknown older man. Always the cut throat. And always with some sort of carny connec—"

"Hello, kids."

We looked up, startled. It was Fred Dean. Today he was wearing a golfing shirt, bright red baggies, and a long-billed cap with HEAVEN'S BAY COUNTRY CLUB stitched in gold thread above the brim. I was a lot more used to seeing him in a suit, where informality consisted of pulling down his tie and popping the top button of his Van Heusen shirt. Dressed for the links, he looked absurdly young. Except for the graying wings of hair at his temples, that was.

"Hello, Mr. Dean," Erin said, standing up. Most of her paperwork—and some of the photographs—were still clutched in one hand. The folder was in the other. "I don't know if you remember me—"

"Of course I do," he said, approaching. "I never forget a Hollywood Girl, but sometimes I *do* mix up the names. Are you Ashley or Jerri?"

She smiled, put her paperwork back in the folder, and handed it to me. I added the photos I was still holding. "I'm Erin."

"Of course. Erin Cook." He dropped me a wink, which was even weirder than seeing him in old-fashioned golfing baggies. "You have excellent taste in young ladies, Jonesy."

"I do, don't I?" It seemed too complicated to tell him that Erin was actually Tom Kennedy's girlfriend. Fred probably wouldn't remember Tom anyway, never having seen him in a flirty green dress and high heels.

"I just stopped by to get the accounts books. Quarterly IRS payments coming up. Such a pain in the hindquarters. Enjoying your little alumna visit, Erin?"

"Yes, sir, very much."

"Coming back next year?"

She looked a trifle uncomfortable at that, but stuck gamely to the truth. "Probably not."

"Fair enough, but if you change your mind, I'm sure Brenda Rafferty can find a place for you." He switched his attention to me. "This boy you plan to bring to the park, Jonesy. Have you set a date with his mother?"

"Tuesday. Wednesday or Thursday if it's rainy. The kid can't be out in the rain."

Erin was looking at me curiously.

"I advise you stick to Tuesday," he said. "There's a storm coming up the coast. Not a hurricane, thank God, but a tropical disturbance. Lots of rain and gale-force winds is what they're saying. It's supposed to arrive mid-morning on Wednesday."

"Okay," I said. "Thanks for the tip."

"Nice to see you again, Erin." He tipped his cap to her and started off toward the back lot.

Erin waited until he was out of sight before bursting into giggles. "Those *pants*. Did you see those *pants*?"

"Yeah," I said. "Pretty wild." But I was damned if I was going to laugh at them. Or him. According to Lane, Fred Dean held Joyland together with spit, baling wire, and account-book wizardry. That being the case, I thought he could wear all the golf baggies he wanted. And at least they weren't checks.

"What's this about bringing some kid to the park?"

"Long story," I said. "I'll tell you while we walk back."

So I did, giving her the Boy-Scout-majoring-in-modesty

version and leaving out the big argument at the hospital. Erin listened without interruption, asking only one question, just as we reached the steps leading up from the beach. “Tell me the truth, Dev—is mommy foxy?”

People kept asking me that.

♥

That night Tom and Erin went out to Surfer Joe’s, a beer-and-boogie bar where they had spent more than a few off-nights during the summer. Tom invited me along, but I heeded that old saying about two being company and three being you-know-what. Besides, I doubted if they’d find the same raucous, party-hearty atmosphere. In towns like Heaven’s Bay, there’s a big difference between July and October. In my role as big brother, I even said so.

“You don’t understand, Dev,” Tom said. “Me n Erin don’t go *looking* for the fun; we *bring* the fun. It’s what we learned last summer.”

Nevertheless, I heard them coming up the stairs early, and almost sober, from the sound of them. Yet there were whispers and muffled laughter, sounds that made me feel a little lonely. Not for Wendy; just for *someone*. Looking back on it, I suppose even that was a step forward.

I read through Erin’s notes while they were gone, but found nothing new. I set them aside after fifteen minutes and went back to the photographs, crisp black-and-white images TAKEN BY YOUR JOYLAND “HOLLYWOOD GIRL.” At first I just shuffled through them; then I sat on the floor and laid them out in a square, moving them from place to place like a guy trying to put a puzzle together. Which was, I suppose, exactly what I was doing.

Erin was troubled by the carny connection and the tattoos that probably weren't real tattoos at all. Those things troubled me as well, but there was something else. Something I couldn't quite get. It was maddening because I felt like it was staring me right in the face. Finally I put all but two of the photos back in the folder. The key two. These I held up, looking first at one, then at the other.

Linda Gray and her killer waiting in line at the Whirly Cups.

Linda Gray and her killer at the Shootin' Gallery.

Never mind the goddam tattoo, I told myself. *It's not that. It's something else.*

But what else could it be? The sunglasses masked his eyes. The goatee masked his lower face, and the slightly tilted bill of the baseball cap shaded his forehead and eyebrows. The cap's logo showed a catfish peering out of a big red C, the insignia of a South Carolina minor league team called the Mudcats. Dozens of Mudcat lids went through the park every day at the height of the season, so many that we called them fishtops instead of dogtops. The bastard could hardly have picked a more anonymous lid, and surely that was the idea.

Back and forth I went, from the Whirly Cups to the Shootin' Gallery and then back to the Whirly Cups again. At last I tossed the photos in the folder and threw the folder on my little desk. I read until Tom and Erin came in, then went to bed.

Maybe it'll come to me in the morning, I thought. *I'll wake up and say, "Oh shit, of course."*

The sound of the incoming waves slipped me into sleep. I dreamed I was on the beach with Annie and Mike. Annie and I were standing with our feet in the surf, our arms around each other, watching Mike fly his kite. He was paying out twine and running after it. He could do that because there was nothing wrong with him. He was fine. I had only dreamed that stuff about Duchenne's muscular dystrophy.

I woke early because I'd forgotten to pull down the shade. I went to the folder, pulled out those two photographs, and stared at them in the day's first sunlight, positive I'd see the answer.

But I didn't.

♥

A harmony of scheduling had allowed Tom and Erin to travel from New Jersey to North Carolina together, but when it comes to train schedules, harmony is the exception rather than the rule. The only ride they got together on Sunday was the one from Heaven's Bay to Wilmington, in my Ford. Erin's train left for upstate New York and Annandale-on-Hudson two hours before Tom's Coastal Express was due to whisk him back to New Jersey.

I tucked a check in her jacket pocket. "Interlibrary loans and long distance."

She fished it out, looked at the amount, and tried to hand it back. "Eighty dollars is too much, Dev."

"Considering all you found out, it's not enough. Take it, Lieutenant Columbo."

She laughed, put it back in her pocket, and kissed me goodbye —another brother-sister quickie, nothing like the one we'd shared that night at the end of the summer. She spent considerably longer in Tom's arms. Promises were made about Thanksgiving at Tom's parents' home in western Pennsylvania. I could tell he didn't want to let her go, but when the loudspeakers announced last call for Richmond, Baltimore, Wilkes-Barre, and points north, he finally did.

When she was gone, Tom and I strolled across the street and had an early dinner in a not-too-bad ribs joint. I was contemplating the dessert selection when he cleared his throat and said, "Listen, Dev."

Something in his voice made me look up in a hurry. His cheeks were even more flushed than usual. I put the menu down.

"This stuff you've had Erin doing…I think it should stop. It's bothering her, and I think she's been neglecting her coursework." He laughed, glanced out the window at the train-station bustle, looked back at me. "I sound more like her dad than her boyfriend, don't I?"

"You sound concerned, that's all. Like you care for her."

"*Care* for her? Buddy, I'm head-over-heels in love. She's the most important thing in my life. What I'm saying here isn't jealousy talking, though. I don't want you to get that idea. Here's the thing: if she's going to transfer and still hold onto her financial aid, she can't let her grades slip. You see that, don't you?"

Yes, I could see that. I could see something else, too, even if Tom couldn't. He wanted her away from Joyland in mind as well as body, because something had happened to him there that he couldn't understand. Nor did he want to, which in my opinion made him sort of a fool. That dour flush of envy ran through me again, causing my stomach to clench around the food it was trying to digest.

Then I smiled—it was an effort, I won't kid you about that—and said, "Message received. As far as I'm concerned, our little research project is over." *So relax, Thomas. You can stop thinking about what happened in Horror House. About what you saw there.*

"Good. We're still friends, right?"

I reached across the table. "Friends to the end," I said.

We shook on it.

♥

The Wiggle-Waggle Village's Story Stage had three backdrops: Prince Charming's Castle, Jack's Magic Beanstalk, and a starry night sky featuring the Carolina Spin outlined in red neon. All three had sun-faded over the course of the summer. I was in the Wiggle-Waggle's small backstage area on Monday morning, touching them up (and hoping not to *fuck* them up—I was no Van Gogh) when one of the part-time gazoonies arrived with a message from Fred Dean. I was wanted in his office.

I went with some unease, wondering if I was going to get a reaming for bringing Erin into the park on Saturday. I was surprised to find Fred dressed not in one of his suits or his amusing golf outfit, but in faded jeans and an equally faded Joyland tee-shirt, the short sleeves rolled to show some real muscle. There was a paisley sweatband cinched around his brow. He didn't look like an accountant or the park's chief employment officer; he looked like a ride-jock.

He registered my surprise and smiled. "Like the outfit? I must admit I do. It's the way I dressed when I caught on with the Blitz Brothers show in the Midwest, back in the fifties. My mother was okay with the Blitzies, but my dad was horrified. And *he* was carny."

"I know," I said.

He raised his eyebrows. "Really? Word gets around, doesn't it? Anyway, there's a lot to do this afternoon."

"Just give me a list. I'm almost done painting the backdrops in the—"

"Not at all, Jonesy. You're signing out at noon today, and I don't want to see you until tomorrow morning at nine, when you turn up with your guests. Don't worry about your paycheck, either. I'll see you're not docked for the hours you miss."

"What's this about, Fred?"

He gave me a smile I couldn't interpret. "It's a surprise."

♥

That Monday was warm and sunny, and Annie and Mike were having lunch at the end of the boardwalk when I walked back to Heaven's Bay. Milo saw me coming and raced to meet me.

"Dev!" Mike called. "Come and have a sandwich! We've got plenty!"

"No, I really shouldn't—"

"We insist," Annie said. Then her brow furrowed. "Unless you're sick, or something. I don't want Mike to catch a bug."

"I'm fine, just got sent home early. Mr. Dean—he's my boss—wouldn't tell me why. He said it was a surprise. It's got something to do with tomorrow, I guess." I looked at her with some anxiety. "We're still on for tomorrow, right?"

"Yes," she said. "When I surrender, I surrender. Just…we're not going to tire him out. Are we, Dev?"

"*Mom,*" Mike said.

She paid him no mind. "*Are* we?"

"No, ma'am." Although seeing Fred Dean dressed up like a carny road dog, with all those unsuspected muscles showing, had made me uneasy. Had I made it clear to him how fragile Mike's health was? I thought so, but—

"Then come on up here and have a sandwich," she said. "I hope you like egg salad."

♥

I didn't sleep well on Monday night, half-convinced that the tropical storm Fred had mentioned would arrive early and wash out Mike's trip to the park, but Tuesday dawned cloudless. I crept down to the parlor and turned on the TV in time to get the six forty-five weathercast on WECT. The storm was still coming, but the only people who were going to feel it today were the ones living in coastal Florida and Georgia. I hoped Mr. Easterbrook had packed his galoshes.

"You're up early," Mrs. Shoplaw said, poking her head in from the kitchen. "I was just making scrambled eggs and bacon. Come have some."

"I'm not that hungry, Mrs. S."

"Nonsense. You're still a growing boy, Devin, and you need to eat. Erin told me what you've got going on today, and I think you're doing a wonderful thing. It will be fine."

"I hope you're right," I said, but I kept thinking of Fred Dean in his work-clothes. Fred, who'd sent me home early. Fred, who had a surprise planned.

♥

We had made our arrangements at lunch the day before, and when I turned my old car into the driveway of the big green Victorian at eight-thirty on Tuesday morning, Annie and Mike were ready to go. So was Milo.

"Are you sure nobody will mind us bringing him?" Mike had asked on Monday. "I don't want to get into trouble."

"Service dogs are allowed in Joyland," I said, "and Milo's going to be a service dog. Aren't you, Milo?"

Milo had cocked his head, apparently unfamiliar with the service dog concept.

Today Mike was wearing his huge, clanky braces. I moved to help him into the van, but he waved me off and did it himself. It took a lot of effort and I expected a coughing fit, but none came. He was practically bouncing with excitement. Annie, looking impossibly long-legged in Lee Riders, handed me the van keys. "You drive." And lowering her voice so Mike wouldn't hear: "I'm too goddam nervous to do it."

I was nervous, too. I'd bulldozed her into this, after all. I'd had help from Mike, true, but I was the adult. If it went wrong, it would be on me. I wasn't much for prayer, but as I loaded Mike's crutches and wheelchair into the back of the van, I sent one up that nothing would go wrong. Then I backed out of the driveway, turned onto Beach Drive, and drove past the bill-board reading BRING YOUR KIDS TO JOYLAND FOR THE TIME OF THEIR LIVES!

Annie was in the passenger seat, and I thought she had never looked more beautiful than she did that October morning, in her faded jeans and a light sweater, her hair tied back with a hank of blue yarn.

"Thank you for this, Dev," she said. "I just hope we're doing the right thing."

"We are," I said, trying to sound more confident than I felt. Because, now that it was a done deal, I had my doubts.

♥

The Joyland sign was lit up—that was the first thing I noticed. The second was that the summertime get-happy music was playing through the loudspeakers: a sonic parade of late sixties and early seventies hits. I had intended to park in one of the Lot A handicapped spaces—they were only fifty feet or so from the park entrance—but before I could do so, Fred Dean stepped through the open gate and beckoned us forward. Today he wasn't wearing just any suit but the three-piecer he saved for the occasional celebrity who rated a VIP tour. The suit I had seen, but never the black silk top hat, which looked like the kind you saw diplomats wearing in old newsreel footage.

"Is this usual?" Annie asked.

"Sure," I said, a trifle giddily. None of it was usual.

I drove through the gate and onto Joyland Avenue, pulling up next to the park bench outside the Wiggle-Waggle Village where Mr. Easterbrook had once sat during my first turn as Howie.

Mike wanted to get out of the van the way he'd gotten in: by himself. I stood by, ready to catch him if he lost his balance, while Annie hoisted the wheelchair out of the back. Milo sat at my feet, tail thumping, ears cocked, eyes bright.

As Annie rolled the wheelchair up, Fred approached in a cloud of aftershave. He was…resplendent. There's really no other word for it. He took off his hat, bowed to Annie, then held out a hand. "You must be Mike's mother." You have to remember that Ms. wasn't common usage back then, and, nervous as I was, I took a moment to appreciate how deftly he had avoided the Miss/Mrs. dichotomy.

"I am," she said. I don't know if she was flustered by his courtliness or by the difference in the way they were dressed—she amusement-park casual, he state-visit formal—but flustered she was. She shook his hand, though. "And this young man—"

"—is Michael." He offered his hand to the wide-eyed boy standing there in his steel supports. "Thank you for coming today."

"You're welcome…I mean, thank *you*. Thank you for having us." He shook Fred's hand. "This place is *huge*."

It wasn't, of course; Disney World is huge. But to a ten-year-old who had never been to an amusement park, it had to look that way. For a moment I could see it through his eyes, see it new, and my doubts about bringing him began to melt away.

Fred bent down to examine the third member of the Ross family, hands on his knees. "And you're Milo!"

Milo barked.

"Yes," Fred said, "and I am equally pleased to meet you." He held out his hand, waiting for Milo to raise his paw. When he did, Fred shook it.

"How do you know our dog's name?" Annie asked. "Did Dev tell you?"

He straightened, smiling. "He did not. I know because this is a magic place, my dear. For instance." He showed her his empty hands, then put them behind his back. "Which hand?"

"Left," Annie said, playing along.

Fred brought out his left hand, empty.

She rolled her eyes, smiling. "Okay, right."

This time he brought out a dozen roses. Real ones. Annie and Mike gasped. Me too. All these years later, I have no idea how he did it.

"Joyland is for children, my dear, and since today Mike is the only child here, the park belongs to him. These, however, are for you."

She took them like a woman in a dream, burying her face in the blooms, smelling their sweet red dust.

"I'll put them in the van for you," I said.

She held them a moment longer, then passed them to me.

"Mike," Fred said, "do you know what we sell here?"

He looked uncertain. "Rides? Rides and games?"

"We sell *fun*. So what do you say we have some?"

♥

I remember Mike's day at the park—Annie's day, too—as if it happened last week, but it would take a correspondent much more talented than I am to tell you how it *felt*, or to explain how it could have ended the last hold Wendy Keegan still held over my heart and my emotions. All I can say is what you already know: some days are treasure. Not many, but I think in almost every life there are a few. That was one of mine, and when I'm blue—when life comes down on me and everything looks tawdry and cheap, the way Joyland Avenue did on a rainy day—I go back to it, if only to remind myself that life isn't always a butcher's game. Sometimes the prizes are real. Sometimes they're precious.

Of course not all the rides were running, and that was okay, because there were a lot of them Mike couldn't handle. But more than half of the park was operational that morning—the lights, the music, even some of the shys, where half a dozen gazoonies were on duty selling popcorn, fries, sodas, cotton candy, and Pup-A-Licious dogs. I have no idea how Fred and Lane pulled it off in a single afternoon, but they did.

We started in the Village, where Lane was waiting beside the engine of the Choo-Choo Wiggle. He was wearing a pillowtick engineer's cap instead of his derby, but it was cocked at the same insouciant angle. Of course it was. "All aboard! This is the ride that makes kids happy, so get on board and make it snappy. Dogs ride free, moms ride free, kids ride up in the engine with me."

He pointed at Mike, then to the passenger seat in the engine. Mike got out of his chair, set his crutches, then tottered on them. Annie started for him.

"No, Mom. I'm okay. I can do it."

He got his balance and clanked to where Lane was standing—a real boy with robot legs—and allowed Lane to boost him into the passenger seat. "Is that the cord that blows the whistle? Can I pull it?"

"That's what it's there for," Lane said, "but watch out for pigs on the tracks. There's a wolf in the area, and they're scared to death of him."

Annie and I sat in one of the cars. Her eyes were bright. Roses all her own burned in her cheeks. Her lips, though tightly pressed together, were trembling.

"You okay?" I asked her.

"Yes." She took my hand, laced her fingers through mine, and squeezed almost tight enough to hurt. "Yes. Yes. Yes."

"Controls green across the board!" Lane cried. "Check me on that, Michael!"

"Check!"

"Watch out for what on the tracks?"

"Pigs!"

"Kid, you got style that makes me smile. Give that yell-rope a yank and we're off!"

Mike yanked the cord. The whistle howled. Milo barked. The airbrakes chuffed, and the train began to move.

Choo-Choo Wiggle was strictly a zamp ride, okay? All the

rides in the Village were zamps, meant mostly for boys and girls between the ages of three and seven. But you have to remember how seldom Mike Ross had gotten out, especially since his pneumonia the year before, and how many days he had sat with his mother at the end of that boardwalk, listening to the rumble of the rides and the happy screams coming from down the beach, knowing that stuff wasn't for him. What *was* for him was more gasping for air as his lungs failed, more coughing, a gradual inability to walk even with the aid of crutches and braces, and finally the bed where he would die, wearing diapers under his PJs and an oxygen mask over his face.

Wiggle-Waggle Village was sort of depopulated with no greenies to play the fairy-tale parts, but Fred and Lane had reactivated all the mechanicals: the magic beanstalk that shot out of the ground in a burst of steam; the witch cackling in front of the Candy House; the Mad Hatter's tea party; the nightcap-wearing wolf who lurked beneath one of the underpasses and sprang at the train as it passed. As we rounded the final turn, we passed three houses all kids know well—one of straw, one of sticks, and one of bricks.

"Watch out for pigs!" Lane cried, and just then they came waddling onto the tracks, uttering amplified oinks. Mike shrieked with laughter and yanked the whistle. As always, the pigs escaped ...barely.

When we pulled back into the station, Annie let go of my hand and hurried up to the engine. "Are you okay, hon? Want your inhaler?"

"No, I'm fine." Mike turned to Lane. "Thanks, Mr. Engineer!"

"My pleasure, Mike." He held out a hand, palm up. "Slap me five if you're still alive."

Mike did, and with gusto. I doubt if he'd ever felt more alive.

"Now I've got to move on," Lane said. "Today I am a man of many hats." He dropped me a wink.

♥

Annie vetoed the Whirly Cups but allowed Mike—not without apprehension—to ride the Chair-O-Planes. She gripped my arm even harder than she had my hand when his chair rose thirty feet above the ground and began to tilt, then loosened up again when she heard him laughing.

"God," she said, "look at his *hair*! How it flies out behind him!" She was smiling. She was also crying, but didn't seem aware of it. Nor of my arm, which had found its way around her waist.

Fred was running the controls, and knew enough to keep the ride at half-speed, rather than bringing it all the way up to full, which would have had Mike parallel to the ground, held in only by centrifugal force. When he finally came back to earth, the kid was too dizzy to walk. Annie and I each took an arm and guided him to the wheelchair. Fred toted Mike's crutches.

"Oh, man." It seemed to be all he could say. "Oh man, oh man."

The Dizzy Speedboats—a land ride in spite of the name—was next. Mike rode over the painted water in one with Milo, both of them clearly loving it. Annie and I took another one. Although I had been working at Joyland for over four months by then, I'd never been on this ride, and I yelled the first time I saw us rushing prow-first at Mike and Milo's boat, only to shear off at the last second.

"*Wimp!*" Annie shouted in my ear.

When we got off, Mike was breathing hard but still not

coughing. We rolled him up Hound Dog Way and grabbed sodas. The gazoonie refused to take the fivespot Annie held out. "Everything's on the house today, ma'am."

"Can I have a Pup, Mom? And some cotton candy?"

She frowned, then sighed and shrugged. "Okay. Just as long as you understand that stuff is still off-limits, buster. Today's an exception. And no more fast rides."

He wheeled ahead to the Pup-A-Licious shy, his own pup trotting beside him. She turned to me. "It's not about nutrition, if that's what you're thinking. If he gets sick to his stomach, he might vomit. And vomiting is dangerous for kids in Mike's condition. They—"

I kissed her, just a gentle brush of my lips across hers. It was like swallowing a tiny drop of something incredibly sweet. "Hush," I said. "Does he look sick?"

Her eyes got very large. For a moment I felt positive that she was going to slap me and walk away. The day would be ruined and it would be my own stupid goddam fault. Then she smiled, looking at me in a speculative way that made my stomach feel light. "I bet you could do better than that, if you had half a chance."

Before I could think of a reply, she was hurrying after her son. It really would have made no difference if she'd hung around, because I was totally flummoxed.

♥

Annie, Mike, and Milo crowded into one car of the Gondola Glide, which crossed above the whole park on a diagonal. Fred Dean and I rode beneath them in one of the electric carts, with Mike's wheelchair tucked in back.

"Seems like a terrific kid," Fred commented.

"He is, but I never expected you to go all-out like this."

"That's for you as much as for him. You've done the park more good than you seem to know, Dev. When I told Mr. Easterbrook I wanted to go big, he gave me the green light."

"You called him?"

"I did indeed."

"That thing with the roses...how'd you pull it off?"

Fred shot his cuffs and looked modest. "A magician never tells his secrets. Don't you know that?"

"Did you have a card-and-bunny-gig when you were with Blitz Brothers?"

"No, sir, I did not. All I did with the Blitzies was ride-jock and drag the midway. And, although I did not have a valid driver's license, I also drove a truck on a few occasions when we had to DS from some rube-ranch or other in the dead of night."

"So where did you learn the magic?"

Fred reached behind my ear, pulled out a silver dollar, dropped it into my lap. "Here and there, all around the square. Better goose it a little, Jonesy. They're getting ahead of us."

♥

From Skytop Station, where the gondola ride ended, we went to the merry-go-round. Lane Hardy was waiting. He had lost the engineer's cap and was once more sporting his derby. The park's loudspeakers were still pumping out rock and roll, but under the wide, flaring canopy of what's known in the Talk as the spinning jenny, the rock was drowned out by the calliope playing "A Bicycle Built for Two." It was recorded, but still sweet and old-fashioned.

Before Mike could mount the dish, Fred dropped to one knee and regarded him gravely. "You can't ride the jenny without a Joyland hat," he said. "We call em dogtops. Got one?"

"No," Mike said. He still wasn't coughing, but dark patches had begun to creep out beneath his eyes. Where his cheeks weren't flushed with excitement, he looked pale. "I didn't know I was supposed to..."

Fred took off his own hat, peered inside, showed it to us. It was empty, as all magicians' top hats must be when they are displayed to the audience. He looked into it again, and brightened. "Ah!" He brought out a brand new Joyland dogtop and put it on Mike's head. "Perfect! Now which beast do you want to ride? A horse? The unicorn? Marva the Mermaid? Leo the Lion?"

"Yes, the lion, please!" Mike cried. "Mom, you ride the tiger right next to me!"

"You bet," she said. "I've always wanted to ride a tiger."

"Hey, champ," Lane said, "lemme help you up the ramp."

While he did that, Annie lowered her voice and spoke to Fred. "Not a lot more, okay? It's all great, a day he'll never forget, but—"

"He's fading," Fred said. "I understand."

Annie mounted the snarling, green-eyed tiger next to Mike's lion. Milo sat between them, grinning a doggy grin. As the merry-go-round started to move, "A Bicycle Built for Two" gave way to "Twelfth Street Rag." Fred put his hand on my shoulder. "You'll want to meet us at the Spin—we'll make that his last ride—but you need to visit the costume shop first. And put some hustle into it."

I started to ask why, then realized I didn't need to. I headed for the back lot. And yes, I put some hustle into it.

♥

That Tuesday morning in October of 1973 was the last time I wore the fur. I put it on in the costume shop and used Joyland Under to get back to the middle of the park, pushing one of the electric carts as fast as it would go, my Howie-head bouncing up and down on one shoulder. I surfaced behind Madame Fortuna's shy, just in time. Lane, Annie, and Mike were coming up the midway. Lane was pushing Mike's chair. None of them saw me peering around the corner of the shy; they were looking at the Carolina Spin, their necks craned. Fred saw me, though. I raised a paw. He nodded, then turned and raised his own paw to whoever was currently watching from the little sound booth above Customer Services. Seconds later, Howie-music rolled from all the speakers. First up was Elvis, singing "Hound Dog."

I leaped from cover, going into my Howie-dance, which was kind of a fucked-up soft-shoe. Mike gaped. Annie clapped her hands to her temples, as if she'd suddenly been afflicted with a monster headache, then started laughing. I believe what followed was one of my better performances. I hopped and skipped around Mike's chair, hardly aware that Milo was doing the same thing, only in the other direction. "Hound Dog" gave way to the Rolling Stones version of "Walking the Dog." That's a pretty short song, which was good—I hadn't realized how out of shape I was.

I finished by throwing my arms wide and yelling: "*Mike! Mike! Mike!*" That was the only time Howie ever talked, and all I can say in my defense is that it really sounded more like a bark.

Mike rose from his chair, opened his arms, and fell forward. He knew I'd catch him, and I did. Kids half his age had given me the Howie-Hug all summer long, but no hug had ever felt so good. I only wished I could turn him around and squeeze him the way I had Hallie Stansfield, expelling what was wrong with him like an aspirated chunk of hotdog.

Face buried in the fur, he said: "You make a really good Howie, Dev."

I rubbed his head with one paw, knocking off his dogtop. I couldn't reply as Howie—barking his name was as close as I could come to that—but I was thinking, *A good kid deserves a good dog. Just ask Milo*.

Mike looked up into Howie's blue mesh eyes. "Will you come on the hoister with us?"

I gave him an exaggerated nod and patted his head again. Lane picked up Mike's new dogtop and stuck it back on his head.

Annie approached. Her hands were clasped demurely at her waist, but her eyes were full of merriment. "Can I unzip you, Mr. Howie?"

I wouldn't have minded, but of course I couldn't let her. Every show has its rules, and one of Joyland's—hard and fast—was that Howie the Happy Hound was *always* Howie the Happy Hound. You never took off the fur where the conies could see.

♥

I ducked back into Joyland Under, left the fur in the cart, and rejoined Annie and Mike at the ramp leading up to the Carolina Spin. Annie looked up nervously and said, "Are you sure you want to do this, Mike?"

"Yes! It's the one I want to do most!"

"All right, then. I guess." To me she added: "I'm not terrified of heights, but they don't exactly thrill me."

Lane was holding a car door open. "Climb aboard, folks. I'm

going to send you up where the air is rare." He bent down and scruffed Milo's ears. "You're sittin this one out, fella."

I sat on the inside, nearest the wheel. Annie sat in the middle, and Mike on the outside, where the view was best. Lane dropped the safety bar, went back to the controls, and reset his derby on a fresh slant. "Amazement awaits!" he called, and up we went, rising with the stately calm of a coronation procession.

Slowly, the world opened itself beneath us: first the park, then the bright cobalt of the ocean on our right and all of the North Carolina lowlands on our left. When the Spin reached the top of its great circle, Mike let go of the safety bar, raised his hands over his head, and shouted, "*We're flying!*"

A hand on my leg. Annie's. I looked at her and she mouthed two words: *Thank you*. I don't know how many times Lane sent us around—more spins than the usual ride, I think, but I'm not sure. What I remember best was Mike's face, pale and full of wonder, and Annie's hand on my thigh, where it seemed to burn. She didn't take it away until we slowed to a stop.

Mike turned to me. "Now I know what my kite feels like," he said.

So did I.

♥

When Annie told Mike he'd had enough, the kid didn't object. He was exhausted. As Lane helped him into his wheelchair, Mike held out a hand, palm up. "Slap me five if you're still alive."

Grinning, Lane slapped him five. "Come back anytime, Mike."

"Thanks. It was so great."

Lane and I pushed him up the midway. The booths on both sides were shut up again, but one of the shys was open: Annie

Oakley's Shootin' Gallery. Standing at the chump board, where Pop Allen had stood all summer long, was Fred Dean in his three-piece suit. Behind him, chain-driven rabbits and ducks traveled in opposite directions. Above them were bright yellow ceramic chicks. These were stationary, but very small.

"Like to try your shooting skill before you exit the park?" Fred asked. "There are no losers today. Today *ev*-rybody wins a prize."

Mike looked around at Annie. "Can I, mom?"

"Sure, honey. But not long, okay?"

He tried to get out of the chair, but couldn't. He was too tired. Lane and I propped him up, one on each side. Mike picked up a rifle and took a couple of shots, but he could no longer steady his arms, even though the gun was light. The beebees struck the canvas backdrop and clicked into the gutter at the bottom.

"Guess I suck," he said, putting the rifle down.

"Well, you didn't exactly burn it up," Fred allowed, "but as I said, today everyone wins a prize." With that, he handed over the biggest Howie on the shelf, a top stuffy that even sharp-shooters couldn't earn without spending eight or nine bucks on reloads.

Mike thanked him and sat back down, looking overwhelmed. That damn stuffed dog was almost as big as he was. "You try, Mom."

"No, that's okay," she said, but I thought she wanted to. It was something in her eyes as she measured the distance between the chump board and the targets.

"Please?" He looked first at me, then at Lane. "She's really good. She won the prone shooting tournament at Camp Perry before I was born and came in second twice. Camp Perry's in Ohio."

"I don't—"

Lane was already holding out one of the modified .22s. "Step right up. Let's see your best Annie Oakley, Annie."

She took the rifle and examined it in a way few of the conies ever did. "How many shots?"

"Ten a clip," Fred said.

"If I'm going to do this, can I shoot two clips?"

"As many as you want, ma'am. Today's your day."

"Mom used to also shoot skeet with my grampa," Mike told them.

Annie raised the .22 and squeezed off ten shots with a pause of perhaps two seconds between each. She knocked over two moving ducks and three of the moving bunnies. The teensy ceramic chicks she ignored completely.

"A crack shot!" Fred crowed. "Any prize on the middle shelf, your pick!"

She smiled. "Fifty percent isn't anywhere near crack. My dad would have covered his face for shame. I'll just take the reload, if that's okay."

Fred took a paper cone from under the counter—a wee shoot, in the Talk—and put the small end into a hole on top of the gag rifle. There was a rattle as another ten beebees rolled in.

"Are the sights on these trigged?" she asked Fred.

"No, ma'am. All the games at Joyland are straight. But if I told you Pop Allen—the man who usually runs this shy—spent long hours sighting them in, I'd be a liar."

Having worked on Pop's team, I knew that was disingenuous, to say the least. Sighting in the rifles was the *last* thing Pop would do. The better the rubes shot, the more prizes Pop had to give away…and he had to buy his own prizes. All the shy-bosses did. They were cheap goods, but not *free* goods.

"Shoots left and high," she said, more to herself than to us. Then she raised the rifle, socked it into the hollow of her right shoulder, and triggered off ten rounds. This time there was no discernable pause between shots, and she didn't bother with the ducks and bunnies. She aimed for the ceramic chicks and exploded eight of them.

As she put the gun back on the counter, Lane used his bandanna to wipe a smutch of sweat and grime from the back of his neck. He spoke very softly as he did this chore. "Jesus Horatio Christ. Nobody gets eight peeps."

"I only nicked the last one, and at this range I should have had them all." She wasn't boasting, just stating a fact.

Mike said, almost apologetically: "Told you she was good." He curled a fist over his mouth and coughed into it. "She was thinking about the Olympics, only then she dropped out of college."

"You really *are* Annie Oakley," Lane said, stuffing his bandanna back into a rear pocket. "Any prize, pretty lady. You pick."

"I already have my prize," she said. "This has been a wonderful, wonderful day. I can never thank you guys enough." She turned in my direction. "And *this* guy. Who actually had to talk me into it. Because I'm a fool." She kissed the top of Mike's head. "But now I better get my boy home. Where's Milo?"

We looked around and saw him halfway down Joyland Avenue, sitting in front of Horror House with his tail curled around his paws.

"Milo, come!" Annie called.

His ears pricked up but he didn't come. He didn't even turn in her direction, just stared at the façade of Joyland's only dark ride. I could almost believe he was reading the drippy, cobweb-festooned invitation: COME IN IF YOU DARE.

While Annie was looking at Milo, I stole a glance at Mike. Although he was all but done in from the excitements of the day, his expression was hard to mistake. It was satisfaction. I know it's crazy to think he and his Jack Russell had worked this out in advance, but I did think it.

I still do.

"Roll me down there, Mom," Mike said. "He'll come with me."

"No need for that," Lane said. "If you've got a leash, I'm happy to go get him."

"It's in the pocket on the back of Mike's wheelchair," Annie said.

"Um, probably not," Mike said. "You can check but I'm pretty sure I forgot it."

Annie checked while I thought, *In a pig's ass you forgot.*

"Oh, Mike," Annie said reproachfully. "Your dog, your responsibility. How many times have I told you?"

"Sorry, Mom." To Fred and Lane he said, "Only we hardly ever use it because Milo *always* comes."

"Except when we need him to." Annie cupped her hands around her mouth. "Milo, come *on*! Time to go home!" Then, in a much sweeter voice: "Biscuit, Milo! Come get a biscuit!"

Her coaxing tone would have brought me on the run—probably with my tongue hanging out—but Milo didn't budge.

"Come *on* Dev," Mike said. As if I were also in on the plan but had missed my cue, somehow. I grabbed the wheelchair's handles and rolled Mike down Joyland Avenue toward the funhouse. Annie followed. Fred and Lane stayed where they were, Lane leaning on the chump board among the laid-out popguns on their chains. He had removed his derby and was spinning it on one finger.

When we got to the dog, Annie regarded him crossly. "What's wrong with you, Milo?"

Milo thumped his tail at the sound of Annie's voice, but didn't look at her. Nor did he move. He was on guard and intended to stay that way unless he was hauled away.

"Michael, *please* make your dog heel so we can go home. You need to get some r—"

Two things happened before she could finish. I'm not exactly sure of the sequence. I've gone over it often in the years since then—most often on nights when I can't sleep—and I'm still not sure. I *think* the rumble came first: the sound of a ride-car starting to roll along its track. But it might have been the padlock dropping. It's even possible that both things happened at the same time.

The big American Master fell off the double doors below the Horror House façade and lay on the boards, gleaming in the October sunshine. Fred Dean said later that the shackle must not have been pushed firmly into the locking mechanism, and the vibration of the moving car caused it to open all the way. This made perfect sense, because the shackle was indeed open when I checked it.

Still bullshit, though.

I put that padlock on myself, and remember the click as the shackle clicked into place. I even remember tugging on it to make sure it caught, the way you do with a padlock. And all that begs a question Fred didn't even *try* to answer: with the Horror House breakers switched off, how could that car have gotten rolling in the first place? As for what happened next…

Here's how a trip through Horror House ended. On the far side of the Torture Chamber, just when you thought the ride was over and your guard was down, a screaming skeleton (nicknamed Hagar the Horrible by the greenies) came flying at you, seemingly on a collision course with your car. When it pulled away, you saw a stone wall dead ahead. Painted there in fluorescent green was a rotting zombie and a gravestone with END OF THE LINE printed on it. Of course the stone wall split open just in time, but that final double-punch was extremely effective. When the car emerged into the daylight, making a semicircle before going back in through another set of double doors and stopping, even grown men were often screaming their heads off. Those final shrieks (always accompanied by gales of oh-shit-you-got-me laughter) were Horror House's best advertisement.

There were no screams that day. Of course not, because when the double doors banged open, the car that emerged was empty. It rolled through the semicircle, bumped lightly against the next set of double doors, and stopped.

"O-*kay*," Mike said. It was a whisper so low that I barely heard it, and I'm sure Annie didn't—all her attention had been drawn to the car. The kid was smiling.

"What made it do that?" Annie asked.

"I don't know," I said. "Short-circuit, maybe. Or some kind of power surge." Both of those explanations sounded good, as long as you didn't know about the breakers being off.

I stood on my tiptoes and peered into the stalled car. The

first thing I noticed was that the safety bar was up. If Eddie Parks or one of his greenie minions forgot to lower it, the bar was supposed to snap down automatically once the ride was in motion. It was a state-mandated safety feature. The bar being up on this one made a goofy kind of sense, though, since the only rides in the park that had power that morning were the ones Lane and Fred had turned on for Mike.

I spotted something beneath the semicircular seat, something as real as the roses Fred had given Annie, only not red.

It was a blue Alice band.

♥

We headed back to the van. Milo, once more on best behavior, padded along beside Mike's wheelchair.

"I'll be back as soon as I get them home," I told Fred. "Put in some extra hours."

He shook his head. "You're eighty-six for today. Get to bed early, and be here tomorrow at six. Pack a couple of extra sandwiches, because we'll all be working late. Turns out that storm's moving a little faster than the weather forecasters expected."

Annie looked alarmed. "Should I pack some stuff and take Mike to town, do you think? I'd hate to when he's so tired, but—"

"Check the radio this evening," Fred advised. "If NOAA issues a coastal evacuation order, you'll hear it in plenty of time, but I don't think that'll happen. This is just going to be your basic cap of wind. I'm a little worried about the high rides, that's all—the Thunderball, the Shaker, and the Spin."

"They'll be okay," Lane said. "They stood up to Agnes last year, and that was a bona fide hurricane."

"Does this storm have a name?" Mike asked.

"They're calling it Gilda," Lane said. "But it's no hurricane, just a little old subtropical depression."

Fred said, "Winds are supposed to start picking up around midnight, and the heavy rain'll start an hour or two later. Lane's probably right about the big rides, but it's still going to be a busy day. Have you got a slicker, Dev?"

"Sure."

"You'll want to wear it."

♥

The weather forecast we heard on WKLM as we left the park eased Annie's mind. The winds generated by Gilda weren't expected to top thirty miles an hour, with occasionally higher gusts. There might be some beach erosion and minor flooding inland, but that was about it. The dj called it "great kite-flying weather," which made us all laugh. We had a history now, and that was nice.

Mike was almost asleep by the time we arrived back at the big Victorian on Beach Row. I lifted him into his wheelchair. It wasn't much of a chore; I'd put on muscle in the last four months, and with those horrible braces off, he couldn't have weighed seventy pounds. Milo once more paced the chair as I rolled it up the ramp and into the house.

Mike needed the toilet, but when his mother tried to take over the wheelchair handles, Mike asked if I'd do it, instead. I rolled him into the bathroom, helped him to stand, and eased down his elastic-waisted pants while he held onto the grab bars.

"I hate it when she has to help me. I feel like a baby."

Maybe, but he pissed with a healthy kid's vigor. Then, as he leaned forward to push the flush handle, he staggered and almost took a header into the toilet bowl. I had to catch him.

"Thanks, Dev. I already washed my hair once today." That made me laugh, and Mike grinned. "I wish we *were* going to have a hurricane. That'd be boss."

"You might not think so if it happened." I was remembering Hurricane Doria, two years before. It hit New Hampshire and Maine packing ninety-mile-an-hour winds, knocking down trees all over Portsmouth, Kittery, Sanford, and the Berwicks. One big old pine just missed our house, our basement flooded, and the power had been out for four days.

"I wouldn't want stuff to fall down at the park, I guess. That's just about the best place in the world. That I've ever been, anyway."

"Good. Hold on, kid, let me get your pants back up. Can't have you mooning your mother."

That made him laugh again, only the laughter turned to coughing. Annie took over when we came out, rolling him down the hall to the bedroom. "Don't you sneak out on me, Devin," she called back over her shoulder.

Since I had the afternoon off, I had no intention of sneaking out on her if she wanted me to stay awhile. I strolled around the parlor, looking at things that were probably expensive but not terribly interesting—not to a young man of twenty-one, anyway. A huge picture window, almost wall-to-wall, saved what would otherwise have been a gloomy room, flooding it with light. The window looked out on the back patio, the boardwalk, and the ocean. I could see the first clouds feathering in from the southeast, but the sky overhead was still bright blue. I remember thinking that I'd made it to the big house after all, although I'd probably never have a chance to count all the bathrooms. I remember thinking about the Alice band, and wondering if Lane would see it when he put the wayward car back under cover. What else was I thinking? That I had seen a ghost after all. Just not of a person.

Annie came back. "He wants to see you, but don't stay long."

"Okay."

"Third door on the right."

I went down the hall, knocked lightly, and let myself in. Once you got past the grab bars, the oxygen tanks in the corner, and the leg braces standing at steely attention beside the bed, it could have been any boy's room. There was no baseball glove and no skateboard propped against the wall, but there were posters of Mark Spitz and Miami Dolphins running back Larry Csonka. In the place of honor above the bed, the Beatles were crossing Abbey Road.

There was a faint smell of liniment. Mike looked very small in the bed, all but lost under a green coverlet. Milo was curled up, nose to tail, beside him, and Mike was stroking his fur absently. It was hard to believe this was the same kid who had raised his hands triumphantly over his head at the apogee of the Carolina Spin. He didn't look sad, though. He looked almost radiant.

"Did you see her, Dev? Did you see her when she left?"

I shook my head, smiling. I had been jealous of Tom, but not of Mike. Never of Mike.

"I wish my grampa had been there. He would have seen her, and heard what she said when she left."

"What *did* she say?"

"Thanks. She meant both of us. And she told you to be careful. Are you sure you didn't hear her? Even a little?"

I shook my head again. No, not even a little.

"But you *know*." His face was too pale and tired, the face of a boy who was very sick, but his eyes were alive and healthy. "You *know*, don't you?"

"Yes." Thinking of the Alice band. "Mike, do you know what happened to her?"

"Someone killed her." Very low.

"I don't suppose she told you…"

But there was no need to finish. He was shaking his head.

"You need to sleep," I said.

"Yeah, I'll feel better after a nap. I always do." His eyes closed, then slowly opened again. "The Spin was the best. The hoister. It's like flying."

"Yes," I said. "It is like that."

This time when his eyes closed, they didn't re-open. I walked to the door as quietly as I could. As I put my hand on the knob, he said, "Be careful, Dev. It's not white."

I looked back. He was sleeping. I'm sure he was. Only Milo was watching me. I left, closing the door softly.

♥

Annie was in the kitchen. "I'm making coffee, but maybe you'd rather have a beer? I've got Blue Ribbon."

"Coffee would be fine."

"What do you think of the place?"

I decided to tell the truth. "The furnishings are a little elderly for my taste, but I never went to interior decorating school."

"Nor did I," she said. "Never even finished college."

"Join the club."

"Ah, but you will. You'll get over the girl who dumped you, and you'll go back to school, and you'll finish, and you'll march off into a brilliant future."

"How do you know about—"

"The girl? One, you might as well be wearing a sandwich board. Two, Mike knows. He told me. He's been *my* brilliant future. Once upon a time I was going to major in anthropology. I was going to win a gold medal at the Olympics. I was going to see strange and fabulous places and be the Margaret Mead of my generation. I was going to write books and do my best to earn back my father's love. Do you know who he is?"

"My landlady says he's a preacher."

"Indeed he is. Buddy Ross, the man in the white suit. He also has a great head of white hair. He looks like an older version of the Man from Glad in the TV ads. Mega church; big radio presence; now TV. Offstage, he's an asshole with a few good points." She poured two cups of coffee. "But that's pretty much true of all of us, isn't it? I think so."

"You sound like someone with regrets." It wasn't the politest thing to say, but we were beyond that. I hoped so, at least.

She brought the coffee and sat down opposite me. "Like the song says, I've had a few. But Mike's a great kid, and give my father this—he's taken care of us financially so I could be with Mike full-time. The way I look at it, checkbook love is better than no love at all. I made a decision today. I think it happened when you were wearing that silly costume and doing that silly dance. While I was watching Mike laugh."

"Tell me."

"I decided to give my father what he wants, which is to be

invited back into my son's life before it's too late. He said terrible things about how God caused Mike's MD to punish me for my supposed sins, but I've got to put that behind me. If I wait for an apology, I'll be waiting a long time...because in his heart, Dad still believes that's true."

"I'm sorry."

She shrugged, as if it were of no matter. "I was wrong about not letting Mike go to Joyland, and I've been wrong about holding onto my old grudges and insisting on some sort of fucked-up *quid pro quo*. My son isn't goods in a trading post. Do you think thirty-one's too old to grow up, Dev?"

"Ask me when I get there."

She laughed. "*Touché*. Excuse me a minute."

She was gone for almost five. I sat at the kitchen table, sipping my coffee. When she came back, she was holding her sweater in her right hand. Her stomach was tanned. Her bra was a pale blue, almost matching her faded jeans.

"Mike's fast asleep," she said. "Would you like to go upstairs with me, Devin?"

♥

Her bedroom was large but plain, as if, even after all the months she had spent here, she'd never fully unpacked. She turned to me and linked her arms around my neck. Her eyes were very wide and very calm. A trace of a smile touched the corners of her mouth, making soft dimples. "'I bet you could do better, if you had half a chance.' Remember me saying that?"

"Yes."

"Is that a bet I'd win?"

Her mouth was sweet and damp. I could taste her breath.

She drew back and said, "It can only be this once. You have to understand that."

I didn't want to, but I did. "Just as long as it's not...you know..."

She was really smiling now, almost laughing. I could see teeth as well as dimples. "As long as it's not a thank-you fuck? It's not, believe me. The last time I had a kid like you, I was a kid myself." She took my right hand and put it on the silky cup covering her left breast. I could feel the soft, steady beat of her heart. "I must not have let go of all my daddy issues yet, because I feel delightfully wicked."

We kissed again. Her hands dropped to my belt and unbuckled it. There was the soft rasp as my zipper went down, and then the side of her palm was sliding along the hard ridge beneath my shorts. I gasped.

"Dev?"

"What?"

"Have you ever done this before? Don't you dare lie to me."

"No."

"Was she an idiot? This girl of yours?"

"I guess we both were."

She smiled, slipped a cool hand inside my underwear, and gripped me. That sure hold, coupled with her gently moving thumb, made all of Wendy's efforts at boyfriend satisfaction seem very minor league. "So you're a virgin."

"Guilty as charged."

"Good."

♥

It *wasn't* just the once, and that was lucky for me, because the first time lasted I'm going to say eight seconds. Maybe nine. I got inside, that much I did manage, but then everything spurted everywhere. I may have been more embarrassed once—the time I blew an ass-trumpet while taking communion at Methodist Youth Camp—but I don't think so.

"Oh God," I said, and put a hand over my eyes.

She laughed, but there was nothing mean about it. "In a weird way, I'm flattered. Try to relax. I'm going downstairs for another check on Mike. I'd just as soon he didn't catch me in bed with Howie the Happy Hound."

"Very funny." I think if I'd blushed any harder, my skin would have caught on fire.

"I think you'll be ready again when I come back. It's the nice thing about being twenty-one, Dev. If you were seventeen, you'd probably be ready now."

She came back with a couple of sodas in an ice bucket, but when she slipped out of her robe and stood there naked, Coke was the last thing I wanted. The second time was quite a bit better; I think I might have managed four minutes. Then she began to cry out softly, and I was gone. But what a way to go.

♥

We drowsed, Annie with her head pillowed in the hollow of my shoulder. "Okay?" she asked.

"So okay I can't believe it."

I didn't see her smile, but I felt it. "After all these years, this bedroom finally gets used for something besides sleeping."

"Doesn't your father ever stay here?"

"Not for a long time, and I only started coming back because

Mike loves it here. Sometimes I can face the fact that he's almost certainly going to die, but mostly I can't. I just turn away from it. I make deals with myself. 'If I don't take him to Joyland, he won't die. If I don't make it up with my father so Dad can come and see him, he won't die. If we just stay here, he won't die.' A couple of weeks ago, the first time I had to make him put on his coat to go down to the beach, I cried. He asked me what was wrong, and I told him it was my time of the month. He knows what that is."

I remembered something Mike had said to her in the hospital parking lot: *It doesn't have to be the last good time*. But sooner or later the last good time would come around. It does for all of us.

She sat up, wrapping the sheet around her. "Remember me saying that Mike turned out to be my future? My brilliant career?"

"Yes."

"I can't think of another one. Anything beyond Michael is just ...blank. Who said that in America there are no second acts?"

I took her hand. "Don't worry about act two until act one is over."

She slipped her hand free and caressed my face with it. "You're young, but not entirely stupid."

It was nice of her to say, but I certainly felt stupid. About Wendy, for one thing, but that wasn't the only thing. I found my mind drifting to those damn pictures in Erin's folder. Something about them...

She lay back down. The sheet slipped away from her nipples, and I felt myself begin to stir again. Some things about being twenty-one *were* pretty great. "The shooting gallery was fun. I forgot how good it is, sometimes, just to have that eye-and-hand thing going on. My father put a rifle in my hands for the first time when I was six. Just a little single-shot .22. I loved it."

"Yeah?"

She was smiling. "Yeah. It was our thing, the thing that worked. The *only* thing, as it turned out." She propped herself up on an elbow. "He's been selling that hellfire and brimstone shit since he was a teenager, and it's not just about the money—he got a triple helping of backroads gospel from his own parents, and I have no doubt he believes every word of it. You know what, though? He's still a southern man first and a preacher second. He's got a custom pickup truck that cost fifty thousand dollars, but a pickup truck is still a pickup truck. He still eats biscuits and gravy at Shoney's. His idea of sophisticated humor is Minnie Pearl and Junior Samples. He loves songs about cheatin and honky-tonkin. And he loves his guns. I don't care for his brand of Jesus and I have no interest in owning a pickup truck, but the guns...that he passed on to his only daughter. I go bang-bang and feel better. Shitty legacy, huh?"

I said nothing, only got out of bed and opened the Cokes. I gave one to her.

"He's probably got fifty guns at his full-time place in Savannah, most of them valuable antiques, and there's another half a dozen in the safe here. I've got two rifles of my own at my place in Chicago, although I hadn't shot at a target for two years before today. If Mike dies..." She held the Coke bottle to the middle of her forehead, as if trying to soothe a headache. "*When* Mike dies, the first thing I'm going to do is get rid of them all. They'd be too much temptation."

"Mike wouldn't want—"

"No, of course not, I know that, but it's not *all* about him. If

I could believe—like my holy-hat father—that I was going to find Mike waiting outside the golden gates to show me in after I die, that would be one thing. But I don't. I tried my ass off to believe that when I was a little girl, and I couldn't. God and heaven lasted about four years longer than the Tooth Fairy, but in the end, I couldn't. I think there's just darkness. No thought, no memory, no love. Just darkness. Oblivion. That's why I find what's happening to him so hard to accept."

"Mike knows it's more than oblivion," I said.

"What? Why? Why do you think that?"

Because she was there. He saw her, and he saw her go. Because she said thank you. And I know because I saw the Alice band, and Tom saw her.

"Ask him," I said. "But not today."

She put her Coke aside and studied me. She was wearing the little smile that put dimples at the corners of her mouth. "You've had seconds. I don't suppose you'd be interested in thirds?"

I put my own Coke down beside the bed. "As a matter of fact..."

She held out her arms.

♥

The first time was embarrassing. The second time was good. The third...man, the third time was the charm.

♥

I waited in the parlor while Annie dressed. When she came downstairs, she was back in her jeans and sweater. I thought of the blue bra just beneath the sweater, and damned if I didn't feel that stirring again.

"Are we good?" she said.

"Yes, but I wish we could be even better."

"I wish that, too, but this is as good as it's ever going to get. If you like me as much as I like you, you'll accept that. Can you?"

"Yes."

"Good."

"How much longer will you and Mike be here?"

"If the place doesn't blow away tonight, you mean?"

"It won't."

"A week. Mike's got a round of specialists back in Chicago starting on the seventeenth, and I want to get settled before then." She drew in a deep breath. "And talk to his grandpa about a visit. There'll have to be some ground rules. No Jesus, for one."

"Will I see you again before you leave?"

"Yes." She put her arms around me and kissed me. Then she stepped away. "But not like this. It would confuse things too much. I know you get that."

I nodded. I got it.

"You better go now, Dev. And thank you. It was lovely. We saved the best ride for last, didn't we?"

That was true. Not a dark ride but a bright one. "I wish I could do more. For you. For Mike."

"So do I," she said, "but that's not the world we live in. Come by tomorrow for supper, if the storm's not too bad. Mike would love to see you."

She looked beautiful, standing there barefooted in her faded jeans. I wanted to take her in my arms, and lift her, and carry her into some untroubled future.

Instead, I left her where she was. *That's not the world we live in*, she'd said, and how right she was.

How right she was.

♥

About a hundred yards down Beach Row, on the inland side of the two-lane, there was a little cluster of shops too tony to be called a strip mall: a gourmet grocery, a salon called Hair's Looking at You, a drugstore, a branch of the Southern Trust, and a restaurant called Mi Casa, where the Beach Row elite no doubt met to eat. I didn't give those shops so much as a glance when I drove back to Heaven's Bay and Mrs. Shoplaw's. If ever I needed proof that I didn't have the gift that Mike Ross and Rozzie Gold shared, that was it.

♥

Go to bed early, Fred Dean had told me, and I did. I lay on my back with my hands behind my head, listening to the waves as I had all summer long, remembering the touch of her hands, the firmness of her breasts, the taste of her mouth. Mostly it was her eyes I thought about, and the fan of her hair on the pillow. I didn't love her the way I loved Wendy—that sort of love, so strong and stupid, only comes once—but I loved her. I did then and still do now. For her kindness, mostly, and her patience. Some young man somewhere may have had a better initiation into the mysteries of sex, but no young man ever had a sweeter one.

Eventually, I slept.

♥

It was a banging shutter somewhere below that woke me. I picked my watch up from the night table and saw it was quarter of one. I didn't think there was going to be any more sleep for me until that banging stopped, so I got dressed, started out the door, then returned to the closet for my slicker. When I got downstairs, I paused. From the big bedroom down the hall from the parlor, I could hear Mrs. S. sawing wood in long, noisy strokes. No banging shutter was going to break her rest.

It turned out I didn't need the slicker, at least not yet, because the rain hadn't started. The wind was strong, though; it had to be blowing twenty-five already. The low, steady thud of the surf had become a muted roar. I wondered if the weather boffins had underestimated Gilda, thought of Annie and Mike in the house down the beach, and felt a tickle of unease.

I found the loose shutter and re-fastened it with the hook-and-eye. I let myself back in, went upstairs, undressed, and lay down again. This time sleep wouldn't come. The shutter was quiet, but there was nothing I could do about the wind moaning around the eaves (and rising to a low scream each time it gusted). Nor could I turn off my brain, now that it was running again.

It's not white, I thought. That meant nothing to me, but it *wanted* to mean something. It wanted to connect with something I'd seen at the park during our visit.

There's a shadow over you, young man. That had been Rozzie Gold, on the day that I'd met her. I wondered how long she had worked at Joyland, and where she had worked before. Was she carny-from-carny? And what did it matter?

One of these children has the sight. I don't know which.

I knew. Mike had seen Linda Gray. And set her free. He had, as they say, shown her the door. The one she hadn't been able to find herself. Why else would she have thanked him?

I closed my eyes and saw Fred at the Shootin' Gallery, resplendent in his suit and magic top hat. I saw Lane holding out one of the.22s chained to the chump board.

Annie: *How many shots?*

Fred: *Ten a clip. As many as you want. Today's your day.*

My eyes flew open as several things came crashing together in my mind. I sat up, listening to the wind and the agitated surf. Then I turned on the overhead light and got Erin's folder out of my desk drawer. I laid the photographs on the floor again, my heart pounding. The pix were good but the light wasn't. I dressed for the second time, shoved everything back into the folder, and made another trip downstairs.

A lamp hung above the Scrabble table in the middle of the parlor, and I knew from the many evenings I'd gotten my ass kicked that the light it cast was plenty bright. There were sliding doors between the parlor and the hall leading to Mrs. S.'s quarters. I pulled them shut so the light wouldn't disturb her. Then I turned on the lamp, moved the Scrabble box to the top of the TV, and laid my photos out. I was too agitated to sit down. I bent over the table instead, arranging and re-arranging the photographs. I was about to do that for the third time when my hand froze. I saw it. I saw *him*. Not proof that would stand up in court, no, but enough for me. My knees came unhinged, and I sat down after all.

The phone I'd used so many times to call my father—always noting down the time and duration on the guest-call honor sheet when I was done—suddenly rang. Only in that windy early morning silence, it sounded more like a scream. I lunged at it and picked up the receiver before it could ring again.

"H-H-Hel—" It was all I could manage. My heart was pounding too hard for more.

"It's you," the voice on the other end said. He sounded both amused and pleasantly surprised. "I was expecting your landlady. I had a story about a family emergency all ready."

I tried to speak. Couldn't.

"Devin?" Teasing. *Cheerful*. "Are you there?"

"I...just a second."

I held the phone to my chest, wondering (it's crazy how your mind can work when it's put under sudden stress) if he could hear my heart at his end of the line. On mine, I listened for Mrs. Shoplaw. I heard her, too: the muted sound of her continuing snores. It was a good thing I'd closed the parlor doors, and a better thing that there was no extension in her bedroom. I put the phone back to my ear and said, "What do you want? Why are you calling?"

"I think you know, Devin...and even if you didn't, it's too late now, isn't it?"

"Are you psychic, too?" It was stupid, but right then my brain and my mouth seemed to be running on separate tracks.

"That's Rozzie," he said. "Our Madame Fortuna." He actually laughed. He sounded relaxed, but I doubt if he was. Killers don't make telephone calls in the middle of the night if they're relaxed. Especially if they can't be sure of who's going to answer the phone.

But he had a story, I thought. *This guy's a Boy Scout, he's crazy but always prepared. The tattoo, for instance. That's what takes your eye when you look at those photos. Not the face. Not the baseball cap.*

"I knew what you were up to," he said. "I knew even before the girl brought you that folder. The one with the pictures in it. Then today...with the pretty mommy and the crippled kid... have you told them, Devin? Did they help you work it out?"

"They don't know anything."

The wind gusted. I could hear it at his end, too...as if he were outside. "I wonder if I can believe you."

"You can. You absolutely can." Looking down at the pictures. Tattoo Man with his hand on Linda Gray's ass. Tattoo Man helping her aim her rifle at the Shootin' Gallery.

Lane: *Let's see your best Annie Oakley, Annie.*

Fred: *A crack shot!*

Tattoo Man in his fishtop cap and dark glasses and sandy blond goatee. You could see the bird tattoo on his hand because the rawhide gloves had stayed in his back pocket until he and Linda Gray were in Horror House. Until he had her in the dark.

"I wonder," he said again. "You were in that big old house for a long time this afternoon, Devin. Were you talking about the pictures the Cook girl brought, or were you just fucking her? Maybe it was both. Mommy's a tasty piece, all right."

"They don't know anything," I repeated. I was speaking low and fixing my gaze on the closed parlor doors. I kept expecting them to open and to see Mrs. S. standing there in her nightgown, her face ghostly with cream. "Neither do I. Not that I could prove."

"Probably not, but it would only be a matter of time. You can't unring the bell. Do you know that old saying?"

"Sure, sure." I didn't, but at that moment I would have agreed with him if he'd declared that Bobby Rydell (a yearly performer at Joyland) was president.

"Here's what you're going to do. You're going to come to Joyland, and we'll talk this out, face to face. Man to man."

"Why would I do that? That would be pretty crazy, if you're who I—"

"Oh, you know I am." He sounded impatient. "And *I* know that if you went to the police, they'd find out I came onboard at Joyland only a month or so after Linda Gray was killed. Then they'd put me with the Wellman show and Southern Star Amusements, and there goes the ballgame."

"So why don't I call them right now?"

"Do you know where I am?" Anger was creeping into his voice. No—venom. "Do you know where I am right now, you nosy little sonofabitch?"

"Joyland, probably. In admin."

"Not at all. I'm at the shopping center on Beach Row. The one where the rich bitches go to buy their macrobiotics. Rich bitches like your girlfriend."

A cold finger began to trace its course—its very slow course—down the length of my spine from the nape of my neck to the crack of my ass. I said nothing.

"There's a pay phone outside the drugstore. Not a booth, but that's okay because it isn't raining yet. Just windy. That's where I am. I can see your girlfriend's house from where I'm standing. There's a light on in the kitchen—probably the one she leaves on all night—but the rest of the house is dark. I could hang up this phone and be there in sixty seconds."

"There's a burglar alarm!" I didn't know if there was or not.

He laughed. "At this point, do you think I give a shit? It won't stop me from cutting her throat. But first I'll make her watch me do it to the little cripple."

You won't rape her, though, I thought. *You wouldn't even if there was time. I don't think you can.*

I came close to saying it, but didn't. As scared as I was, I knew that goading him right now would be a very bad idea.

"You were so nice to them today," I said stupidly. "Flowers… prizes…the rides…"

"Yeah, all the rube shit. Tell me about the car that came popping out of the funhouse shy. What was *that* about?"

"I don't know."

"I think you do. Maybe we'll discuss it. At Joyland. I know

your Ford, Jonesy. It's got the flickery left headlight and the cute little pinwheel on the antenna. If you don't want me in that house cutting throats, you're going to get in it right now, and you're going to drive down Beach Row to Joyland."

"I—"

"Shut up when I'm talking to you. When you pass the shopping center, you'll see me standing by one of the park trucks. I'll give you four minutes to get here from the time I hang up the phone. If I don't see you, I'll kill the woman and the kid. Understand?"

"I..."

"*Do you understand?*"

"Yes!"

"I'll follow you to the park. Don't worry about the gate; it's already open."

"So you'll either kill me or them. I get to choose. Is that it?"

"Kill you?" He sounded honestly surprised. "I'm not going to kill you, Devin. That would only make my position worse. No, I'm going to do a fade. It won't be the first time, and it probably won't be the last. What I want is to talk. I want to know how you got onto me."

"I could tell you that over the phone."

He laughed. "And spoil your chance to overpower me and be Howie the Hero again? First the little girl, then Eddie Parks, and the pretty mommy and her crippled-up brat for the exciting climax. How could you pass that up?" He stopped laughing. "Four minutes."

"I—"

He hung up. I stared down at the glossy photos. I opened the drawer in the Scrabble table, took out one of the pads, and fumbled for the mechanical pencil Tina Ackerley always insisted on using to keep score. I wrote: *Mrs. S. If you're reading this, something has happened to me. I know who killed Linda Gray. Others, too.*

I wrote his name in capital letters.

Then I ran for the door.

♥

My Ford's starter spun and sputtered and did not catch. Then it began to slow. All summer I'd been telling myself I had to get a new battery, and all summer I'd found other things to spend my money on.

My father's voice: *You're flooding it, Devin.*

I took my foot off the gas and sat there in the dark. Time seemed to be racing, racing. Part of me wanted to run back inside and call the police. I couldn't call Annie because I didn't have her fucking phone number, and given her famous father, it would be unlisted. Did *he* know that? Probably not, but he had the luck of the devil. As brazen as he was, the murdering son of a bitch should have been caught three or four times already, but hadn't been. Because he had the luck of the devil.

She'll hear him breaking in and she'll shoot him.

Only the guns were in the safe, she'd said so. Even if she got one, she'd probably find the bastard holding his straight-razor to Mike's throat when she confronted him.

I turned the key again, and with my foot off the accelerator and the carb full of gas, my Ford started up at once. I backed down the driveway and turned toward Joyland. The circular red neon of the Spin and the blue neon swoops of the Thunderball stood out against low, fast-running clouds. Those two rides were always lit on stormy nights, partly as a beacon for ships at sea, partly to warn away any low-flying small aircraft bound for the Parish County Airport.

Beach Row was deserted. Sheets of sand blew across it with every gust of wind, some of those gusts strong enough to shake my car. Dunelets were already starting to build up on the macadam. In my headlights, they looked like skeleton fingers.

When I passed the shopping center, I saw a single figure standing in the middle of the parking lot next to one of the Joyland maintenance trucks. He raised a hand to me as I went past and gave a single solemn wave.

The big Victorian on the beach side came next. There *was* a light on in the kitchen. I thought it was the fluorescent over the sink. I remembered Annie coming into the room with her sweater in her hand. Her tanned stomach. The bra almost the same color as her jeans. *Would you like to go upstairs with me, Devin?*

Lights bloomed in my rearview mirror and pulled up close. He was using his brights and I couldn't see the vehicle behind them, but I didn't have to. I knew it was the maintenance truck, just as I knew he had been lying when he said he wasn't going to kill me. The note I'd left for Mrs. Shoplaw would still be there in the morning. She would read it, and the name I had written there. The question was how long it would take her to believe it. He was such a charmer, him with his rhyming patter, winning smile, and cocked derby lid. Why, all the women loved Lane Hardy.

♥

The gates were open, as promised. I drove through them and tried to park in front of the now-shuttered Shootin' Gallery. He gave his horn a brief blip and flashed his lights: *Drive on*. When I got to the Spin, he flashed his lights again. I turned off my

Ford, very aware that I might never start it again. The hoister's red neon cast a blood-colored light over the dashboard, the seats, my own skin.

The truck's headlights went out. I heard the door open and shut. And I heard the wind blowing through the Spin's struts—tonight that sound was a harpy's screech. There was a steady, almost syncopated rattling sound, as well. The wheel was shaking on its tree-thick axle.

The Gray girl's killer—and DeeDee Mowbray's, and Claudine Sharp's, and Darlene Stamnacher's—walked to my car and tapped on the window with the barrel of a pistol. With his other hand he made a beckoning gesture. I opened the door and got out.

"You said you weren't going to kill me." It sounded as weak as my legs felt.

Lane smiled his charming smile. "Well…we'll see which way the flow's gonna go. Won't we?"

Tonight his derby was cocked to the left and pulled down tight so it wouldn't fly off. His hair, let loose from its workday ponytail, blew around his neck. The wind gusted and the Spin gave an unhappy screech. The red glow of the neon flickered across his face as it shook.

"Don't worry about the hoister," he said. "If it was solid it might blow over, but the wind shoots right through the struts. You've got other things to worry about. Tell me about the funhouse car. That's what I really want to know. How'd you do that? Was it some kind of remote gadget? I'm very interested in those things. They're the wave of the future, that's what I think."

"There was no gadget."

He didn't seem to hear me. "Also what was the point? Was it

supposed to flush me out? If it was, you didn't need to bother. I was already flushed."

"*She* did it," I said. I didn't know if that was strictly true, but I had no intention of bringing Mike into this conversation. "Linda Gray. Didn't you see her?"

The smile died. "Is that the best you can manage? The old ghost-in-the-funhouse story? You'll have to do a little better than that."

So he hadn't seen her any more than I had. But I think he knew there was *something*. I'll never know for sure, but I think that was why he offered to go after Milo. He hadn't wanted us anywhere near Horror House.

"Oh, she was there. I saw her headband. Remember me looking in? It was under the seat."

He lashed out so suddenly I didn't even have a chance to get my hand up. The barrel of the gun slammed across my forehead, opening a gash. I saw stars. Then blood poured into my eyes and I saw only that. I staggered back against the rail beside the ramp leading to the Spin and gripped it to keep from falling down. I swiped at my face with the sleeve of my slicker.

"I don't know why you'd bother trying to spook me with a campfire story at this late date," he said, "and I don't appreciate it. You know about the headband because there was a picture of it in the folder your nosy college-cunt girlfriend brought you." He smiled. There was nothing charming about this one; it was all teeth. "Don't kid a kidder, kiddo."

"But...you didn't *see* the folder." The answer to that one was a simple deduction even with my head ringing. "Fred saw it. And told you. Didn't he?"

"Yep. On Monday. We were having lunch together in his

office. He said that you and the college cunt were playing Hardy Boys, although he didn't put it quite that way. He thought it was sort of cute. I didn't, because I'd seen you stripping off Eddie Parks's gloves after he had his heart attack. That's when *I* knew you were playing Hardy Boys. That folder...Fred said the cunt had pages of notes. I knew it was only a matter of time before she put me with Wellman's and Southern Star."

I had an alarming picture of Lane Hardy riding the train to Annandale with a straight razor in his pocket. "Erin doesn't know anything."

"Oh, relax. Do you think I'm going after her? Apply some strain and use your brain. And take a little stroll while you do it. Up the ramp, champ. You and I are going for a ride. Up there where the air is rare."

I started to ask him if he was crazy, but that would have been sort of a stupid question at this late date, wouldn't it?

"What have you got to grin about, Jonesy?"

"Nothing," I said. "You don't really want to go up with the wind blowing like this, do you?" But the Spin's engine was running. I hadn't been aware of it over the wind, the surf, and the eerie scream of the ride itself, but now that I was listening, I heard it: a steady rumble. Almost a purr. Something fairly obvious came to me: he was probably planning to turn the gun on himself after he finished with me. Maybe you think that should have occurred to me sooner, because crazy people have a way of doing that—you read about it in the paper all the time. Maybe you'd be right. But I was under a lot of stress.

"Old Carolina's safe as houses," he said. "I'd go up in her if the wind was blowing sixty instead of just thirty. It blew at least that hard when Carla skimmed past the coast two years ago, and she was just fine."

"How are you going to put it in gear if we're both in the car?"

"Get in and see. Or..." He lifted the gun. "Or I can shoot you right here. I'm good with it either way."

I walked up the ramp, opened the door of the car currently sitting at the loading station, and started to climb in.

"No, no, no," he said. "You want to be on the outside. Better view. Stand aside, Clyde. And put your hands in your pockets."

Lane sidled past me, the gun leveled. More blood was trickling into my eyes and down my cheeks, but I didn't dare take a hand from my slicker pocket to wipe it off. I could see how white his finger was on the trigger of the pistol. He sat down on the inside of the car.

"*Now* you."

I got in. I didn't see any choice.

"And close the door, that's what it's there for."

"You sound like Dr. Seuss," I said.

He grinned. "Flattery will get you nowhere. Close the door or I'll put a bullet in your knee. You think anyone will hear it over this wind? I don't."

I closed the door. When I looked at him again, he had the pistol in one hand and a square metal gadget in the other. It had a stubby antenna. "Told you, I love these gadgets. This one's your basic garage door-opener with a couple of small modifications. Sends a radio signal. Showed it to Mr. Easterbrook this spring, told him it was the perfect thing for wheel maintenance when there wasn't a greenie or a gazoonie around to run the groundside controls. He said I couldn't use it because it hasn't been safety-approved by the state commission. Cautious old sonofabitch. I was going to patent it. Too late now, I guess. Take it."

I took it. It *was* a garage door opener. A Genie. My dad had one almost exactly like it.

"See the button with the up arrow?"

"Yes."

"Push it."

I put my thumb on the button, but didn't push it. The wind was strong down here; how much stronger up there, where the air was rare? *We're flying!* Mike had shouted.

"Push it or take one in the knee, Jonesy."

I pushed the button. The Spin's motor geared down at once, and our car began to rise.

"Now throw it over the side."

"*What?*"

"Throw it over the side or you get one in the knee and you'll never two-step again. I'll give you a three-count. One…t—"

I threw his controller over the side. The wheel rose and rose into the windy night. To my right I could see the waves pounding in, their crests marked by foam so white it looked phosphorescent. On the left, the land was dark and sleeping. Not a single set of headlights moved on Beach Row. The wind gusted. My blood-sticky hair flew back from my forehead in clumps. The car rocked. Lane threw himself forward, then back, making the car rock more…but the gun, now pointed at my side, never wavered. Red neon skimmed lines along the barrel.

He shouted, "*Not so much like a grandma ride tonight, is it, Jonesy*?"

It sure wasn't. Tonight the staid old Carolina Spin was terrifying. As we reached the top, a savage gust shook the wheel so hard I heard our car rattling on the steel supports that held it. Lane's derby flew off into the night.

"Shit! Well, there's always another one."

Lane, how are we going to get off? The question rose behind my lips, but I didn't ask. I was too afraid he'd tell me we weren't, that if the storm didn't blow the Spin over and if the power didn't go out, we'd still be going around and around when Fred got here in the morning. Two dead men on Joyland's chump-hoister. Which made my next move rather obvious.

Lane was smiling. "You want to try for the gun, don't you? I can see it in your eyes. Well, it's like Dirty Harry said in that movie—you have to ask yourself if you feel lucky."

We were going down now, the car still rocking but not quite so much. I decided I didn't feel lucky at all.

"How many have you killed, Lane?"

"None of your fucking business. And since I have the gun, I think I should get to ask the questions. How long have you known? Quite a while, right? At least since the college cunt showed you the pictures. You just held off so the cripple could get his day at the park. Your mistake, Jonesy. A rube's mistake."

"I only figured it out tonight," I said.

"Liar, liar, pants on fire."

We swept past the ramp and started up again. I thought, *He's probably going to shoot me when the car's at the top. Then he'll either shoot himself or push me out, slide over, and jump onto the ramp when the car comes back down. Take his chances on not breaking a leg or a collarbone.* I was betting on the murder-suicide scenario, but not until his curiosity was satisfied.

I said, "Call me stupid if you want, but don't call me a liar. I kept looking at the pictures, and I kept seeing something in them, something familiar, but until tonight I couldn't quite figure out what it was. It was the hat. You were wearing a fishtop baseball cap in the photos, not a derby, but it was tilted one way when you and the Gray girl were at the Whirly Cups, and the other when you were at the Shootin' Gallery. I looked at the rest, the ones where the two of you are only in the background, and saw the same thing. Back and forth, back and forth. You do it all the time. You don't even think about it."

"That's *all*? A fucking tilted cap?"

"No."

We were reaching the top for the second time, but I thought I was good for at least one more turn. He wanted to hear this. Then the rain started, a hard squall that turned on like a shower spigot. *At least it'll wash the blood off my face*, I thought. When I looked at him, I saw that wasn't all it was washing off.

"One day I saw you with your hat off and I thought your hair was showing the first strands of white." I was almost yelling to be heard over the wind and the rush of the rain. It was coming sideways, hitting us in the face. "Yesterday I saw you wiping the back of your neck. I thought it was dirt. Then tonight, after I got the thing about the cap, I started thinking about the fake bird tattoo. Erin saw how the sweat made it run. I guess the cops missed that."

I could see my car and the maintenance truck, growing larger as the Spin neared the bottom of its circle for the second time. Beyond them, something large—a wind-loosened swatch of canvas, maybe—was blowing up Joyland Avenue.

"It wasn't dirt you were wiping off, it was dye. It was running, just like the tattoo ran. Like it's running now. It's all over your neck. It wasn't strands of white hair I saw, it was strands of *blond*."

He wiped his neck and looked at the black smear on his palm. I almost went for him then, but he raised the gun and all at once I was looking into a black eye. It was small but terrible.

"I *used* to be blond," he said, "but under the black I'm mostly gray now. I've lived a stressful life, Jonesy." He smiled ruefully, as though this were some sad joke we were both in on.

We were going up again, and I had just a moment to think that the thing I'd seen blowing up the midway—what I'd taken for a big square of loose canvas—could have been a car with its headlights out. It was crazy to hope, but I hoped, anyway.

The rain slashed at us. My slicker rippled. Lane's hair flew like a ragged flag. I hoped I could keep him from pulling the trigger for at least one more spin. Maybe two? Possible but not probable.

"Once I let myself think of you as Linda Gray's killer—and it wasn't easy, Lane, not after the way you took me in and showed me the ropes—I could see past the hat and sunglasses and face-hair. I could see *you*. You weren't working here—"

"I was running a forklift in a warehouse in Florence." He wrinkled his nose. "Rube work. I hated it."

"You were working in Florence, you met Linda Gray in Florence, but you knew all about Joyland over here in NC, didn't you? I don't know if you're carny-from-carny, but you've never been able to stay away from the shows. And when you suggested a little road trip, she went along with it."

"I was her secret boyfriend. I told her I had to be. Because I was older." He smiled. "She bought it. They all do. You'd be surprised how much the young ones will buy."

You sick fuck, I thought. *You sick, sick fuck.*

"You brought her to Heaven's Bay, you stayed at a motel, and then you killed her here at Joyland even though you must have known about the Hollywood Girls running around with their cameras. Bold as brass. That was part of the kick, wasn't it? Sure it was. You did it on a ride full of conies—"

"Rubes," he said. The hardest gust yet shook the Spin, but he seemed not to feel it. Of course, he was on the inside of the wheel where things were a little calmer. "Call em what they are. They're just rubes, all of them. They see nothing. It's like their eyes are connected to their assholes instead of their brains. Everything goes right through."

"You get off on the risk, don't you? That's why you came back and hired on."

"Not even a month later." His smile widened. "All this time I've been right under their noses. And you know what? I've been...you know, good...ever since that night in the funhouse. All the bad stuff was behind me. I could have gone on being good. I like it here. I was building a life. I had my gadget, and I was going to patent it."

"Oh, I think sooner or later you would have done it again." We were back at the top. The wind and rain pelted us. I was shivering. My clothes were soaked; Lane's cheeks were dark with hair-dye. It ran down his skin in tendrils. *His mind is like that*, I thought. *On the inside, where he never smiles.*

"No. I was cured. I have to do you, Jonesy, but only because you stuck your nose in where it doesn't belong. It's too bad, because I liked you. I really did."

I thought he was telling the truth, which made what was happening even more horrible.

We were going back down. The world below was windy and rain-soaked. There had been no car with its headlights out, only a blowing piece of canvas that for a moment looked like that to my yearning mind. The cavalry wasn't coming. Thinking it was would only get me killed. I had to do this myself, and the only chance I had was to make him mad. *Really* mad.

"You get off on risk, but you don't get off on rape, do you? If you did, you would have taken them to some isolated place. I think what your secret girlfriends have between their legs scares you limp. What do you do later? Lie in bed and jack off thinking about how brave you are, killing defenseless girls?"

"Shut up."

"You can fascinate them, but you can't fuck them." The wind shouted; the car rocked. I was going to die and at that moment I didn't give shit one. I didn't know how angry I was making him, but I was angry enough for both of us. "What happened to make you this way? Did your mother put a clothespin on your peepee when you went weewee in the corner? Did Uncle Stan make you give him a blowjob? Or was it—"

"*Shut up!*" He rose into a crouch, gripping the safety bar in one hand and pointing the gun at me with the other. A stroke of lightning lit him up: staring eyes, lank hair, working mouth. And the gun. "*Shut your dirty mou—*"

"*DEVIN, DUCK!*"

I didn't think about it, I just did it. There was a whipcrack report, an almost liquid sound in the blowing night. The bullet must have gone right past me, but I didn't hear it or feel it, the way characters do in books. The car we were in swept past the loading point and I saw Annie Ross standing on the ramp with a rifle in her hands. The van was behind her. Her hair was blowing around her bone-white face.

We started up again. I looked at Lane. He was frozen in his crouch, his mouth ajar. Black dye ran down his cheeks. His eyes were rolled up so only the bottom half of the irises showed. Most of his nose was gone. One nostril hung down by his upper lip, but the rest of it was just a red ruin surrounding a black hole the size of a dime.

He sat down on the seat, hard. Several of his front teeth rattled out of his mouth when he did. I plucked the gun from his hand and tossed it over the side. What I was feeling right then was…nothing. Except in some very deep part of me, where I had begun to realize this might not be my night to die, after all.

"Oh," he said. Then he said "Ah." Then he slumped forward, chin on chest. He looked like a man considering his options, and very carefully.

There was more lightning as the car reached the top. It illuminated my seatmate in a stutter of blue fire. The wind blew and the Spin moaned in protest. We were coming down again.

From below, almost lost in the storm: "*Dev, how do I stop it?*"

I first thought of telling her to look for the remote control gadget, but in the storm she could hunt for half an hour and still not find it. Even if she did, it might be broken or lying shorted out in a puddle. Besides, there was a better way.

"*Go to the motor!*" I shouted. "*Look for the red button! RED BUTTON, ANNIE! It's the emergency stop!*"

I swept past her, registering the same jeans and sweater she'd worn earlier, both now soaked and plastered to her. No jacket, no hat. She had come in a hurry, and I knew who had sent her. How much simpler it would have been if Mike had focused on Lane at the start. But Rozzie never had, even though she'd known him for years, and I was to find out later that Mike never focused on Lane Hardy at all.

I was going back up again. Beside me, Lane's soaking hair

was dripping black rain into his lap. "*Wait until I come back down!*"

"*What*?"

I didn't bother trying again; the wind would have drowned it out. I could only hope she wouldn't hammer on the red button while I was at the top of the ride. As the car rose into the worst of the storm the lightning flashed again, and this time there was an accompanying crack of thunder. As if it had roused him—perhaps it had—Lane lifted his head and looked at me. *Tried* to look at me; his eyes had come back level in their sockets, but were now pointing in opposite directions. That terrible image has never left my mind, and still comes to me at the oddest times: going through turnpike tollbooths, drinking a cup of coffee in the morning with the CNN anchors baying bad news, getting up to piss at three AM, which some poet or other has rightly dubbed the Hour of the Wolf.

He opened his mouth and blood poured out. He made a grinding insectile sound, like a cicada burrowing into a tree. A spasm shook him. His feet tap-danced briefly on the steel floor of the car. They stilled, and his head dropped forward again.

Be dead, I thought. *Please be dead this time*.

As the Spin started down again, a bolt of lightning struck the Thunderball; I saw the tracks light up briefly. I thought, *That could have been me*. The hardest gust of wind yet struck the car. I held on for dear life. Lane flopped like a big doll.

I looked down at Annie—her white face staring up, her eyes squinted against the rain. She was inside the rail, standing next to the motor. So far, so good. I put my hands around my mouth. "*The red button!*"

"*I see it!*"

"Wait until I tell you!"

The ground was coming up. I grabbed the bar. When the late (at least I hoped he was) Lane Hardy was at the control stick, the Spin always came to an easy halt, the cars up top swaying gently. I had no idea what an emergency stop would be like, but I was going to find out.

"Now, Annie! Push it now!"

It was a good thing I was holding on. My car stopped dead about ten feet from the unloading point and still five feet above the ground. The car tilted. Lane was thrown forward, his head and torso flopping over the bar. Without thinking, I grabbed his shirt and pulled him back. One of his hands flopped into my lap and I flung it away with a grunt of disgust.

The bar wouldn't unlock, so I had to wriggle out from beneath it.

"Be careful, Dev!" Annie was standing beside the car, holding up her hands, as if to catch me. She had propped the rifle she'd used to end Hardy's life against the motor housing.

"Step back," I said, and threw one leg over the side of the car. More lightning flashed. The wind howled and the Spin howled back. I got hold of a strut and swung out. My hands slipped on the wet metal and I dropped. I went to my knees. A moment later she was pulling me to my feet.

"Are you all right?"

"Yes."

I wasn't, though. The world was swimming, and I was on the edge of a faint. I lowered my head, gripped my legs just above the knees, and began taking deep breaths. For a moment it could have gone either way, but then things began to solidify. I stood up again, careful not to move too fast.

It was hard to tell with the rain bucketing down, but I was

pretty sure she was crying. "I had to do it. He was going to kill you. Wasn't he? Please, Dev, say he was going to kill you. Mike *said* he was, and—"

"You can quit worrying about that, believe me. And I wouldn't have been his first. He's killed four women." I thought of Erin's speculation about the years when there had been no bodies—none discovered, at least. "Maybe more. *Probably* more. We have to call the police. There's a phone in—"

I started to point toward Mysterio's Mirror Mansion, but she grabbed my arm. "No. You can't. Not yet."

"Annie—"

She thrust her face close to mine, almost kissing distance, but kissing was the last thing on her mind. "How did I get here? Am I supposed to tell the police that a ghost showed up in my son's room in the middle of the night and told him you'd die on the Ferris wheel if I didn't come? Mike can't be a part of this, and if you tell me I'm being an overprotective mom, I'll…I'll kill you myself."

"No," I said. "I won't tell you that."

"So how did I get here?"

At first I didn't know. You have to remember that I was still scared myself. Only scared doesn't cover it. Scared isn't even in the ballpark. I was in shock. Instead of Mysterio's, I led her to her van and helped her sit behind the wheel. Then I went around and got in on the passenger side. By then I had an idea. It had the virtue of simplicity, and I thought it would fly. I shut the door and took my wallet out of my hip pocket. I almost dropped it on the floor when I opened it; I was shaking like crazy. Inside there were plenty of things to write on, but I had nothing to write with.

"Please tell me you have a pen or a pencil, Annie."

"Maybe in the glove compartment. *You'll* have to call the police, Dev. I have to get back to Mike. If they arrest me for leaving the scene or something…or for murder…"

"Nobody's going to arrest you, Annie. You saved my life." I was pawing through the glove compartment as I talked. There was an owner's manual, piles of gasoline credit card receipts, Rolaids, a bag of M&Ms, even a Jehovah's Witnesses pamphlet asking if I knew where I was going to spend the afterlife, but no pen or pencil.

"You can't wait…in a situation like that…that's what I was always told…" Her words came in chunks because her teeth were chattering. "Just aim…and squeeze before you can…you know…second-guess yourself…it was supposed to go between his eyes, but…the wind…I guess the wind…"

She shot out a hand and gripped my shoulder hard enough to hurt. Her eyes were huge.

"Did I hit you, too, Dev? There's a gash in your forehead and blood on your shirt!"

"You didn't hit me. He pistol-whipped me a little, that's all. Annie, there's nothing in here to write w—"

But there was: a ballpoint at the very back of the glove compartment. Printed on the barrel, faded but still legible, was LET'S GO KROGERING! I won't say that pen saved Annie and Mike Ross serious police trouble, but I know it saved them a lot of questions about what had brought Annie to Joyland on such a dark and stormy night.

I passed her the pen and a business card from my wallet, blank side up. Earlier, sitting in my car and terribly afraid that my failure to buy a new battery was going to get Annie and Mike killed, I'd thought I could go back into the house and call her...only I didn't have her number. Now I told her to write it down. "And below the number, write *Call if plans change*."

While she did, I started the van's engine and turned the heater on full blast. She returned the card. I tucked it into my wallet, shoved the wallet back into my pocket, and tossed the pen into the glove compartment. I took her in my arms and kissed her cold cheek. Her trembling didn't stop, but it eased.

"You saved my life," I said. "Now let's make sure nothing happens to you *or* Mike because you did. Listen very carefully."

She listened.

♥

Six days later, Indian summer came back to Heaven's Bay for a brief final fling. It was perfect weather for a noon meal at the end of the Ross boardwalk, only we couldn't go there. Newsmen and photographers had it staked out. They could do that because, unlike the two acres surrounding the big green Victorian, the beach was public property. The story of how Annie had taken out Lane Hardy (known then and forever after as The Carny Killer) with one shot had gone nationwide.

Not that the stories were bad. Quite the opposite. The Wilmington paper had led with DAUGHTER OF EVANGELIST BUDDY ROSS BAGS CARNY KILLER. The *New York Post* was more succinct: HERO MOM! It helped that there were file photos from Annie's salad days where she looked not just gorgeous but smoking hot. *Inside View*, the most popular of the supermarket tabloids back then, put out an extra edition. They had unearthed a photo of Annie at seventeen, taken after a shooting competition at Camp Perry. Clad in tight jeans, an NRA tee-shirt, and cowboy boots, she was standing with an antique Purdey shotgun broken over one arm and holding up a blue ribbon in her free hand. Next to the smiling girl was a mug-shot of Lane Hardy at twenty-one, after an arrest in San Diego—under his real name, which was Leonard Hopgood—for indecent exposure. The two pix made a terrific contrast. The headline: BEAUTY AND THE BEAST.

Being a minor hero myself, I got some mention in the North Carolina papers, but in the tabloids I was hardly mentioned. Not sexy enough, I guess.

Mike thought having a HERO MOM was cool. Annie loathed the whole circus and couldn't wait for the press to move on to the next big thing. She'd gotten all the newspaper coverage she wanted in the days when she had been the holy man's wild child, famous for dancing on the bars in various Greenwich Village dives. So she gave no interviews, and we had our farewell picnic in the kitchen. There were actually five of us, because Milo was under the table, hoping for scraps, and Jesus—on the face of Mike's kite—was propped in the extra chair.

Their bags were in the hall. When the meal was done, I would drive them to Wilmington International. A private jet, laid on by Buddy Ross Ministries, Inc., would fly them back to Chicago and out of my life. The Heaven's Bay police department (not to mention the North Carolina State Police and maybe even the FBI) would undoubtedly have more questions for her, and she'd probably be back at some point to testify before a grand jury, but she'd be fine. She was the HERO MOM, and thanks to that promotional pen from Kroger's in the back of the van's glove compartment, there would never be a photo of Mike in the *Post* below a headline reading PSYCHIC SAVIOR!

Our story was simple, and Mike played no part in it. I had gotten interested in the murder of Linda Gray because of the legend that her ghost haunted the Joyland funhouse. I had enlisted the help of my research-minded friend and summer co-worker, Erin Cook. The photographs of Linda Gray and her killer had reminded me of someone, but it wasn't until after Mike's day at Joyland that the penny dropped. Before I could call the police, Lane Hardy had called me, threatening to kill Annie and Mike if I didn't come to Joyland on the double. So much truth, and only one little lie: I had Annie's phone number so I could call her if plans for Mike's visit to the park changed. (I produced the card for the lead detective, who barely glanced at it.) I said I called Annie from Mrs. Shoplaw's before leaving for Joyland, telling her to lock her doors, call the cops, and stay put. She *did* lock the doors, but didn't stay put. Nor did she call the police. She was terrified that if Hardy saw blue flashing lights, he'd kill me. So she'd taken one of the guns from the safe and followed Lane with her headlights off, hoping to surprise him. Which she did. Thus, HERO MOM.

"How's your father taking all this, Dev?" Annie asked.

"Aside from saying he'd come to Chicago and wash your cars for life, if you wanted?" She laughed, but my father had actually said that. "He's fine. I'm heading back to New Hampshire next month. We'll have Thanksgiving together. Fred asked me to stay on until then, help him get the park buttoned up, and I agreed. I can still use the money."

"For school?"

"Yeah. I guess I'll go back for the spring semester. Dad's sending me an application."

"Good. That's where you need to be, not painting rides and replacing lightbulbs in an amusement park."

"You'll really come to see us in Chicago, right?" Mike asked. "Before I get too sick?"

Annie stirred uneasily, but said nothing.

"I have to," I said, and pointed to the kite. "How else am I going to return that? You said it was just a loan."

"Maybe you'll get to meet my grandpa. Other than being crazy about Jesus, he's pretty cool." He gave his mother a sideways glance. "*I* think so, anyway. He's got this great electric train set in his basement."

I said, "Your grandfather may not want to see me, Mike. I almost got your mother in a whole peck of trouble."

"He'll know you didn't mean to. It wasn't your fault that you worked with that guy." Mike's face grew troubled. He put down his sandwich, picked up a napkin, and coughed into it. "Mr. Hardy seemed really nice. He took us on the rides."

A lot of girls thought he was really nice, too, I thought. "You never had a…a vibe about him?"

Mike shook his head and coughed some more. "No. I liked him. And I thought he liked me."

I thought of Lane on the Carolina Spin, calling Mike a crippled brat.

Annie put a hand on Mike's wand of a neck and said, "Some people hide their real faces, hon. Sometimes you can tell when they're wearing masks, but not always. Even people with powerful intuitions can get fooled."

I had come for lunch, and to take them to the airport, and to say goodbye, but I had another reason, as well. "I want to ask you something, Mike. It's about the ghost who woke you up and told you I was in trouble at the park. Is that okay? Will it upset you?"

"No, but it's not like on TV. There wasn't any white see-through thing floating around and going *whooo-ooo*. I just woke up…and the ghost was there. Sitting on my bed like a real person."

"I wish you wouldn't talk about this," Annie said. "Maybe it's not upsetting him, but it's sure as hell upsetting me."

"I just have one more question, and then I'll let it go."

"Fine." She began to clear the table.

Tuesday we had taken Mike to Joyland. Not long after midnight on Wednesday morning, Annie had shot Lane Hardy on the Carolina Spin, ending his life and saving mine. The next day had been taken up by police interviews and dodging reporters. Then, on Thursday afternoon, Fred Dean had come to see me, and his visit had nothing to do with Lane Hardy's death.

Except I thought it did.

"Here's what I want to know, Mike. Was it the girl from the funhouse? Was she the one who came and sat on your bed?"

Mike's eyes went wide. "Gosh, no! She's gone. When they go, I don't think they ever come back. It was a *guy*."

♥

In 1991, shortly after his sixty-third birthday, my father suffered a fairly serious heart attack. He spent a week in Portsmouth General Hospital and was then sent home, with stern warnings about watching his diet, losing twenty pounds, and cutting out the evening cigar. He was one of those rare fellows who actually followed the doctor's orders, and at this writing he's eighty-five and, except for a bad hip and dimming eyesight, still good to go.

In 1973, things were different. According to my new research assistant (Google Chrome), the average stay back then was two weeks—the first in ICU, the second on the Cardiac Recovery floor. Eddie Parks must have done okay in ICU, because while Mike was touring Joyland on that Tuesday, Eddie was being moved downstairs. That was when he had the second heart attack. He died in the elevator.

♥

"What did he say to you?" I asked Mike.

"That I had to wake up my mom and make her go to the park right away, or a bad man was going to kill you."

Had this warning come while I was still on the phone with Lane, in Mrs. Shoplaw's parlor? It couldn't have come much later, or Annie wouldn't have made it in time. I asked, but Mike didn't know. As soon as the ghost went—that was the word Mike used; it didn't disappear, didn't walk out the door or use the window, it just *went*—he had thumbed the intercom beside his bed. When Annie answered his buzz, he'd started screaming.

"That's enough," Annie said, in a tone that brooked no refusal. She was standing by the sink with her hands on her hips.

"I don't mind, Mom." *Cough-cough*. "Really." *Cough-cough-cough*.

"She's right," I said. "It's enough."

Did Eddie appear to Mike because I saved the bad-tempered old geezer's life? It's hard to know anything about the motivations of those who've Gone On (Rozzie's phrase, the caps always implied by lifted and upturned palms), but I doubt it. His reprieve only lasted a week, after all, and he sure didn't spend those last few days in the Caribbean, being waited on by topless honeys. But…

I had come to visit him, and except maybe for Fred Dean, I was the only one who did. I even brought him a picture of his ex-wife. Sure, he'd called her a miserable scolding backbiting cunt, and maybe she was, but at least I'd made the effort. In the end, so had he. For whatever reason.

As we drove to the airport, Mike leaned forward from the back seat and said, "You want to know something funny, Dev? He never once called you by name. He just called you the kiddo. I guess he figured I'd know who he meant."

I guessed so, too.

Eddie fucking Parks.

♥

Those are things that happened once upon a time and long ago, in a magical year when oil sold for eleven dollars a barrel. The year I got my damn heart broke. The year I lost my virginity. The year I saved a nice little girl from choking and a fairly nasty old man from dying of a heart attack (the first one, at least). The year a madman almost killed me on a Ferris wheel. The year I wanted to see a ghost and didn't…although I guess at least one of them saw me. That was also the year I learned to talk a secret language, and how to dance the Hokey Pokey in a dog costume. The year I discovered that there are worse things than losing the girl.

The year I was twenty-one, and still a greenie.

The world has given me a good life since then, I won't deny it, but sometimes I hate the world, anyway. Dick Cheney, that apologist for waterboarding and for too long chief preacher in the Holy Church of Whatever It Takes, got a brand-new heart while I was writing this—how about that? He lives on; other people have died. Talented ones like Clarence Clemons. Smart ones like Steve Jobs. Decent ones like my old friend Tom Kennedy. Mostly you get used to it. You pretty much have to. As W. H. Auden pointed out, the Reaper takes the rolling in money, the screamingly funny, and those who are very well hung. But that isn't where Auden starts his list. He starts with the innocent young.

Which brings us to Mike.

♥

I took a seedy off-campus apartment when I went back to school for the spring semester. One chilly night in late March, as I was cooking a stir-fry for myself and this girl I was just about crazy for, the phone rang. I answered it in my usual jokey way: "Wormwood Arms, Devin Jones, proprietor."

"Dev? It's Annie Ross."

"Annie! Wow! Hold on a second, just let me turn down the radio."

Jennifer—the girl I was just about crazy for—gave me an inquiring look. I shot her a wink and a smile and picked up the phone. "I'll be there two days after spring break starts, and you can tell him that's a promise. I'm going to buy my ticket next wee—"

"Dev. Stop. Stop."

I picked up on the dull sorrow in her voice and all my happiness at hearing from her collapsed into dread. I put my forehead against the wall and closed my eyes. What I really wanted to close was the ear with the phone pressed to it.

"Mike died last evening, Dev. He..." Her voice wavered, then steadied. "He spiked a fever two days ago, and the doctor said we ought to get him into the hospital. Just to be safe, he said. He seemed to be getting better yesterday. Coughing less. Sitting up and watching TV. Talking about some big basketball tournament. Then...last night..." She stopped. I could hear the rasp of her breath as she tried to get herself under control. I was also trying, but the tears had started. They were warm, almost hot.

"It was very sudden," she said. Then, so softly I could barely hear: "My heart is breaking."

There was a hand on my shoulder. Jennifer's. I covered it

with my own. I wondered who was in Chicago to put a hand on Annie's shoulder.

"Is your father there?"

"On a crusade. In Phoenix. He's coming tomorrow."

"Your brothers?"

"George is here now. Phil's supposed to arrive on the last flight from Miami. George and I are at the...place. The place where they...I can't watch it happen. Even though it's what he wanted." She was crying hard now. I had no idea what she was talking about.

"Annie, what can I do? Anything. Anything at all."

She told me.

♥

Let's end on a sunny day in April of 1974. Let's end on that short stretch of North Carolina beach that lies between the town of Heaven's Bay and Joyland, an amusement park that would close its doors two years later; the big parks finally drove it to bankruptcy in spite of all Fred Dean's and Brenda Rafferty's efforts to save it. Let's end with a pretty woman in faded jeans and a young man in a University of New Hampshire sweatshirt. The young man is holding something in one hand. Lying at the end of the boardwalk with his snout on one paw is a Jack Russell terrier who seems to have lost all his former bounce. On the picnic table, where the woman once served fruit smoothies, there's a ceramic urn. It looks sort of like a vase missing its bouquet. We're not quite ending where we began, but close enough.

Close enough.

♥

"I'm on the outs with my father again," Annie said, "and this time there's no grandson to hold us together. When he got back from his damn crusade and found out I'd had Mike cremated, he was furious." She smiled wanly. "If he hadn't stayed for that last goddam revival, he might have talked me out of it. Probably would have."

"But it's what Mike wanted."

"Strange request for a kid, isn't it? But yes, he was very clear. And we both know why."

Yes. We did. The last good time always comes, and when you see the darkness creeping toward you, you hold on to what was bright and good. You hold on for dear life.

"Did you even ask your dad…?"

"To come? Actually I did. It's what Mike would have wanted. Daddy refused to participate in what he called 'a pagan ceremony.' And I'm glad." She took my hand. "This is for us, Dev. Because we were here when he was happy."

I raised her hand to my lips, kissed it, gave it a brief squeeze, then let it go. "He saved my life as much as you did, you know. If he hadn't woken you up…if he'd even hesitated—"

"I know."

"Eddie couldn't have done anything for me without Mike. I don't see ghosts, or hear them. Mike was the medium."

"This is hard," she said. "Just…so hard to let him go. Even the little bit that's left."

"Are you sure you want to go through with it?"

"Yes. While I still can."

She took the urn from the picnic table. Milo raised his head to look at it, then lowered it back to his paw. I don't know if he understood Mike's remains were inside, but he knew Mike was gone, all right; that he knew damned well.

I held out the Jesus kite with the back to her. There, as per Mike's instructions, I had taped a small pocket, big enough to hold maybe half a cup of fine gray ash. I held it open while Annie tipped the urn. When the pocket was full, she planted the urn in the sand between her feet and held out her hands. I gave her the reel of twine and turned toward Joyland, where the Carolina Spin dominated the horizon.

I'm flying, he'd said that day, lifting his arms over his head. No braces to hold him down then, and none now. I believe that Mike was a lot wiser than his Christ-minded grandfather. Wiser than all of us, maybe. Was there ever a crippled kid who didn't want to fly, just once?

I looked at Annie. She nodded that she was ready. I lifted the kite and let it go. It rose at once on a brisk, chilly breeze off the ocean. We followed its ascent with our eyes.

"You," she said, and held out her hands. "This part is for you, Dev. He said so."

I took the twine, feeling the pull as the kite, now alive, rose above us, nodding back and forth against the blue. Annie picked up the urn and carried it down the sandy slope. I guess she dumped it there at the edge of the ocean, but I was watching the kite, and once I saw the thin gray streamer of ash running away from it, carried into the sky on the breeze, I let the string go free. I watched the untethered kite go up, and up, and up. Mike would have wanted to see how high it would go before it disappeared, and I did, too.

I wanted to see that, too.

August 24, 2012

THE
END

AUTHOR'S NOTE

Carny purists (I'm sure there are such) are even now preparing to write and inform me, with varying degrees of outrage, that much of what I call "the Talk" doesn't exist: that rubes were never called conies, for instance, and that pretty girls were never called points. Such purists would be correct, but they can save their letters and emails. Folks, that's why they call it fiction.

And anyway, most of the terms here really are carnival lingo, an argot both rich and humorous. The Ferris wheel was known as the chump-hoister or the simp-hoister; kiddie rides were known as zamp rides; leaving town in a hurry was indeed called burning the lot. These are just a few examples. I am indebted to *The Dictionary of Carny, Circus, Sideshow & Vaudeville Lingo*, by Wayne N. Keyser. It's posted on the internet. You can go there and check out a thousand other terms. Maybe more. You can also order his book, *On the Midway*.

Charles Ardai edited this book. Thanks, man.

Stephen King